Blood
on the
Moon

Blood
on the
Moon

by
James Ellroy

THE MYSTERIOUS PRESS
New York

Library of Congress Catalogue Number: 83-63039
   ISBN: 0-89296-069-8 Trade Edition

Designed by Kingsley Parker at the Angelica Design Group, Ltd.

Jacket illustration copyright © 1983 by John Gamache

FIRST EDITION

In Memory of
KENNETH MILLAR
1915–1983

The bay trees in our country are all withered,
and meteors fright the fixed stars of heaven;
the pale face moon looks bloody on the earth,
and lean look'd prophets whisper fearful change.

Shakespeare
Richard II

PART ONE
FIRST TASTES OF BLOOD

CHAPTER ONE

Friday, June 10th, 1964 was the start of a KRLA golden oldie weekend. The two conspirators scouting the territory where the "kidnaping" would take place blasted their portable radio at full volume to drown out the sound of power saws, hammers and crowbars — the noise of the third floor classroom renovation and the music of the Fleetwoods battling for audial supremacy.

Larry "Birdman" Craigie, the radio held close to his head, marveled at the irony of this construction work taking place a scant week before school was to close for the summer. Just then, Gary U. S. Bonds came over the airwaves, singing: "School is out at last, and I'm so glad I passed," and Larry fell to the sawdust covered linoleum floor, convulsed with laughter. School was maybe gonna be out, but he wasn't gonna pass, and his name was Chuck and he didn't give a fuck. He rolled on the floor, heedless of his recently swiped purple fuzzy Sir Guy shirt.

Delbert "Whitey" Haines started to get disgusted and mad. The Birdman was either psycho or faking it, which meant that his long time stooge was smarter than him, which meant that he was laughing *at* him. Whitey waited until Larry's laughter wound down and he propped himself into push-up position. He knew what was coming next: A series of lurid remarks about doing push-ups on Ruthie Rosenberg, how Larry was going to make her blow him while he hung from the rings in the girls' gym.

Larry's laughter trailed off, and he opened his mouth to speak. Whitey didn't let him get that far; he liked Ruthie

3

and hated to hear nice girls blasphemed. He nuzzled the toe of his boot into Larry's shoulder blades, right where he knew the zits were really bad. Larry screeched and hopped to his feet, cradling the radio into his chest.

"You didn't have to do that."

"No," Whitey said, "but I did. I can read your mind, psycho. Phony psycho. So don't say no nasty things about nice girls. We got the punk to deal with, not nice girls."

Larry nodded; that he was included in such important plans took the sting out of the attack. He walked to the nearest window and looked out and thought of the punk in his saddle shoes and his argyle sweaters and his pretty boy looks and his poetry review that he printed up in the camera shop on Aluarado where he lived, sweeping up the store in exchange for room and board.

The *Marshall High Poetry Review* — punk, sissy poems; gooey love stuff that everyone knew was dedicated to that stuck-up Irish parochial school transfer girl and the stuck-up snooty bitches in her poet crowd, and vicious fucking attacks on him and Whitey and all the *righteous* homeboys at Marshall. When Larry had gotten zonked on glue and cherry bombed the Folk Song Club, the *Review* had commemorated the occasion with line drawings of him in a storm trooper's outfit and maiming prose: "We now have a brownshirt named Birdman — illiterate, not much of a wordman. His weapons are stealth, and poor mental health; he's really much more like a turdman."

Whitey had fared even worse: after kicking Big John Kafesjian's ass in a fair fight in the Rotunda Court, the punk had devoted an entire copy of the *Review* to an "epic" poem detailing the event, calling Whitey a "white trash loser provocateur" and ending with a prediction of his fate, phrased like an epitaph:

"No autopsy can e'er reveal, what his darkest heart did most conceal; that shallow muscleman void,

defined by terror and hate—Let that be the requiem
for this light-weight."

Larry had volunteered to give Whitey a swift revenge,
doing himself a favor in the process: The Boys' V.P. had
said that he would be expelled for one more fight or cherry
bomb episode, and the idea of no more school nearly made
him cream in his jeans. But Whitey had nixed the notion of
quick retribution, saying, "No, it's too easy. The punk has
got to suffer like we did. He made us laughing stocks.
We're gonna return the compliment, and then some."

So their plan of disrobing, beating, genital painting, and
shaving was hatched. Now, if it all worked out, was the
time. Larry watched Whitey trace swastikas in the sawdust with a two by four. The Del-Viking's rendition of
"Come Go With Me" ended and the news came on, meaning it was three o'clock. Larry heard the whoops a moment
later, then watched as the workmen gathered up their
handtools and power equipment and bustled off down the
main staircase, leaving them alone to wait for the poet.

Larry swallowed and nudged Whitey, afraid of upset-
ting his silent artwork.

"Are you sure he'll come? What if he figures out the
note's a phony?"

Whitey looked up and kicked out at a half-opened wall
locker door, snapping it off at its hinges. "He'll be here. A
note from that Irish cunt? He'll think it's some kind of
fucking lovers' rendezvous. Just relax. My sister wrote the
note. Pink stationery, a girl's handwriting. Only it ain't
gonna be no lovers' rendezvous. You know what I mean,
homeboy?"

Larry nodded; he knew.

The conspirators waited in silence, Larry daydreaming,
Whitey rummaging through the abandoned lockers, looking for left-behinds. When they heard footsteps on the

second floor corridor below them, Larry grabbed a pair of jockey shorts from a brown paper bag and pulled a tube of acetate airplane glue from his pocket. He squeezed the tube's entire contents onto the shorts, then flattened himself against the row of lockers nearest to the stairwell. Whitey crouched beside him, homemade knuckle dusters coiled in his right fist.

"Sweetheart?"

The endearment, whispered hesitantly, preceded the sound of footsteps that seemed to grow bolder as they neared the third story landing. Whitey counted to himself, and when he calculated that the poet was within grabbing range he pushed Larry out of the way and stationed himself next to the edge of the stairs.

"Darling?"

Larry started to laugh, and the poet froze in mid-step, his hand on the stair rail. Whitey grabbed the hand and jerked upwards, sending the poet sprawling over the last two steps. He yanked again, relieving the pressure at just the right angle to twist the poet into a kneeling position. When his adversary was staring up at him with impotent, beseeching eyes, Whitey kicked him in the stomach, then pulled him to his feet as he trembled uncontrollably.

"Now, Birdman!" Whitey screeched.

Larry wrapped the glue-streaked jockey shorts around the poet's mouth and nostrils and pushed until his tremors became gurgling sounds and the skin around his temples went from pink to red to blue and he started to gasp for breath.

Larry relinquished his grip and backed away, the jockey shorts falling to the floor. The poet writhed on his feet, then fell backward, crashing into a half open locker door. Whitey stood his ground, both fists cocked, watching the poet retch for breath, whispering, "We killed him. We honest to fucking god killed him."

Larry was on his knees, praying and making the sign of

the cross, when the poet's gasps finally caught oxygen and he expelled a huge ball of glue covered phlegm, followed by a screeching syllable, "*sc-sc-sc.*"

"Scum!"

He got the word out in a rush of new breath, the color in his face returning to normal as he drew himself slowly to his knees. "Scum! Dirty white trash, low-life scum! Stupid, mean, ugly, wanton!"

Whitey Haines started to laugh as relief flooded through him. Larry Craigie began to dry-sob in relief and molded his prayer forming hands into fists. Whitey's laughter became hysterical, and the poet, on his feet now, turned his fury on him: "Muscle-bound auto mechanic peckerwood trash! No woman would ever touch you! The girls I know all laugh at you and your two inch dick! No dick, no sex fool. No——"

Whitey went red, and started to shake. He pulled his foot back and sent it full-force into the poet's genitals. The poet screamed and fell to his knees. Whitey yelled, "Turn the radio on, full blast!"

Larry obeyed, and the Beachboys flooded the corridor as Whitey kicked and pummeled the poet, who drew himself into a fetal ball, muttering, "scum, scum" as the blows rained into him.

When the poet's face and bare arms were covered with blood, Whitey stepped back to savor his revenge. He pulled down his fly to deliver a warm liquid *coup de grace*, and discovered he was hard. Larry noticed this, and looked to his leader for some clue to what was supposed to happen. Suddenly Whitey was terrified. He looked down at the poet, who moaned "scum," and spat out a stream of blood onto the steel-toed paratrooper boots. Now Whitey knew what his hardness meant, and he knelt beside the poet and pulled off his Levi cords and boxer shorts and spread his legs and blunderingly plunged himself into him. The poet screamed once as he entered; then his breathing settled into something strangely like ironic laughter. Whitey finished, withdrew and looked to his shock-stilled underling for support. To make it easy for him, he turned up the volume on the radio until Elvis Presley wailed into a garbled screech; then he watched as Larry delivered his ultimate acquiescence.

They left him there, bereft of tears or the will to feel anything beyond the hollowness of his devastation. As they walked away, "Cathy's Clown," by the Everly Brothers, came on the radio. They had both laughed, and Whitey had kicked him one last time.

He lay there until he was certain the quad would be deserted. He thought of his true love and imagined that she was with him, her head resting on his chest, telling him how much she loved the sonnets he composed for her.

Finally, he got to his feet. It was hard to walk; each step shot a rending pain through his bowels up into his chest. He felt at his face; it was covered with dried matter that had to be blood. He scrubbed his face furiously with his sleeve until the abrasions ran with fresh trickles of blood over smooth skin. This made him feel better, and the fact that he hadn't betrayed tears made him feel better still.

Except for a few odd groups of kids hanging out and playing catch, the quad was deserted, and the poet made his way across it in slow, painful steps. Gradually, he became aware of a warm liquid running down his legs. He pulled up his right trouser leg and saw that his sock was soaked in blood laced with white matter. Taking off his socks, he hobbled toward the "Arch of Fame," a marble inlaid walkway that commemorated the school's previous graduating classes. The poet wiped the bloody handfuls of cotton over mascots depicting the Athenians of '63 all the way back through the Delphians of '31, then strode barefoot, gaining strength and purpose with each step, out the school's south gate and onto Griffith Park Boulevard, his mind bursting with odd bits of poetry and sentimental rhymes; all for her.

When he saw the florist's shop at the corner of Griffith Park and Hyperion, he knew that this was his destination. He steeled himself for human contact and went in and purchased a dozen red roses, to be sent to an address he knew by heart but had never visited. He selected a blank card to go with them, and scribbled on the back some musings about love being etched in blood. He paid the florist, who smiled and assured him that the flowers would be delivered within the hour.

The poet walked outside, realizing that there were still two hours of daylight left, and that he had no place to go. This frightened him, and he tried composing an ode to waning daylight to keep his fear at bay. He tried, and tried, but his mind wouldn't click in and his fear became terror and he fell to his knees, sobbing for a word or phrase to make it right again.

CHAPTER TWO

When Watts burst into flames on August 23, 1965, Lloyd Hopkins was building sand castles on the beach at Malibu and inhabiting them with members of his family and fictional characters out of his own brilliant imagination.

A crowd of children had gathered around the gangly twenty-three year old, eager to be entertained, yet somehow deferential to the great mind that they sensed in the big young man whose hands so deftly molded drawbridges, moats, and parapets. Lloyd was at one with the children and with his own mind, which he viewed as a separate entity. The children watched, and he sensed their eagerness and desire to be with him and knew instinctively when to gift them with a smile or waggle his eyebrows so that they would be satisfied and he could return to his real play.

His Irish Protestant ancestors were fighting with his lunatic brother Tom for control of the castle. It was a battle between the good loyalists of the past and Tom and his rabblerousing paramilitary cohorts who thought that Negroes should be shipped back to Africa and that all roadways should be privately owned. The loonies had the upper hand temporarily — Tom and his backyard arsenal of hand grenades and automatic weaponry were formidable — but the good loyalists were staunch-hearted where Tom and his band were craven, and led by about-to-be police officer Lloyd, the Irish band had surmounted technology and was now raining flaming arrows into the midst of Tom's hardware, causing it to explode. Lloyd envisioned flames in the sand in front of him, and wondered for the eight thousandth time that day what the Academy would be like. Tougher than basic training? It would have to be, or the city of Los Angeles was in deep trouble.

Lloyd sighed. He and his loyalists had won the battle and his parents, inexplicably lucid, had come to praise the victorious son and heap scorn on the loser.

"You can't beat brains, Doris," his father told his mother. "I wish it weren't true, but they rule the world. Learn another language, Lloydy; Tom can commune with those low-lifes in that phone sales racket, but you solve puzzles and rule the world." His mother nodded mutely; the stroke had destroyed her ability to talk.

Tom just glowered in defeat.

Out of nowhere, Lloyd heard the music and very slowly, very consciously forced himself to turn in the direction from which the raucous sound was coming.

A little girl was holding a radio, cradled preciously into herself, attempting to sing along. When Lloyd saw the little girl, his heart melted. *She* didn't know how he hated music, how it undercut his thought processes. He would have to be gentle with her, as he was with women of all ages. He caught the little girl's attention, speaking softly, even as his headache grew: "Do you like my castle, sweetheart?"

"Y . . . Yes," the little girl said.

"It's for you. The Good Loyalists fought the battle for a fair damsel, and that damsel is you."

The music was growing deafening; Lloyd thought briefly that the whole world could hear it. The little girl shook her head coquettishly, and Lloyd said, "Can you turn the radio off, sweetie? Then I'll take you on a tour of your castle." The child complied, and fumbled the volume switch the wrong way just as the music stopped and a stern-voiced announcer intoned: "And Governor Edmund G. Brown has just announced that the National Guard has been ordered into South Central Los Angeles in force to stop the two day reign of looting and terror that has already left four dead. All members of the following units are to report immediately . . ."

The little girl fiddled the radio off just as Lloyd's headache metamorphosed into a perfect stillness. "You ever read *Alice in Wonderland,* sweetheart?" he asked.

"My mommy read me from the picture book," the little girl said.

"Good. Then you know what it means to follow the rabbit down the hole?"

"Does it mean what Alice did when she went into Wonderland?"

"That's right; and that's what old Lloyd has to do now — the radio just said so."

"Are you 'Old Lloyd'?"

"Yes."

"Then what's going to happen to your castle?"

"You inherit it, fair damsel — it's yours to do with as you please."

"Really?"

"Really."

The little girl hopped into the air and came down square

on top of the castle, obliterating it. Lloyd ran for his car and what he hoped would be his baptism by fire.

In the Armory, Staff Sergeant Beller took his prize cadre aside and told them that for a few bucks they could appreciably cut down the odds of getting eaten alive in niggerland and maybe have a few laughs, besides.

He motioned Lloyd Hopkins and two other P.F.C.s into the lavatory and displayed his wares and elaborated: ".45 automatic. Your classic officer's sidearm. Guaranteed to drop any firebreathing nigger at thirty yards, regardless of where it hits him. Strictly illegal for E.M., and a valuable asset in its own right — but these babies are fully automatic — machine pistols, with my specially devised elephant clip — twenty shots, reload in five seconds flat, The piece overheats, but I throw in a glove. The piece, two elephant clips and the glove — an even C-note. Takers?" He proffered the sidearms around. The two motor pool P.F.C.s eyed them longingly and hefted them with love, but declined.

"I'm broke, Sarge," the first P.F.C. said.

"I'm staying behind at the command post with the half-tracks, Sergeant," the second P.F.C. said.

Beller sighed, and looked up at Lloyd Hopkins, who gave him the creeps. "The Brain," the guys in the company called him. "Hoppy, what about you?"

"I'll take them both," Lloyd said.

Dressed in Class C fatigues, leggings, full bandoliers and helmet liners, Co. A of the 2nd Battalion, 46th Division, California National Guard stood at parade rest in the main meeting hall of the Glendale Armory, waiting to be briefed. Their battalion commander, a forty-four year old Pasadena dentist who held the reserve rank of Lieutenant Colonel, formulated his thoughts and orders into what he hoped would be considered a fierce brevity and spoke into the microphone. "Gentlemen, we are going into the fire-storm. The Los Angeles police have just informed us that a forty-eight square mile portion of South Central Los Angeles is engulfed in flames, and that entire commercial blocks have been pillaged and then set on fire. We are being sent in to protect the lives of the firemen battling those fires and to divert through our presence the looting and other criminal activity taking place. This is the sole regular infantry company in an otherwise armored division. You men, I'm sure, will be the spearhead of this peace-keeping force of civilian soldiers. You will be briefed further when we reach our objective. Good day, and God be with you!"

Nobody mentioned God as the convoy of armored half tracks and personnel carriers rolled out of Glendale toward the Golden State Freeway southbound. The main topics of conversation were guns, sex, and Negroes, until P.F.C. Lloyd Hopkins, sweltering in the canvas covered half-track, took off his fatigue jacket and introduced fear and immortality:

"First of all, you have to say it to yourselves, get it out in the air, say it—'I'm afraid. I don't wanna die!' You got that? No, don't say it out loud, that takes the power out of it. Say it to yourselves. There. Two, say this, too—I'm a nice white boy going to college who joined the fucking National Guard to get out of two years active duty, right?"

The civilian soldiers, whose average age was twenty, started to drift in to Lloyd's drift, and a few of them muttered, "Right."

"I can't hear you!" Lloyd bellowed, imitating Sergeant Beller.

"Right!" the guardsmen yelled in unison.

Lloyd laughed, and the others, relieved at the break in the tension, followed suit. Lloyd breathed out, letting his big frame go slack in an imitation of a Negro's shuffle. "And you all be afraid of de colored man?" he said in broad dialect.

Silence greeted the question, followed by a general breakout of hushed conversations. This angered Lloyd; he felt his momentum was drifting away, destroying this transcendent moment of his life.

He banged the butt end of his M-14 into the metal floorboard of the half-track. "Right!" he screamed. "Right, you dumb-fuck, pussy-whipped, nigger-scared, chickenshit motherfuckers! Right?" He banged his rifle again. "Right? Right? Right? Right?"

"*Right*!!!" The half-track exploded with the word, the *feeling*, the new pride in candor, and the laughter that followed grew deafening in its freedom and bravado.

Lloyd slammed his rifle butt one last time, to call the group to order. "Then they can't hurt us. Do you know that?" He waited until he was rewarded by a nod of the head from every man present, then pulled his bayonet from its scabbard and cut a large hole in the canvas top of the half-track. Being tall, he was able to peer out the top with ease. In the distance he could see the flatlands of his beloved L.A. Basin awash in smog. Spirals of flame and smoke covered its southern perimeter. Lloyd thought it was the most beautiful thing he had ever seen.

The division bivouacked at McCallum Park on Florence and 90th Street, a mile from the heart of the firestorm. Trees were downed to provide space for the hundred-odd military vehicles that would cruise the streets of Watts that night, filled with men armed to the teeth, and C-rations were distributed from the back of a five ton truck while platoon leaders briefed their men on their assignments.

Rumors abounded, fed by a cadre of L.A.P.D. and Sheriff's liaison officers: The Black Muslims were coming out in force, in whiteface, bent on hitting the profusion of discount appliance stores near Vermont and Slauson; scores of Negro youth gangs on pep pills were stealing cars and forming "kamikaze" squads and heading for Beverly

Hills and Bel-Air; Rob "Magawambi" Jones and his Afro-Americans for Goldwater had taken a distinct left turn and were demanding that Mayor Yorty grant them eight commercial blocks on Wilshire Boulevard as reparation for "L.A.P.D. Crimes Against Humanity." If their terms were not met within twenty-four hours, those eight blocks would be incinerated by firebombs hidden deep within the bowels of the LaBrea Tar Pits.

Lloyd Hopkins didn't believe a word of it. He understood the hyperbole of fear and understood further that his fellow civilian soldiers and cops were hyping themselves up to kill and that a lot of poor black bastards out to grab themselves a color TV and a case of booze were going to die.

Lloyd gobbled his C-rations and listened to his platoon leader, Lt. Campion, the night manager of a Bob's Big Boy Restaurant, explain orders that had come down to him from several other higher echelon civilian soldiers: "Being infantry, we will provide foot patrol, walking point for the armored guys—checking out doorways, alleys, letting our presence be known; bayonets fixed, combat stance, that kind of shit. Look tough. The armored platoon we trained with last summer at camp will be the platoon we hang with tonight. Questions? Everyone know who their squad leader is? Any new men with questions?"

Sergeant Beller, stretched out on the grass at the back of the platoon, raised his hand and said: "Loot, you know that the platoon is hanging in at four men over strength? Fifty-four men?"

Campion cleared his throat. "Yes...uh...yes, Sergeant, I do."

"Sir, do you also know that we got three men who got special M.O.S.s? Three men who ain't regular grunts?"

"You mean..."

"I mean, *sir*, that myself, Hopkins, and Jensen are infantry scouts, and I'm sure you'll agree we could be

15

of more value to this operation by running far point ahead of the armor. Right, *sir*?"

Lloyd saw the Lieutenant start to waver, and suddenly realized that *he* wanted it as bad as Beller did. Raising his hand, he said, "Sir, Sergeant Beller is right; we can walk far point *and* protect the platoon better *and* make it more autonomous. The platoon is over strength, and..."

The Lieutenant capitulated. "All right then," he said, "Beller, Hopkins and Jensen, you walk point two hundred yards ahead of the convoy. Be careful—stay sharp. No more questions? Platoon dismissed."

Lloyd and Beller found each other just as the tanks and half-tracks were starting their engines, flooding the twilight air with the sound of volatile combustion. Beller smiled; Lloyd smiled back in silent complicity.

"*Far* point, Sergeant?"

"*Far, far* point, Hoppy."

"What about Jensen?"

"He's just a kid. I'll tell him to hang back with the armor. *We're* covered. We've got carte blanche; that's the important thing."

"Opposite sides of the street?"

"Sounds right to me. Whistle twice if it gets hairy. Why do they call you 'The Brain'?"

"Because I'm very intelligent."

"Intelligent enough to know that the niggers are destroying the whole fucking country?"

"No, too intelligent for that shit. Anyone with half a brain knows that this is just a temporary blow-out and that when it's over it'll be business as usual. I'm here to see about saving innocent lives."

Beller said scornfully, "That's a crock. It just proves brains are over-rated. Guts are what counts."

"Brains rule the world."

"But the world's all fucked up."

"I don't know. Let's see what it's like out there."

"Yeah, let's do that." Beller began to worry about his ass. Hoppy was starting to sound like a nigger lover.

They ditched the division completely, walking south towards where the flames rose the highest and the gunfire sounded its loudest echoes.

Lloyd took the north side of 93rd Street and Beller the south, rifles at high port with bayonets fixed and sharpened, eyes scanning row after row of cheap white clapboard houses where Negro families peered from lighted windows and sat on porches, drinking, smoking, chattering and waiting for something to *happen*.

They hit Central. Lloyd gulped and felt a trickle of sweat run down into his skivvies, which hung below his hipbones, weighted down by the two specially constructed automatics jammed into his waistband.

Beller whistled from across the street and pointed forward. Lloyd nodded as he felt a whiff of smoke hit his nostrils. They walked south, and it took long moments for Lloyd's head to click into place and assimilate the epiphanies, the perfect logic of the self-destruction he was viewing:

Liquor stores, night clubs, process parlors and storefront churches interspersed with vacant lots covered with abandoned cars burned out from the inside. Gutted storefront after gutted storefront spilling profusions of broken liquor bottles; broken glass everywhere; the gutters filled with cheap electric ware — non-hockable items obviously looted in haste and discarded when the looters realized they were valueless.

Lloyd poked his M-14 into smashed-in windows, squinting into the darkness, cocking his ears the way he had seen dogs do it, listening for the slightest sound or presence of movement. There was nothing — only the wail of sirens and the crack of gunshots in the distance.

Beller trotted across the street just as an L.A.P.D. black-

and-white turned onto Central from 94th. Two flak-coated officers jumped out, the driver running up to Lloyd and demanding: "What the fuck are you *doing* here?"

Beller answered, startling the cops, who swiveled to face him, reaching for their .38s. "Far point, officer! My buddy and I been assigned to run ahead of our company and search out snipers. We're infantry scouts."

Lloyd knew that the cops didn't buy it and that he *had* to pursue the violent wonder of Watts without his low-life partner. He sent a sharp look Beller's way and said, "I think we're lost. We were only supposed to go out three blocks ahead, but we took a wrong turn somewhere. All the houses on these numbered streets look alike." He hesitated, trying to look bewildered.

Beller caught the drift and said, "Yeah. All these houses look alike. All these niggers on their steps sloppin' up juice look alike, too."

The older of the two cops nodded, then pointed south and said, "You guys with that artillery down near 102nd? The heavy-duty coon hunting?"

Lloyd and Beller looked at each other. Beller licked his lips to try to keep from laughing. "Yes," they said in unison.

"Then get in the car. You ain't lost no more."

As they highballed it southbound without lights or siren, Lloyd told the cops he was flagged for the October class at the academy and that he wanted the riot to be his *solo* training ground. The younger cop whooped and said, "Then this riot *is* a preordained training ground for you. How tall are you, six-four? Six-five? With your size, you're gonna get sent straight to 77th Street Division, Watts, these self-same fucking streets we're cruising right now. After the smoke clears and the fucking liberals run off at the mouth about the niggers being victims of poverty, there's gonna be the job of maintaining order over some very agitated bad-ass niggers who've had a distinct taste of blood. What's your name, kid?"

"Hopkins."

"You ever kill anyone, Hopkins?"

"No, sir."

"Don't call me 'sir.' You ain't a cop yet, and I'm a plain old patrolman. Well, I killed lots of guys in Korea. Lots and *lots,* and it changed me. Things look different now. Real different. I've talked about it to other guys who've lost their cherry, and we all agree: You appreciate different things. You see innocent people, like little kids, and you want them to stay that way because you got no innocence yourself. Little things like little kids and their toys and pets get to you, 'cause you know they're heading straight into this big fucking shitstorm and you don't want them to. Then you see people who got no regard for gentle things, for decent things, and you gotta come down hard on them. You gotta protect what two cents worth of innocence there is in the world. That's why I'm a cop. You look cherry to me, Hopkins. You look eager, too. You understand what I'm saying?"

Lloyd nodded, tingling with a pins and needles sensation. He smelled smoke through the open patrol car window, and the feeling began to numb as he realized the cop was talking instinctively about Lloyd's Irish Protestant ethos. "I understand exactly what you're saying," he said.

"Good, kid. Then it starts tonight. Pull over, partner."

The older cop braked and drew up to the curb.

"It's all yours, kid," the younger cop said, reaching over and banging Lloyd's helmet. "We'll take your buddy back to your outfit. You see if you can stir up anything on your own."

Lloyd tumbled out of the patrol car so fast that he never got to thank his mentor. They hit the siren by way of farewell.

102nd and Central was a chaos of smoldering ruins, the hiss of fire hoses, the squeal of tires on the now wet pavement, all modulated by police helicopters that hovered overhead, casting broad searchlights into storefronts to give the firemen light to work by.

Lloyd walked into the maelstrom, grinning broadly, still suffused with the eloquent recapitulation of his philosophy. He watched an armored half-track move slowly down the street, a fifty caliber machine gun mounted in its bed. A guardsman in the cab barked into a powerful bullhorn: "Curfew in five minutes! This area is under martial law! Anyone found on the streets after nine o'clock will be arrested. Anyone attempting to cross official police barriers will be shot. Repeat, curfew in five minutes!"

The words, clearly enunciated with force and malice, echoed loudly down the street, resulting in a flurry of activity. Within seconds Lloyd saw dozens of young men dart from burnt-out buildings, running full speed in any direction not caught by the searchlights. He rubbed his eyes and squinted to see if the men were carrying pilfered merchandise, only to discover they had disappeared before he could yell out or train his M-14 on them.

Lloyd shook his head and walked past a group of firemen milling around in front of a ravaged liquor store. They all noticed him, but no one seemed puzzled by the anomaly of a lone guardsman on foot patrol. Emboldened, Lloyd decided to check out life indoors.

He liked it. The darkness inside the burned-out store was soothing and Lloyd sensed that the shadow-shrouded silence was there to inform him with essential knowledge. He stopped and took a roll of friction tape from his fatigue jacket pocket and fixed his flashlight to the bottom edge of his bayonet. He swung his rifle in a figure eight arc and admired the results: wherever the M-14 pointed, there would be light.

Mounds of charred wood; piles of insulation stuffing; crushed booze bottles. Used condoms everywhere. Lloyd chuckled at the thought of subterranean liquor store coupling, then felt himself go dead cold as his chuckle was returned, followed by a hideous low moan.

He moved his M-14 around in a three hundred sixty degree arc, the muzzle at waist level. Once, then twice. On the third time around he was rewarded: an old man lay crumpled atop a mound of wadded up insulation fiber. Lloyd's heart melted. The old bastard was withered to prune dimensions and was obviously a threat to no one. He walked to the old man and handed him his canteen. The old man grasped it with shaking hands, raised it to his lips, then threw it to the ground, screeching:

"That not be what I need! I needs my Lucy! I gots to have my Lucy!"

Lloyd was befuddled. Was the old geezer crying out for his wife or some long lost love?

He removed the flashlight from his bayonet housing and shined it in the old man's face, then winced; the mouth and chin of that face were covered with congealed blood, from which glass shards stuck out like crystalline porcupine quills. Lloyd recoiled, then pointed his light into the old man's lap and recoiled further: the withered hands were cut to the bone, and three fingers of the right hand had been ground down to bloody stubs. The gnarled left hand held the shattered remnants of a bottle of Thunderbird wine.

"My Lucy! Gimme my Lucy!" the old man wailed, spitting globules of blood out with each word.

Lloyd took his flashlight and went crashing through the glass strewn ruins, brushing tears from his eyes, searching for an intact bottle of liquid salvation. Finally he found one, partially hidden by an overturned ceiling beam—a pint of six-year-old Seagram's 7.

Lloyd carried the bottle over and fed the old man, holding his head by the short nap of his grey hair, keeping the bottle a few inches from his bloody lips lest he try to ingest the entire thing. Thoughts of going for medical attention crossed his mind, but he pushed them away. He knew that the old man wanted to die, that he deserved to die drunk and that this service he was performing was the wartime equivalent of the many hours he had spent talking to his mute, brain-damaged mother.

The old man made slurping sounds, sucking convulsively at the bottle each time it touched his lips. After a few minutes had passed and half the pint was consumed, his tremors subsided and he pushed Lloyd's hand away.

"Dis be de start of World War Three," he said.

Lloyd ignored the comment and said, "I'm P.F.C. Hopkins, California National Guard. Do you want medical attention?"

The old man laughed, coughing up huge wads of blood-streaked sputum.

"I think you're bleeding internally," Lloyd said. "I can get you to an ambulance. Do you think you can walk?"

"I can do anything I wants to," the old man shrieked, "but I wants to die! Ain't no place for me in this war — I gots to make the scene on de other side!"

The bloodshot, filmy old brown eyes importuned Lloyd as if he were an idiot child. He fed the old man again, watching some kind of liquid acceptance course through the ancient body. When the bottle was finished the old man said, "You gots to do me a favor, white boy."

"Name it," Lloyd said.

"I'm gonna die. You gots to go over to my room and get my books and maps and things out and sell dem so I can have a decent burial. Christian like, you dig?"

"Where's your room?"

"It in Long Beach."

"I can go there when the riot is over. Not until then."

The old man shook his head furiously, until his body shook with it, rag-doll like, all the way down to his toes. "You gots to! They gonna lock me out tomorrow 'cause I behind on the rent! Then de po-lice gonna throw me in de sewer with the rats! You gots to!"

"Hush," Lloyd said. "I can't go that far. Not now. Don't you have any friends here I can talk to? Someone who can go to Long Beach for you?"

The old man considered the offer. Lloyd watched his wheels turn slowly. "You goes to de mission on Avalon an' one hundred and sixth. De African church. You talk to Sister Sylvia. You tell her she got to go to Famous Johnson's crib and get his shit and sell it. She gots my birthday in de church records. I wants a nice headstone. You tells her I loves Jesus, but I loves sweet Lucy more."

Lloyd stood up. "How bad do you want to die?" he asked.

"Bad, man, bad."

"Why?"

"Ain't no place for me in dis war, man."

"What war?"

"World War Three, you dumb motherfucker!"

Lloyd thought of his mother and reached for his rifle, but couldn't do it.

Lloyd ran all the way to 106th and Avalon, composing epitaphs for Famous Johnson en route. His chest was heaving and his arms and shoulders ached from holding his rifle at high port, and when he saw the neon sign proclaiming the "United African Episcopal Methodist Church" he took in last gulps of air to bring his raging heartbeat down to a low ebb; he wanted to be the very picture of armed dignity on a mission of mercy.

The church was storefront, two stories high, with lights shining in violation of the curfew. Lloyd walked in, to be confronted by a pandemonium that was part prayer meeting, part coffee klatch. Large tables had been set up lengthwise between rows of wooden pews, and middle aged and elderly Negroes were kneeling in prayer and helping themselves to coffee and donuts.

Lloyd moved slowly along with walls, which were festooned with paintings of a black Christ, weeping, blood dripping from his crown of thorns. He started looking to the faces of the kneelers for signs of holiness or compassion. All he saw was fear.

Until he noticed a fat black woman in a white robe who seemed to be smiling inwardly as she dispensed shoulder taps to the people who knelt by the pews nearest the aisle. When the woman noticed Lloyd she shouted, "Welcome, soldier," above the other hubbub and walked up to him, hand extended.

Startled, Lloyd shook the hand and said, "I'm P.F.C. Hopkins. I'm here on a mission of mercy for one of your parishioners."

The woman dropped Lloyd's hand and said, "I'm Sister Sylvia. This church is strictly for the Afro-American folk, but tonight is sort of special. Did you come to pray for the victims of this Armageddon? Do that be your mission?"

Lloyd shook his head. "No, I came to ask a favor. Famous Johnson is dead. Before he died, he asked me to come here and tell you to sell his belongings so he can have a proper burial. He told me you know the address of his place in Long Beach and his birthdate. He wants a nice headstone. He told me to tell you he loves Jesus." Lloyd was startled to see Sister Sylvia shaking her head ironically, a grin starting to form at the corners of her mouth. "I don't think it's funny," he said.

"You don't!" Sister Sylvia bellowed. "Well, I does! Famous Johnson was trash, young white man! He deserved to be called what he was—a nigger! And that room in Long Beach? That nothing but fantasy! Famous Johnson lived out of his car, with his sin things in the back seat! He used to come by this church for the donuts and coffee, but that all! Famous Johnson didn't have nothin' to sell!"

"But I . . ."

"You comes with me, young man. I shows you, so you forget all about In-famous Johnson with a clean conscience."

Lloyd decided not to protest; he wanted to see the fat woman's definition of sin.

It was a high-finned, chopped and lowered 1947 Cadillac, what Crazy Tom would have called a "Coon-Mobile."

Lloyd flashed his light into the back seat as Sister Sylvia stood triumphantly next to him, legs spread stolidly, her arms wrapped around her midsection in an "I told you so" attitude. He swung the door open. The tuck and roll upholstered seats were covered with empty soda pop bottles and pornographic photographs, most of them depicting Negro couples engaged in fellatio. Lloyd felt a sudden wave of pity; the sucker and suckee were overweight and middle-aged, and the tawdriness of the photos was a far cry from the *Playboy* magazines he had collected since high school. He didn't want it to be; it was too rotten a legacy for any human being.

"I told you so!" Sister Sylvia barked. "This is In-famous Johnson's house! You gonna sell them pictures and return them empties, and get you a fast dollar ninety-eight, which ain't gonna get you nothin' but two bottles o' T-Bird to pour over In-famous's pauper grave!"

Lloyd shook his head. Radio noise from a block away pounded him, causing the whole ugly moment to sway in his vision. "But you don't understand, ma'am," he said. "Famous entrusted this job to *me*. It's my *job*. It's my *duty*. It's my..."

"I don't wanna hear nothin' 'bout that sinner! You hears me? I wouldn't bury that trash in our cemetery for all the tea in China. You hears me?" Sister Sylvia didn't wait for an answer; she strode angrily back in the direction of her church, leaving Lloyd alone on the sidewalk, wishing the gunshots in the distance would escalate to the point where they drowned out the radio noise.

He sat down on the curb and thought of the two wretched people in the photographs, and of Janice who wouldn't blow him, but who did the final deed on their first date two weeks before high school graduation, leaving Lloyd Hopkins, Marshall High Class of '59, aglow with wonder at the love in his future. Now, six years later, Lloyd Hopkins, *summa cum laude* graduate of Stanford University, graduate of the Fort Polk Infantry School and the Evelyn Wood Speed Reading Class and six year lover of Janice Marie Rice, sat on a curb in Watts wondering why he couldn't get what a fat Negro slob probably got all the time. Lloyd shined his light in the back seat window again. It was as he suspected; the guy's dick was at least two inches bigger than his. He decided it was God and commitment. The jerk in the photo had a low I.Q. and a bad build, so God threw him a big wang to slide through life on. It all worked out.

Janice would take him orally when he graduated the academy and they got married. The last thought made him sex-flushed and sad. Janice made him sad. Then he thought of the daughters they would create. Janice, five foot eleven barefoot, slender, but with a robust set to her hips, was made for bearing exceptional children. Daughters. They would have to be daughters, made to be nurtured by the love in his Irish Protestant credo...

Lloyd took his Janice-daughter fantasies to ends of fulfillment both good and bad, then shifted his mind to women in general — women pure, wanton, vulnerable, needy, strong; all the ambivalences of his mother, now silent in her strength, rendered dumb by years of giving shelter to her lunatic male brood, from which only he emerged sane and capable of providing solace himself.

Lloyd heard a burst of gunshots in the near distance. Automatic weapon fire. At first he thought it was the radio or TV, but it was too real, too right, and it was coming from the direction of the African Church. He picked up his M-14 and ran to the corner. As he rounded it he heard screams, and turned to look in the shattered storefront window. When he saw the devastation inside, he screamed himself. Sister Sylvia and three male parishioners lay on the linoleum floor in a mass of tangled flesh, melded together in a river of blood. From somewhere within the twisted mound of bodies a severed artery shot up a red geyser. Lloyd, transfixed, watched it die and felt his scream metamorphose into the single word, "What! What! What!"

He screeched it until he was able to will his eyes from the bodies to the rest of the cordite-reeking church. The tops of dark heads peered above pews. Dimly, Lloyd perceived that the people were terrified of him. Tears streaming down his face, he dropped his rifle to the pavement and screamed, "What? What? What?", only to be answered by a score of voices hurling, "Killer, killer, murderer!" in horror and outrage.

It was then that he heard it, faintly but plainly, back off to his left, clicking in so succinctly that he knew it was real, not electronic: "*Auf weidersehen,* niggers. *Auf weidersehen,* jungle bunnies. See ya in hell."

It was Beller.

Lloyd knew what he had to do. He tossed the Negroes huddled behind their pews his sternest resolve and went after him, leaving his rifle behind on the pavement, crouching his long frame low behind parked cars as he made his way toward the destroyer of innocence.

Beller was running slowly north, unaware that he was being followed. Lloyd could see him framed plainly in the glow of those streetlights not destroyed, turning every few moments to look back and savor his triumph. He checked the second hand on his watch and calculated. It was obvious: Beller's unconscious was telling him to turn around and scan his blind side every twenty seconds.

Lloyd sprinted full out, counting to himself, and hit the pavement prone just as Beller would turn and peer backwards. He was within fifty yards of the killer when Beller ducked into an alleyway and started screaming, "Freeze, nigger, freeze!" A burst of shots followed, fully automatic. Lloyd knew it was the elephant clip .45.

He reached the alley and halted, catching his breath. There was a dark shape near the end of the cul-de-sac. Lloyd squinted and discerned that it was clad in fatigue green. He heard Beller's voice a moment later, spitting out garbled epithets.

Lloyd entered the alley, inching his way along a brick wall. He pulled one of his .45s from his waistband and flipped off the safety. He was almost within firing distance when his foot hit a tin can, the sound reverberating like hollow thunder.

He fired just as Beller did, and the flash from their gun barrels lit up the alley blindingly, illuminating Beller, crouched over a dead Negro man, the man headless, blown apart at the shoulders, his neck a massive cavity of bloody, charred tissue. Lloyd screamed as the recoil from his .45 lifted him into the air and slammed him back to the ground. A dozen shots tore into the wall above him, and he rolled frantically on the glass strewn pavement as Beller fired another burst at the ground, causing glass and black-top shrapnel to explode before his eyes.

Lloyd started to sob. He flung his arm over his eyes and prayed for courage and the chance to be a good husband to Janice. His prayers were interrupted by the sound of foot-steps running away from him. His mind clicked in: Beller was out of ammo and was running for his life. Lloyd willed himself to stand upright. His legs wobbled, but his mind was steadfast. He was right: Beller's empty M-14 lay across the torso of the dead man, and the .45, spent and burning to the touch, lay a few feet away.

Lloyd deep breathed, reloaded and listened for sounds of flight. He caught them; off to his left he heard the scuffle of feet and strained breathing. He followed the sounds by the shortest possible route, scaling the cement alleyway wall and coming down into a weed-strewn back yard, where the breath-noise mixed with the sound of a radio playing jazz.

Lloyd blundered through the yard, mumbling prayers to

engulf the music. He found a walkway leading to the street, and the light from the adjoining house let him pick out a trail of freshly spilled blood. He saw that the blood led into a huge vacant lot, pitch dark and eerily silent.

Lloyd listened, willing himself to assume the ears of a highly attuned animal. Just as his eyes became accustomed to the darkness and let him pick out objects in the lot, he heard it: a snapping of metal on metal, coming from the direction of a portable construction toilet. It was unmistakable: Beller was still armed with one of his evil customized .45s, and he knew Lloyd was near.

Lloyd hurled a rock at the outhouse. The door creaked open and three single shots rang out, followed by the sound of doors slamming all the way down the block.

Lloyd got an idea. He walked down the street, scanning front porches until he found what he was looking for, nestled among an evening's array of potato chip bags and empty beer cans — a portable radio. Steeling himself, he turned on the volume and was bombarded by rhythmic soul music. Despite his headache, he smiled, then turned the volume down. It was poetic justice for Staff Sergeant Richard A. Beller.

Lloyd carried the radio into the vacant lot and placed it on the ground ten yards in back of the construction toilet, then flipped the volume dial and ran in the opposite direction.

Beller burst out the door of the outhouse seconds later, screaming, "Nigger! Nigger! Nigger!" Blindly, he fired off a series of shots. The light from his muzzle bursts illuminated him perfectly. Lloyd raised his .45 and aimed slowly, pointing at Beller's feet to allow for recoil. He squeezed the trigger, the gun kicked and the elephant clip emptied. Beller screamed. Lloyd dug into the dirt, stifling his own screams. The radio blasted rhythm and blues, and Lloyd ran toward the sound, the butt end of his .45 extended. He stumbled in the darkness, then got down on his hands and knees and bludgeoned the music to death.

Lloyd stood up unsteadily, then walked to the remains of Richard Beller. He felt strangely calm as he carried first the entrails of the former civilian soldier to the outhouse, then the lower body, then the disembodied arms. Beller's head was nothing but splattered bone and brain debris, and Lloyd let them lie in the dirt.

Muttering, "God please, please, God, rabbit down the hole," Lloyd walked out to the street, noting with his animal antennae that there was no one about — the locals were either scared shitless by the gunfire or inured to it. He emptied his canteen into the gutter and found a length of surgical tubing in his bayonet case — good strangling cord, Beller had once told him. There was a '61 Ford Fairlane at the curb. Deftly manipulating the tubing and canteen, Lloyd managed to siphon a solid pint of gas from the tank. He walked back to the outhouse and doused what remained of Beller, than reloaded his .45 and paced off ten yards. He fired, and the outhouse exploded. Lloyd walked back to Avalon Boulevard. When he turned around, the entire lot was engulfed in flames.

Two days later, the Watts Riot was over. Order had been restored to the devastated underbelly of South Central Los Angeles. Forty-two lives were lost — forty rioters, one deputy sheriff and one National Guardsman whose body was never found, but who was presumed dead.

The riot was attributed to many causes. The N.A.A.C.P. and the Urban League attributed it to racism and poverty. The Black Muslim Party attributed it to police brutality. Los Angeles Chief of Police William H. Parker attributed it to a "breakdown in moral values." Lloyd Hopkins considered all these theories fatuous nonsense. He attributed the Watts Riot to the death of the innocent heart, most specifically the heart of an old black wino named Famous Johnson.

When it was over, Lloyd retrieved his car from the parking lot of the Glendale Armory and drove to Janice's apartment. They made love, and Janice provided what comfort she could, but refused the oral comfort Lloyd begged for. He left her bed at three in the morning and went looking for it.

He found a Negro prostitute at the corner of Western and Adams who was willing to do the deed for ten dollars, and they drove to a side street and parked. Lloyd screamed when he came, frightening the hooker, who bolted out of the car before she could collect her money.

Lloyd cruised aimlessly until dawn, then drove to his parents' house in Silverlake. He could hear his father snoring as he unlocked the door, and he saw light coming from under the door to Tom's room. His mother was in her den, sitting in her bentwood rocker. All the lights in the room were off, except for the colored light from the fish tank. Lloyd sat down on the floor and told the mute, prematurely old woman his entire life story, ending with the killing of the killer of innocence and how he could now protect innocent people as never before. Absolved and fortified, he kissed his mother's cheek and wondered how he would kill the eight weeks before he entered the Academy.

Tom was waiting for him outside the house, stationed firmly on the pathway leading to the sidewalk. When he saw Lloyd, he laughed and opened his mouth to speak. Lloyd didn't let him. He pulled a .45 automatic from his waistband and placed it against Tom's forehead. Tom started to tremble, and Lloyd said very softly, "If you ever mention niggers, commies, kikes, or any of that shit to me ever again, I'll kill you." Tom's florid face went pale, and Lloyd smiled and walked back to the shattered remains of his own innocence.

PART TWO
TORCH SONGS

CHAPTER THREE

He cruised west on Ventura Boulevard, savoring the newness of daylight-saving time, the clarity of the extra-long afternoons and the unseasonably warm spring weather that had the harlots dressed in tank tops and bare-midriff halters and the real women in a profusion of demure summer pastels: pink, light blue and green, pale yellow.

It had been many months since the last time, and he attributed this hiatus to the shifting weather patterns that had his head in a tizzy: warm one day, cold and rainy the next, you never knew how women were going to dress, so it was hard to get a fix on one to rescue — you couldn't feel the colors, the texture of what a woman was until you viewed her in a context of consistency. God knows that when the planning started the little fluxes of her life became all too evident; if he lost love for her then, the resultant pity reaffirmed the spiritual aspects of his purpose and gave him the detachment necessary to do the job.

But the planning was at *least* half of it, the part that edified, that cleansed *him*, that gave him abstention from minor chaos and precarious impunity from a world that gobbled up the refined and sensitive and spit them out like so much waste fluid.

Deciding to drive through Topanga Canyon on his way back to the city, he killed the air-conditioning and put a meditation tape on the cassette player, one that stressed his favorite theme: the silent mover, self-assured and accepting, armed with a compassionate purpose. He listened as the minister with the countrified voice spoke of the necessity of goals. "What sets the man of movement apart from the man dwelling in the netherworld of stasis is the road, both inward and outward bound, toward worthwhile goals. Traveling this road is both the journey and the destination, the gift both given and received. You can change your life forever if you will follow this simple thirty day program. First, think of what you want most at this moment—it can be anything from spiritual enlightenment to a new car. Write that goal down on a piece of paper, and write today's date next to it. Now, for the next thirty days, I want you to concentrate on achieving that goal, and allow no thoughts of failure to enter your mind. If these thoughts intrude, banish them! Banish all but the good pure thoughts of achieving your goal, and miracles will happen!"

He believed it; he had made it work for him. There were now twenty pieces of carefully folded paper attesting to the fact that it worked.

He had first played the tape fifteen years before, in 1967, and was impressed. But he didn't know what he wanted. Three days later he saw her, and knew. Jane Wilhelm was her name. Grosse Point born and bred, she had fled Bennington in her senior year, hitching west in search of new values and friends. She had drifted, oxford shirt and penny loafer clad, to the dope scene on the Sunset Strip. He had first seen her outside the Whisky Au Go Go, talking to a bunch of hippie low lifers, obviously trying to downplay her intelligence and good breeding. He picked her up and told her of his tape and piece of paper. She was touched, but laughed aloud for several moments. If he wanted to ball, why didn't he just ask? Romanticism was corny, and she was a liberated woman.

It was then, in his refusal, that he took his first moral stand. He now knew the exactitude of his immediate goal and all his future ones: the salvation of female innocence.

He kept Jane Wilhelm under loose surveillance until the end of the thirty-day period prescribed by the minister, watching her make the rounds of love-ins, crash pads and rock concerts. Shortly after midnight on the thirty-first day, Jane stumbled away alone from Gazzari's Disco. From his car, parked just south of Sunset, he watched her weave across the street. He turned on his high beams, catching her full in the face, committing to memory her drug-puffed features and dilated eyes. It was her final debasement. He strangled her right there on the sidewalk, then threw her body into the trunk of his car.

Three nights later he drove north to the farmland outside of Oxnard. After a roadside prayer service that featured his salvation tape, he buried Jane in the soft earth adjoining a rock quarry. So far as he knew, her body was never found.

He turned onto Topanga Canyon Road, recalling the methodology that had allowed him to save twenty women without the excitable mass media or fuzz ever seizing on him. It was simple. He became his women, spending months assimilating the details of their lives, savoring every nuance, cataloguing every perfection and imperfection before deciding on the method of elimination, which was then tailored to fit the persona, indeed the very soul, of his intended. Thus the planning was the courtship, and the killing the betrothal.

The thought of courtship brought forth a huge rush of ardent imagery, all revolving around prosaic detail, the small intimacies that only a lover could appreciate.

Elaine from 1969, who had loved baroque music; who, although pretty, had spent virtually all her free time listening to Bach and Vivaldi with the windows of her garage apartment open, even in the coldest weather— wanting to share the beauty she felt with a world deadset on ignoring her. Night after night he had listened with a boom receiver from a nearby rooftop, picking up muttered declarations of loneliness beneath the music, almost weeping as their hearts fused in the strains of the Brandenburg Concerti.

Twice he walked through the apartment, collating directions that would indicate the proper way to salvage Elaine's soul. He had decided to wait, to meditate on the end of this woman's life, when he found underneath her sweaters an application for a computer dating service. That Elaine had succumbed to that vulgarity was the final indicator.

He spent a month studying her handwriting, and a week composing a suicide note in that hand. One cold night after Thanksgiving he climbed in through a window and opened three grain and a half Seconal capsules into the bottle of orange juice that he knew Elaine drank from every night before retiring. Later, he watched through a telescope as she took death's communion, then gave her two hours of sleep before entering the apartment, leaving the note and turning on the gas. As a final act of love he put a Vivaldi flute concerto on the stereo to provide accompaniment to Elaine's departure.

Blinding memories of other lovers caused his eyes to well with tears as he pictured their moments of culmination: Karen the horse lover, whose house was a virtual testament to her equine passion; Karen who rode bareback in the hills above Malibu and who died astride her strawberry roan as he ran from cover and bludgeoned the horse over the edge of a cliff; Monica, of the exquisite taste in small things, who clad the polio-riddled body she hated in the finest of silk and wool. As he continued to steal glimpses of her diary and watched her loathing of her body grow, he knew that dismemberment would be the ultimate mercy. After strangling Monica in her Marina Del Ray apartment, he rent her with a power saw and dumped her plastic encased parts into the ocean near Manhattan Beach. Police attributed the death to the "Trashbag Killer."

He dashed tears from his eyes, feeling the memories snowball into yearning. It was time again.

He drove into Westwood Village, paid to park and went walking, deciding not to be hasty, yet also not unduly cautious. Late dusk was falling, bringing with it a corresponding drop in temperature, and the Village streets were bursting with female vitality: women everywhere; snuggling into sweaters, hugging close to storefronts as they waited to enter movie theatres, browsing through bookstores, walking around him, past him, almost through him, it seemed.

Late dusk became night, and with darkness the streets had thinned to the point where individual women stood out in all their uniqueness. It was then that he saw her, standing in front of Hunter's Book Store, peering into the window as if in search of a vision. She was tall and slender, wearing a minimum of make-up on a soft face that tried hard to project a no-nonsense air. Late twenties — a seeker — a good-natured artificer with a sense of humor, he decided; she would enter the book store, check out the best sellers first, then the quality paperbacks, finally settling on a gothic romance or detective novel. She was lonely. She needed him.

The woman pulled her hair into a bun and slid a barette over the loose ends. She sighed and pushed open the door of the bookstore, then strode purposefully to a display table covered with books on self-improvement. Everything from *Creative Divorce* to *Winning Through Dynamic Yoga* was represented, and the woman hesitated, then grabbed a copy of *Force-Field Synergistics Can Save Your Life*, and carried it back to the cashier.

He was a discreet distance behind her all the way, and when she pulled out a checkbook to pay for her purchase, he memorized the name and address printed on her checks:

Linda Deverson
3583 Mentone Avenue
Culver City, Calif. 90408

He didn't wait to hear Linda Deverson converse with the cashier. He ran out of the store and all the way to his car, seized by love and the territorial imperative: the poet wanted to see the ground of his new courtship.

Linda Deverson was many things, he thought three weeks later as he developed the latest batch of photos. Pulling them out of the solution and hanging them up, he watched her spring to life in vivid black and white. There was Linda leaving the office where she worked as a real estate salesperson; Linda scowling as she attempted to pump her own gas; Linda jogging down San Vicente Boulevard; Linda staring out of her living room window, smoking a cigarette.

He locked the shop, took the photos and went upstairs to his apartment. As always when he walked through his darkened kingdom, he felt proud. Proud that he had had the patience to save and persevere and never relent in his determination to own this place that had given him the finest moments of his youth.

When his parents died and left him homeless at fourteen, the owner of Silverlake Camera had befriended him, giving him twenty dollars a week to sweep out the store at closing every night, and allowing him to sleep on the floor and study in the customers' bathroom. He studied hard and made the owner proud of him. The owner was a horse lover and gambler, and used the store as a bookie drop. He had always thought that his benefactor, who suffered from congestive heart disease and was familyless, would leave the store to him; but he was wrong — when he died the shop was taken over by the bookies to whom he owed money. They promptly ran it to hell — hiring nothing but incompetents, turning the quiet little shop into a low-life hangout — running football pools, booking horses, and selling dope.

When he realized what had been done to his sanctuary, he knew that he had to act to save it, whatever the price.

He had been making a good living as a free-lance photographer, shooting weddings and banquets and communions, and he had saved more than enough money to buy the store should it go on the market. But he knew that the scum who owned it would never sell — it was turning too great an illicit profit. This vexed him so much that he completely forgot about his fourth courtship and threw all his energy toward permanent ownership of his despoiled safe harbor.

Batteries of anonymous phone calls to the police and district attorney did no good; they would not act on the malfeasance at Silverlake Camera. Desperate now, he searched out other means.

Through surveillance, he knew that the new owner got drunk every night at a bar on Sunset. He knew that the man had to be poured into a cab at closing time, and that the cabbie who met him at the door of the bar each night at two a.m. was a compulsive horse player who was heavily in his debt. With the same diligence that marked his courtships, he went to work, first acquiring an ounce of uncut heroin, then approaching the cab driver and making him an offer. The cabbie accepted the offer, and left Los Angeles the following day.

Two nights later, *he* was the one behind the wheel of the cab in front of the Short Stop Bar at closing time. At precisely two a.m., the owner of Silverlake Camera staggered outside and flopped into the back seat, promptly passing out. He drove the man to Sunset and Alvarado, and stuffed a plastic bag bursting with heroin into his coat pocket. He then hauled the unconscious drunk over to Silverlake Camera and placed him in a sitting position, half in and half out the front door, the key in his right hand.

He drove to a pay phone, called the Los Angeles Police Department and told them of a burglary in progress. They took care of the rest. Three patrol cars were dispatched to Sunset and Alvarado. As the first car screeched to a halt outside Silverlake Camera, the man in the doorway came awake, got to his feet and reached inside his coat pocket. Misinterpreting his gesture, the two patrolmen shot and killed him. Silverlake Camera went into receivership the following week and *he* picked it up for a song.

The camera shop and the three-room apartment above it became *his* song, and he renovated it into a symphony; a complete aesthetic statement of purpose, one steeped in his own past and the clandestine histories of the three people who had given him the terrible catharsis that set him free to salvage female innocence.

One whole wall was devoted to his attackers — a photographic collage that updated their warped progress in life: the musclebound one a Los Angeles County Deputy Sheriff, his sniveling lackey a male prostitute. Their brief, violent transit with him had shaped their lives for the negative — the acquisition of money and cheap one-on-one power the only balm for their spiritual emptiness. The candid snapshots on the wall spelled it out plainly: The Birdman, stationed at curbside on a "Boy's Town" street, hip outthrust, hungry eyes trawling for wretched lonely men to bring him a few dollars and ten minutes of selfhood; and Muscles, overweight and florid-faced, staring out the window of his patrol car at his West Hollywood constituency — the hip gays that he was sworn to protect, but who disdained his "protection" and ridiculed him as "Officer Pig."

The opposite wall held blown-up yearbook photographs of his original beloved; her innocence preserved forever by the extraordinary clarity of his art. He had clipped the photographs on graduation day 1964, and it wasn't until over a decade later, when he was a master photographer, that he felt confident enough to embark on a complex blow-up and reproduction process in an attempt to make them larger than life. Taped next to the blow-ups were gnarled, shriveled and twisted rose branches — twenty of them — the detritus of the floral tributes that he sent to his beloved after claiming a woman in her name.

He had set out to turn his sanctuary into a *total* sensory testament to the three, but for years the methodology had eluded him. He had claimed his visual access, but he wanted to hear these people *breathe*.

The solution came to him in a dream. Young women were tied to the spindle of a giant recording turntable. He sat at the control board of an elaborate electrical system, pushing buttons and flipping levers in a futile effort to make the women scream. Himself near the point of screaming, he had somehow willed the ability to quash his frustration by waving his arms in the simulation of flight. As his limbs treaded air, he ran out of breath and was close to suffocating when his hands touched free floating streams of magnetic tape. He grabbed the tape and used it as ballast to return to the control board. All the lights on the panel had gone off during his flight, and when he began pushing buttons the lights switched on, then short-circuited and burst with blood. He began to stuff the bloody holes with tape. The tape slithered through the apertures, onto the turntable and around the spindle, crushing the young women who were held captive there. Their screams awoke him from his dream, dissolving into his own scream when he discovered that his groin had exploded into his clenched hands.

That morning he purchased two state-of-the-art transistorized tape recorders, two condensor microphones, three hundred feet of wire, and a transistor power pack. Within a week the apartments of both Officer Pig and his original beloved had been outfitted with brilliantly concealed listening devices; and his access to their lives was complete. He would make weekly runs to change the tapes, almost exploding as he returned home and looked at the pictures on the wall and listened to their breathing compliment, learning intimacies that not even the dearest of lovers would know.

Those intimacies validated his judgment straight down the line: His first beloved took her flesh lovers with caution — they were sensitive-sounding men who loved her and capitulated to her subtle will absolutely. He could tell that she was lonely beneath her sometimes strident Feminist facade, but that was natural: she was a poet, one of growing local renown, and loneliness was the bane of all creative people. Officer Pig was, of course, corruption incarnate — an up-for-grabs cop who took bribes from the male prostitutes of Boy's Town, allowing them to ply their wicked craft while he and his sleazy cop buddies looked the other way. The Birdman was his liaison, and hours of listening to the two old high school buddies gloat over their picayune crime scams had convinced him that the wretchedness of their lives was *his* revenge.

His years of listening passed, long evenings where he would touch himself in total darkness as the tapes unfurled into his headphones. He grew even bolder in his desire to be in total sync with those who had brought about his rebirth, and on the anniversary of the beginning that he rarely thought of anymore, he staged betrothals artificed as suicides to celebrate his own act of submission in a sawdust covered high school corridor. Four times; twice in Officer Pig's veritable backyard, once in his own apartment building. The love he had felt in those moments of symbiotic reverie had made his clenched hand explosions magnify tenfold, and he knew that every gauntlet of camera art and breath and blood that he ran would only serve to make his song more inviolate.

Back in the present, he thought again of the many things Linda Deverson was, then felt his mind go blank as he tried to find a narrative line to impose on the welter of images that constituted his new love.

He sighed and locked the door of his apartment behind him, then took the photographs of Linda and taped them to the Tiffany glass window that fronted his writing desk. Sighing again, he wrote:

5–17–82

Three weeks into the courtship and as yet no access to her apartment, much less her heart — triple locks on the one door, it will take a bold gambit to get inside — I will have to risk it soon — Linda remains so elusive. Or maybe not; what has caught me so far is her sense of humor — the rueful smile that lights up her face as she pulls a cigarette out of her sweatsuit after jogging three miles down San Vicente; her firm but humorous refusals to go out with the obdurate young salesman who shares a cubicle with her at the real estate office; the way she talks to herself when she thinks no one is looking and the broad way she covers her mouth when a passerby catches her in the act. Two nights ago I followed her to the Force Field Synergistics seminar. That same rueful smile when she wrote the check for registration and again at the first "grouping" when they told her she couldn't smoke. I think that Linda possess the same detachment I have noticed in writers — the desire to commune with humanity, to have a common ground or dream — yet the concurrent need to remain aloof, to hold her intrinsic truths (however universal) above those of the collective. Linda is a subtle woman. While the first grouping (ambiguous jive talk about unity and energy) was going on, I snuck back to the registration office and stole her application. I now know this about my beloved:

1. Name: Linda Holly Deverson
2. Birthdate: 4/29/52
3. Birthplace: Goleta, California
4. Education: High school 1 2 3(4)

College 1②3 4
Advanced degrees? No.
5. How did you find out about F.F.S.? — I read your book.
6. Which four of these words best describe you?
      1. Ambitious
      2. Athletic
      3. Aggressive
      ④ Enlightened
      ⑤ Tuned In
      6. Befuddled
      7. Inquisitive
      ⑧ Passive
      9. Angry
      ⑩ Sensitive
      11. Passionate
      12. Aesthetic
      13. Physical
      14. Moral
      15. Generous
7. Why did you come to the F.F.S. Institute? — I can't honestly say. Some of the things in your book struck me as truthful things that could help me to better myself.
8. Do you think F.F.S. can change your life? — I don't know.

A subtle woman. I can change your life, Linda; I am the only one who can.

Three nights later he broke into her apartment.
It was carefully thought out and bold. He knew that she would be attending the second Synergistics Seminar, which was scheduled to last from eight o'clock until midnight. At seven forty-five he was stationed across the street from the F.F.S. Institute on 14th and Montana in Santa Monica,

armed with a matchbook sized circuit breaker and wearing skin-tight rubber gloves.

He smiled as Linda pulled into the parking lot, exchanged guarded greetings with other arriving F.F.S.ers and wolfed down a last cigarette before running into the large red brick building. He waited ten minutes, then sprinted over to her '69 Camaro, opened the hood and attached the circuit breaker to the underside of the car's distributor housing. Should anyone attempt to start the Camaro, it would turn over once and die. Laughing at the small perfection of it, he slammed the hood and ran back to his own car, then drove to the home of his beloved.

It was a pitch-dark spring night, and warm winds gave added audial cover. Parking a block away, he padded over to 3583 Mentone Avenue, carrying a flat-handled lug wrench and a transistor radio in a brown paper bag. Just as a huge gust of wind came up, he placed the radio on the ground outside Linda's living room window and turned the volume up full blast. Punk Rock bombarded the night, and he slammed the lug wrench full force into the window, grabbed the radio and ran back to his car.

He waited for twenty minutes, until he was certain that no one had heard the noise and no silent alarm had been sounded. Then he walked back and vaulted into the dark apartment.

Drawing curtains over the broken window, he deep-breathed and let his eyes become accustomed to the darkness, then followed his most urgent curiosity straight back toward where the bathroom had to be. He turned on a light and then rummaged through the medicine cabinet; checked out the make-up kit on top of the toilet; even went through the dirty clothes hamper. His soul sighed in relief. No contraceptive devices of any kind; his beloved was chaste.

He left the door ajar and walked into the bedroom.

Quickly noting that there was no overhead light, he turned on the lamp next to the bed. Its diffused glow gave him light to work by, and he flung open the walk-in closet door, hungry to touch the fabric of his beloved's life.

The closet was packed with garments on hangers, and he swept them up in a giant armful and carried them into the bathroom. There were mostly dresses, in a variety of fabrics and styles. Trembling, he fondled polyester suits and cotton shifts, pseudo-silk culottes and businesslike tweed; stripes, plaids, tattersall checks — all feminine and all pointing to the subtle, searching nature of Linda Deverson. She doesn't know who she is, he said to himself; so she buys clothes to reflect all the different things she *could* be.

He carried the bundle of clothing back to the closet and arranged it as it had been, then went looking for further evidence of Linda's chastity. He found it on her telephone stand — all the phone numbers in her address book belonged to women. Heart leaping with joy, he went into the kitchen and rummaged beneath the sink until he found a can of black paint and a stiff paint brush. He pried the can open and drew out a big glob of paint and smeared "Clanton 14 St. — Culver City — Viva La Raza" on the kitchen wall. To make it look even better, he grabbed a toaster and portable cassette player and took them with him.

Fondling the toaster on the seat beside him, he drove back to the F.F.S. Institute and removed the circuit breaker from Linda Deverson's car, then went home to meditate on the subtlety of his woman.

The following Wednesday night was the first F.F.S. "Question and Answer" grouping. He had purchased his ticket two days before at the Ticketron outlet near his shop and was curious as to how Linda would query the F.F.S. programmers, who had thus far brooked no feedback from their trainees. He was certain his beloved would interpose intelligent, skeptical questions.

There was a cordon of religious zealots outside the institute, brandishing signs that read "*Syn*ergistics is sin! Jesus is the only way!" He laughed as he walked into them; he thought Jesus was vulgar. One of the zealots noticed the ironic smile on his face and asked him if he had been saved.

"Twenty times," he replied.

The zealot's jaw dropped; he had been on the butt end of many sacrilegious one-liners, but this was a new one. He stood aside and let the nondescript heretic enter the building.

Once inside, he gave his ticket to the security guard, who handed him a large cushion and pointed in the direction of the assembly room. He walked through a hallway adorned with photographs of celebrity F.F.S.ers and into a huge room where knots of people milled around anxiously, chattering and sizing up the new arrivals. At the back of the room he wadded his cushion up and sat down with his eyes glued to the door.

She came in a moment later, setting her cushion down just a few feet away from him. His heart shuddered and pounded so hard that he thought it would drown out all the excited psychobabble that was floating through the room. Staring into his lap, he assumed a meditation pose that he hoped would forestall any conversation she might attempt. He shut his eyes so hard and wrenched his hands so tightly that he felt like a shrapnel bomb about to explode.

Then the lights in the room were dimmed twice, indicating the session was about to begin. A hush came over the assembly as the lights went out completely and candles were lit and placed in strategic positions throughout the room. The sudden darkness gripped him and held him like a lover. He turned his head and caught a glance of Linda silhouetted in candlelight. Mine, he said to himself, mine.

Sitar chords came over the P.A. system, winding down into a soft male voice. "Feel the fields that separate you from your greater self start to dissipate. Feel your inner self mix with the synergy of other tuned-in force fields to produce true energy and union. Feel the synthesis of yourself and everything good in the cosmos."

The voice lowered itself to a whisper. "Today I am here to relate to you personally, to help you apply the principles of Force Field Synergistics to your personal lives. This is your third workshop; you have the ammunition necessary to change your lives forever, but I am sure you have many questions. That is why I am here. Lights, please!"

The lights went on, jarring him. Carefully modulating his breathing to keep his control at optimum, he watched a silver-haired young man in a blue blazer walk to a flower draped lectern at the front of the room. He was greeted with wild applause and bliss-filled gazes.

"Thank you," the man said. "Questions?"

An elderly man at the front of the room raised his hand and said, "Yeah, I got a question. What are you gonna do about the niggers?"

The man at the lectern went beet red beneath his silver coiffure and said, "Well, I don't think that's germane to the issues at hand. I think — "

"Well, I do!" the old man bellowed. "You people took this building over from the Moose, and you got a civic responsibility to address yourself to the nigger problem!" The old man looked around for support and got nothing but embarrassed shrugs and hostile looks. The man at the lectern snapped his fingers and two burly, blazer-clad teenagers entered the room.

The old man ranted on. "I was a member of the Moose Lodge for thirty-eight years, and I rue the day we sold out to you bimbos! I'm gonna call for a meeting of the zoning board, and get an ordinance passed to keep all niggers and religious crackpots south of Wilshire. I'm a member in good..." The teenagers grabbed the old man by his arms and legs and carried him, kicking, biting, and screaming, out of the room.

The man at the lectern called for quiet, raising his hands in a supplicating gesture to quell the relieved hubbub that followed in the old man's wake. Running a hand through his silver hair, he said, "Now there's someone with a low karma synergy! Racism is low chakra! Now..."

Linda Deverson raised her hand forcefully and said, "I have a question. It relates to that old man. What if his inner self is bad and all his native force fields are so twisted with fear and anger that meanness is all he can relate to? What if he has just one germ of kindness, of curiosity, and that's what brought him here tonight? He *paid* to attend this meeting tonight, he—"

"His money will be refunded," the man at the lectern interjected.

"That's not what I'm talking about!" Linda shouted. "That's not what I mean! Don't you understand that that man can't be dismissed with a cheap crack about low chakra? Don't you..." Linda slammed her hands into her cushion, then got to her feet and rushed to the front door.

"Let her go!" the group leader said. "Her misery will be refunded if she leaves our program. Let her pay for her chakra!"

Barely containing his excitement, he got up to follow her and was almost knocked over by a tall buxom woman in a corduroy pantsuit. When he got outside to the parking lot, he found her conferring with Linda, who was smoking a cigarette and brushing angry tears out of her eyes. Shielded by a tall hedgerow, he could hear their conversation plainly.

"Shit, shit, shit," Linda was muttering.

51

"Just forget about it," the woman answered. "You win a few, you lose a few. I've been searching for a few years longer than you; listen to the voice of experience."

Linda laughed. "You're probably right. God, could I use a drink!"

"I wouldn't mind one myself," the woman said. "Do you mind scotch?"

"No, I love it!"

"Good. I've got a bottle of Chivas at home. I live in the Palisades. Did you bring your car?"

"Yes."

"Want to follow me?"

Linda nodded and ground out her cigarette. "Sure."

He was right behind them as they drove the twisting roads of Santa Monica Canyon up to a quiet block of large houses fronted by broad lawns. He watched as the first car hit its right-hand directional and pulled into a long circular driveway. Linda followed suit, parking directly behind. He drove on and parked at the corner, then walked casually over to the house the woman had entered.

The lawn extended around both sides of the house, with towering hibiscus plants forming its perimeters. He threaded his way along them, staying in the shadows, making a complete circuit of the house before catching sight of the two women sitting in adjoining easy chairs in a warmly appointed den. Crouching low, he watched Linda sip scotch and laugh in pantomime, imagining that she was being regaled by him, by his wit and the humorous verse that he wrote only for her. The other woman was laughing too, slapping her knee and freshening Linda's glass every few minutes from the bottle on the coffee table.

He was staring into the window, lost in Linda's laughter, when he suddenly became aware that something was drastically wrong. His instinct never failed him, and just as he was about to hit on the cause of his uneasiness, he saw the two women move toward each other very slowly and in perfect synchronization kiss on the lips, first tentatively, then hungrily, knocking over the bottle of scotch as they moved into a fierce embrace. He started to scream, then stifled the sound by jamming his hand into his mouth. He raised his other fist to smash the window, but reason took tenuous hold and he smashed the ground instead.

He looked in the window again. The women were nowhere to be seen. Frantically, he pressed his face to the glass and craned his neck almost off its axis, until he saw two pair of nude legs wrapped together, twisting and straining on the floor. Then he did scream, and the other-worldly sound of his own terrified voice propelled him out to the street. He ran until his lungs burned and his legs started to wobble. Then he fell to his knees and was perfectly still as comforting images of the twenty others washed over him. He thought of them at their moments of salvation, and of how much they looked like the ones who had betrayed his original true love so many years before.

Restored by the righteousness of his purpose, he got up and walked back to his car.

Performing the rituals of life allowed him to operate over the next week, keeping images of the betrayal from bludgeoning him into desperate action.

He minded the store from morning until late afternoon, then fielded calls that came in from his answering service. Wedding assignments were picking up, as they did each spring, and this year he could afford to be choosy, spending his early evenings interviewing the doting parents of engaged young couples who thought they were interviewing him. No uglies, he decided; no porkers. Only slender, good-looking young people would stand before his camera. He owed himself that.

After conducting business he would drive to the Palisades and watch Linda Deverson and Carol March make love. Dressed in black, he would scale a shadow-shrouded telephone pole and peer down through the upstairs bedroom window as the woman coupled on a quilt-covered waterbed. At about midnight, when his arms were weary from hours of hugging the rough wood of the phone pole, he would watch the sated Linda get up from the bed and dress as Carol importuned her to spend the night. It was always the same; his brain, willfully shut off as he viewed the lovemaking, would snap to life with speculation as Linda took her leave. Why was Linda leaving? Was buried guilt coming to the surface? Regret at the way she had debased herself?

He would then jump down from the pole and run for his car, pulling up without lights behind Linda's Camaro just as she walked out the door. Then he would follow the glow of her taillights as she drove home via the most scenic route possible, almost as if she needed an injection of beauty after her night of debauchery. Keeping a safe distance behind, he would let her part at the intersection of Sunset and the Pacific Coast Highway, wondering how and when he could bring her salvation.

After two more weeks of extensive surveillance, he wrote in his diary:

6–7–82

Linda Deverson is a tragic victim of these times. Her sensuality is self-destructive, but indicative of stong parental need. The March woman capitalizes on this; she is a viper. Linda remains unsatisfied in both her sensuality and search for a mother (the March woman is at least fifteen years her senior!). Her midnight excursions through the most soulful parts of Pacific Palisades and Santa Monica speak volumes on her guilt and subtle searching nature. Her need for beauty is *so* strong in the aftermath of her self destruction. I must take her at this moment — that must be the precise time of her salvation.

Emboldened by knowledge of the place, he put the time out of his mind, losing himself in his courtship. But the late nights were taking their toll in little portents of slippage in his work life — rolls of film clumsily shot, then stupidly exposed to sunlight; appointments forgotten, photo orders misplaced. The slippage had to stop, and he knew how to do it. He had to consummate his courtship of Linda Deverson.

He set the date: Tuesday, June 14th, three days hence. His tremors of expectation began to grow.

On Monday, June 13th, he went to an auto supply store in the Valley and bought a case of motor oil, then drove to a junkyard and told the owner he was looking for chrome hood ornaments. While the owner scurried about looking for them, he scraped up several huge handfuls of iron filings from the ground and loaded them into a paper bag. The junkman came running back a few minutes later, waving a chrome bulldog. Feeling generous, he offered the man ten dollars for it. The man accepted. Driving back over the Cahuenga Pass to his shop, he threw the bulldog out the window and laughed as it clattered over to the edge of the roadway.

His consummation day was carefully planned and honed down to the second. Upon rising he placed the "Closed Due To Illness" sign in the window, then returned to his apartment, where he played his meditation tape and stared at the photos of Linda Deverson. Next he destroyed the pages in his diary that pertained to her and took a long walk through the neighborhood, all the way over to Echo Park, where he spent hours rowing around the lake and feeding the ducks. At nightfall he packed his consummation tools into the trunk of his car and drove to his first and last rendezvous with his beloved.

At 8:45 he was parked four doors down from Carol March's house, alternately shifting his gaze from the darkened street to his dashboard clock. At 9:03 Linda

Deverson pulled into the driveway. He swooned at the perfection of it; she was right on time.

He drove to Santa Monica Canyon, to the intersection of West Channel Road and Biscayne, where West Channel bisected and the right fork led into a small campground filled with picnic tables and swings. If his calculations were correct, Linda would be driving through at precisely ten minutes of midnight. He pulled his car off to the side of the road on the edge of the park proper, where it was shielded from street view by a row of sycamore trees. Then he went for a long walk.

He returned at 11:40 and got his equipment out of the trunk, first donning his park ranger's outfit of Smoky The Bear hat, green wool shirt and field belt, then assembling his sawhorse detour signs and carrying them over to the intersection.

Next he hauled his five gallon can of motor oil and iron filings to the middle of the street and poured them smoothly over the pavement, until the blacktop just before the detour signs was a slippery purple ooze glinting with sharp steel. Then all he could do was wait.

At 11:52 he heard her car approaching. As her headlights appeared, his body shuddered and he had to will himself to contain his bowels and bladder.

The car slowed as it neared the detour signs, braking and going into a right turn, then fishtailing and sliding into the saw horses as it hit the pool of oil. There was a crash of wood on metal, then two loud ka-plops! as the rear tires blew out. The car came to a stop and Linda got out, slamming the door and muttering, "Oh shit, oh fuck," then going around to the back of the car to examine the damage.

Steeling himself with all the courtliness he could muster, he walked from the trees and called out, "Are you okay, miss? That was a nasty slide you took."

Linda called back, "Yes, I'm okay. But my car!"

He pulled a flashlight from his field belt and shined it

into the darkness, arcing it over the campground several times before letting the beam rest on his beloved. Linda blinked against the glare, raising a hand to shield her face. He walked toward her, pointing his light at the ground.

She smiled as she noticed his hat — Smoky The Bear to the rescue; it was good that she had smoked her last cigarette at Carol's. "Oh God, I'm glad you're here," she said. "I saw that detour sign and then skidded on something. I think two of my tires blew out."

"That's no problem," he said. "my service shack is right over here; we'll call an all-night gas station."

"Oh God, what a pain in the ass," Linda said, fumbling in gratitude for the arm of her savior. "You don't know how glad I am to see you."

He faltered at her touch; joy consumed him and he said, "I've loved you for so long. Since we were kids. Since all tho..."

Linda gasped. "What the he..." she said. "Who the he..."

She started to back away, then tripped and fell to the ground. He reached out a hand to help her up. She hesitated. "No, please," she whimpered, moving backwards. He fumbled at his field belt and unclipped a two edged fire axe. He bent down again, grabbing Linda at the wrist and yanking her up just as he brought the axe down in a high, rail-splitting swing. Linda's skull crashed inward as his love went into slow motion and blood and brain fragments burst into the air, suspending the moment into a thousand eternities. He brought the axe down again and again until he was drenched in blood and blood had splattered onto his face and into his mouth and through his brain and his entire soul was a bright lover's red; the bright red of flowers he would send his true love tomorrow. For you, for you, all for you, the poet muttered as he left the remains of Linda Deverson and walked to his car; my soul, my life for you.

CHAPTER FOUR

Detective Sergeant Lloyd Hopkins celebrated the
seventeenth anniversary of his appointment to the Los
Angeles Police Department in his usual manner, grabbing
a computer print-out of recent crimes and field
interrogation reports filed by Rampart Division, then
driving to the old neighborhood to breathe past and
present from the vantage point of seventeen years of
protecting innocence.

The October day was smoggy and just short of hot.
Lloyd got his unmarked Matador from the lot at Parker
Center and drove westbound on Sunset, reminiscing: over
a decade and a half and the fulfillment of his major dreams
—the job, the wife, and the three wonderful daughters.
The job thrilling and sad in excess of fulfillment; the
marriage strong in the sense of the strong people he and
Janice had become; the daughters pure joy and reason for
living in themselves. The exultant feelings were the only
thing lacking, and in the magnanimity of nostalgia Lloyd
chalked up their absence to maturity—he was forty now,
not twenty-three; if his seventeen years as a policeman had
taught him anything, it was that your expectations
diminished as you realized how thoroughly fucked-up the
bulk of humanity was, and that you had to go on a
hundred seemingly contradictory discourses to keep the
major dreams alive.

That the discourses were always women and in direct
violation of his Presbyterian marriage vows was the
ultimate irony, he thought, stopping for the light at Sunset
and Echo Park and rolling up the windows to keep the

street noise out. An irony that staunch, strong Janice would never understand. Feeling that his reverie was recklessly overstepping its bounds, Lloyd plunged ahead, anxious to voice it flat out, to himself and the vacant air around him: "It wouldn't work between us, Janice, if I couldn't cut loose like that. Little things would accumulate and I'd explode. And you'd hate me. The girls would hate me. That's why I do it. That's why I...." Lloyd couldn't bring himself to say the word "cheat."

He stopped his musings and pulled into the parking lot of a liquor store, then dug the computer sheets out of his pocket and settled in to think.

The sheets were pale pink with black typescript, edged with seemingly random perforations. Lloyd fingered through them, arranging them in chronological order, starting with the ones dated 9-15-82. Beginning with the crime reports, he let his perfectly controlled blank mind drift through brief accounts of rapes, robberies, purse snatchings, shopliftings, and vandalism. Suspect descriptions and weaponry from shotguns to baseball bats were recounted in crisp, heavily abbreviated sentences. Lloyd read through the crime reports three times, feeling the disparate facts and figures sink in deeper with each reading, blessing Evelyn Wood and her method that allowed him to gobble up the printed word at the rate of three thousand per minute.

Next he turned to the field interrogation reports. These were accounts of people stopped on the street, briefly detained and questioned, then released. Lloyd read through the F.I.s four times, *knowing* with each reading that there was a connection to be made. He was about to give each stack of print-outs another go round when he snapped to the buried ellipsis that was crying out to him. Furiously shuffling through the pink rolls of paper, he found his match-up: Crime Report #10691, 10-6-82. Armed robbery.

At approximately 11:30 p.m., Thursday, October 6, the Black Cat Bar on Sunset and Vendome was held up by two male Mexicans. They were of undetermined age, but presumed young. They wore silk stockings to disguise their appearances, carried "large" revolvers, and ransacked the cash register before making the proprietor lock up the bar. They then forced the patrons to lie on the floor. While prone, the robbers relieved them of wallets, billfolds and jewelry. They fled a moment later, warning their victims that the "back-up" would be outside with a shotgun for twenty minutes. They slashed the two phone lines before they left. The bartender ran outside five minutes later. There was no back-up.

Stupid fools, Lloyd thought, risking half a dime minimum for a thousand dollars tops. He read over the F.I. report, filed by a Rampart patrolman: 10-7-82, 1:05 a.m. — "Questioned two w.m. outside res. at 2269 Tracy. They were drinking vodka and sitting on top of late model Firebird, Lic. #HBS 027. Explained that car was not theirs, but that they lived in house. Partner and I searched them — clean. Got hot call before we could run warrant check." The officer's name was printed below.

Lloyd kicked the last bits of information around in his head, thinking it sad that he should have greater intimate knowledge of a neighborhood than the cops who patrolled it. 2269 Tracy Street was a low-life holdover from his high school days over twenty years before, when it had been a halfway house for ex-cons. The charismatic ex-gangster who had run the operation on State funds had embezzled a bundle from local Welfare agencies before selling the house to an old buddy from Folsom, then hightailing it to the border, never to be seen again. The buddy promptly hired a good lawyer to help him keep the house. He won his court battle and dealt quality dope out of the old wood-framed dwelling. Lloyd recalled how his high school pals had bought reefers there back in the late 50s. He knew that the house had been sold to a succession of local hoods and had acquired the neighborhood nickname of "Gangster Manor."

Lloyd drove to the Black Cat Bar. The bartender immediately made him for a cop. "Yes, officer?" he said. "No complaints, I hope."

"None," Lloyd said. "I'm here about the robbery of October 6th. Were you tending bar that night?"

"Yeah, I was here. You got any leads? Two detectives came in the next day, but that was it."

"No real leads yet. Do. . . ."

Lloyd was distracted by the sound of the jukebox snapping on, beginning to spill out a disco tune. "Turn that off, will you?" he said. "I can't compete with an orchestra."

The barman laughed. "That's no orchestra, that's 'The Disco Doggies.' Don't you like them?"

Lloyd couldn't tell if the man was being pleasant or trying to vamp him; homosexuals were hard to read. "Maybe I'm behind the times. Just turn it off, okay? Do it now."

The bartender caught the edge in Lloyd's voice and complied, creating a small commotion as he yanked the cord on the jukebox. Returning to the bar he said warily, "Just what was it you wanted to know?"

Relieved by the music's termination, Lloyd said, "Only one thing. Are you certain the two robbers were Mexican?"

"No, I'm not certain."

"Didn't you. . . ."

"They wore masks, officer. What I told the cops is that they talked English with Mexican accents. That's what I said."

"Thank you," Lloyd said, and ran out to his car.

He drove straight to 2269 Tracy Street — Gangster Manor. As he expected, the old house was deserted. Cobwebs, dust, and used condoms covered the warped wood floor, and sets of footprints that Lloyd knew had to be recent were clearly outlined. He followed them into the kitchen. All the fixtures were ripped out and the floor was covered with rodent droppings. Lloyd opened cabinets and drawers, finding only dust, spider webs, and mildewed, maggot-infested groceries. Then he opened a floral patterned bread basket and jumped into the air, dunking imaginary baskets and whooping when he saw what he found: a brand new box of Remington hollow point .38 shells and two pair of Sheer Energy pantyhose. Lloyd whooped again. "Thank you, o' nesting grounds of my youth!" he shouted.

Phone calls to the California Department of Motor Vehicles and L.A.P.D. Records and Information confirmed his thesis. A 1979 Pontiac Firebird, license number HBS 027 was registered to Richard Douglas Wilson of 11879 Saticoy Street, Van Nuys. R. & I. supplied the rest: Richard Douglas Wilson, white male, age thirty-four was a two-time convicted armed robber who had recently been paroled from San Quentin after serving three and a half years of a five year sentence.

Heart bursting, and snug in his soundless phone booth, Lloyd dialed a third number, the home of his one-time mentor and current follower, Captain Arthur Peltz.

"Dutch? Lloyd. What are you doing?"

Peltz yawned into the mouthpiece, "I'm taking a nap, Lloyd. I'm off today. I'm an old man and I need a siesta in the afternoon. What's up? You sound jazzed."

Lloyd laughed. "I am jazzed. You want to take a couple of armed robbers?"

"All by ourselves?"

"Yeah. What's the matter? We've done it a million times."

"At least a million — more like a million and a half. Stake out?"

"Yeah, at the guy's pad in Van Nuys. Van Nuys Station in an hour?"

"I'll be there. You realize that if this thing is a washout, you're buying me dinner?"

"Anywhere you want," Lloyd said, and hung up the phone.

Arthur Peltz was the first Los Angeles policeman to recognize and herald Lloyd Hopkins's genius. It happened when Lloyd was a twenty-seven year old patrolman working Central Division. The year was 1969, and the hippie era of love and good vibes had dwindled out, leaving a backwash of indigent, drug-addicted youngsters floating through the poorer sections of Los Angeles, begging for spare change, shoplifting, sleeping in parks, back yards and doorways and generally contributing to a drastic rise in misdemeanor arrests and felony arrests for possession of narcotics.

Fear of hippie nomads was rife among solid citizen Angelenos, particularly after the Tate-LaBianca slayings were attributed to Charles Manson and his hirsute band. The L.A.P.D. was importuned to come down hard on the destitute minstrels of love; which it did — raiding hippie campgrounds, frequently stopping vehicles containing furtive-looking longhairs and generally letting them know that they were *personae non gratas* in Los Angeles. The results were satisfying — there was a general hippie move toward eschewing outdoor living and "cooling it." Then five longhaired young men were shot to death on the streets in Hollywood over a period of three weeks.

Sergeant Arthur "Dutch" Peltz, then a forty-one year old Homicide detective, was assigned to the case. He had very little to work on, except a strong instinct that the murders of the unacquainted young men were drug related and that the so-called "ritual markings" on their bodies — an xed out letter H — were put there as subterfuge.

Investigation into the recent pasts of the victims proved fruitless; they were transients existing in a subculture of transients. Dutch Peltz was baffled. He was also an intellectual given to contemplative pursuits, so he decided to take his two-week vacation smack in the middle of his case. He came back from fishing in Oregon clearheaded, spiritually renewed, and pleased to find that there were no new victims of the "Hippie Hunter," as the press had dubbed him. But dire things were happening in Los Angeles. The basin had been flooded with a particularly high-quality Mexican brown heroin, its source unknown. Instinct told Dutch Peltz that the heroin onslaught and the murders were connected. But he didn't have the slightest idea how.

On a cold night around this time, Officer Lloyd Hopkins told his partner he was hungry for sweets, and suggested they stop at a market or liquor store for cookies or cupcakes. His partner shook his head; nothing open this late except Donut Despair, he said. Lloyd weighed the pros and cons of a raging sweet-tooth versus the world's worst donuts served up by either sullen or obsequious wetbacks.

His sweet-tooth won, but there were no wetbacks. Lloyd's jaw dropped as he took a seat at the counter. Donut Despair (or Donut Deelite, open all nite!), as it was known to the world at large, hired nothing but illegal aliens at *all* its locations. It was the policy of the chain's owner, Morris Dreyfus, a former gangland czar, to employ illegals and pay them below the minimum wage, but make up the difference by providing them with flop-out space at his many Southside tenements. Now this!

Lloyd watched as a sullen hippie youth placed a cup of coffee and three glazed donuts in front of him, then retreated to a back room, leaving the counter untended. He then heard furtive whispers, followed by the slamming of a back door and the starting of a car engine. The hippie counterman reappeared a moment later and couldn't meet Lloyd's eyes; and Lloyd knew it was more than his blue uniform. He knew something was *wrong*.

The following day, armed with a copy of the Los Angeles Yellow Pages, Lloyd, in civilian clothes, made a circuit of over twenty Donut Despairs, to find the counters manned by longhaired white men at all locations. Twice he sat down and ordered coffee, letting the counterman see — as if by accident — his off-duty .38. In both instances the reaction was cold, stark terror.

Dope, Lloyd said to himself as he drove home that night. Dope. Dope. But. But any streetwise fool would know that anyone as big as I am, with my short haircut and square look is a cop. Those two kids made me for one the second I walked in the door. But it was my *gun* that scared them.

It was then that Lloyd thought of the Hippie Hunter and the seemingly unrelated heroin influx. When he got home he called Hollywood Station, gave his name and badge number and asked to talk to a Homicide dick.

Dutch Peltz was more impressed with the huge young cop himself than he was with the fact that they had been thinking along almost identical lines. Now he had a hypothesis — that Big Mo Dreyfus was pushing smack out of his donut stands, and that somehow people were getting killed because of it. But it was young Hopkins himself, so undeniably infused with a brilliance of instinct for the darkness in life, that had him awestruck.

Peltz listened for hours as Lloyd told of his desire to protect innocence and how he had trained his mind to pick out conversations in crowded restaurants and how he could read lips and memorize with time and place any face that he glimpsed for only a second. When he went home, Dutch Peltz said to his wife, "I met a genius tonight. I don't think I'll ever be the same."

It was a prophetic remark.

The following day Peltz began an investigation into the financial dealings of Morris Dreyfus. He learned that Dreyfus had been converting his stocks and bonds into

65

cash and that he was contacting former gangland associates with offers to sell the Donut Deelite chain dirt cheap. Further investigation showed that Dreyfus had recently applied for a passport and had sold his homes in Palm Springs and Lake Arrowhead.

Peltz began a surveillance of Dreyfus, watching him make steady rounds of his donut stands, where he would motion the longhaired counterman into the back room and depart a moment later. That night Peltz and a veteran narcotics detective tailed Dreyfus to the Benedict Canyon home of Reyes Medina, a Mexican reputed to be the liaison between poppy-growing combines in southern Mexico and scores of heavyweight stateside heroin dealers. Dreyfus was inside for two hours, and left looking distraught.

The following morning, Peltz drove to the Donut Deelite on 43rd and Normandie. He parked across the street and waited until the stand was empty of customers, then walked in and flashed his badge at the youth behind the counter, telling him he wanted information, and not on donut recipes. The youth tried running out the back way, but Peltz wrestled him to the floor, whispering, "Where's the smack? Where's the shit, you hippie fuck?" until the youth began to blubber out the story that he expected.

Mo Dreyfus was pushing Mexican brown heroin to medium-level local dealers, who were turning it over for a huge profit. What Peltz didn't expect was the news that Dreyfus was dying of cancer and was accruing capital to take exorbitantly expensive treatments by a Brazillian doctor-medicine man. The word had come down that all drug sales out of all Donut Deelite locations were to stop the following week, when the new owner took over. Big Mo would be on his way to Brazil by then, and all the countermen-pushers would be contacted by a "rich Mexican" who would give them their "going away" bonuses.

After uncovering three ounces of heroin underneath a

meat locker, Peltz handcuffed the youth and took him downtown to the central jail, where he was booked as a material witness. Peltz then took the elevator to the eighth floor offices of the L.A.P.D.'s Narcotics Division.

Two hours later, after obtaining search and arrest warrants, four shotgun-wielding detectives burst into the home of Morris Dreyfus and arrested him for possession of heroin, possession with intent to sell, sales of dangerous drugs and criminal conspiracy. In his jail cell, against his attorney's advice, Morris Dreyfus made the connection that convinced Dutch Peltz beyond *any* doubt of Lloyd Hopkins's genius: In hushed tones, Dreyfus told how a "death squad" of militant illegal aliens was behind the killing of the five hippies and how they were now demanding $250,000 from him for firing his immigrant work force *en masse*. The hippies were killed as a terror tactic; their random selection a ruse to keep attention from being focused on the Donut Deelite chain.

The following morning a dozen black and whites cordoned off both sides of the 1100 block of Wabash Street in East Los Angeles. Flak-jacketed officers surrounded the building that housed the death squad. Armed with fully automatic AK-47s, they broke through the front door, firing warning bursts above the heads of four men and three women quietly eating breakfast. The seven stoically submitted to handcuffing and a search team was deployed to check the rest of the house. A total of eleven illegal aliens was arrested. After a gruelling series of interrogations, three men admitted to the Hollywood killings. They were indicted on five counts of first-degree murder and ultimately received life sentences.

The day after the confessions were secured, Dutch Peltz went looking for Lloyd Hopkins. He found him going off duty in the parking lot at Central Division. Unlocking his car, Lloyd felt a tap on his shoulder. He turned around and found Peltz shuffling his feet nervously, gazing up at him with a look that he could only think of as pure love.

"Thanks, kid," the older cop said. "You've made me. I was going to tell——"

"No one would believe you," Lloyd interrupted. "Let it go down the way it is."

"Don't you want——"

"You did the work, Sergeant. I just supplied the theory."

Peltz laughed until Lloyd thought he would keel over of a heart attack. As his laughter subsided, Peltz regained his breath and said, "Who are you?"

Lloyd flicked the antenna of his car and said softly, "I don't know. I Jesus fucking Christ don't know."

"I can teach you things," Dutch Peltz said. "I've been a Homicide dick for eleven years. I can give you a lot of solid, practical information, the benefit of a lot of experience."

"What do you want from me?" Lloyd asked.

Peltz took a moment to consider the question. "I think I just want to know you," he said.

The two men stared at each other in silence. Then Lloyd slowly extended his hand, sealing their fates.

It was Lloyd who was the teacher; almost from the start. Dutch would provide knowledge and experience in the form of anecdotes and Lloyd would find the hidden human truth and hold it up for magnification. Hundreds of hours were spent talking, rehashing old crimes and discussing topics as diverse as women's clothing and how it reflected character to dog-walking burglars who used their pets as subterfuge. The men discovered safe harbors in each other—Lloyd knew that he had found the one cop who would never look at him strangely when he retreated at the sound of a radio or begrudge him when he insisted on doing it *his* way; Dutch knew that he had found the supreme police intellect. When Lloyd passed the Sergeant's exam, it was Dutch who pulled strings to get him assigned to the Detective Division, calling in a career's worth of unreturned favors.

It was then that Lloyd Hopkins was able to manifest his intellect and produce astounding results — the greatest number of felony arrests and convictions of any Los Angeles police officer in the history of the department, all within a period of five years. Lloyd's reputation grew to the point where he asked for and was granted almost complete autonomy, deferred to by even the most sternminded, traditionalist cops. And Dutch Peltz proudly watched it happen, content to play in the august light of genius provided by a man he loved more than his own life.

Lloyd found Dutch Peltz in the muster room at Van Nuys Station, pacing the walls and reading the crime reports tacked to the bulletin boards. He cleared his throat and the older cop wheeled and threw up his hands in mock surrender.

"Jesus, Lloyd," he said, "when in God's name will you learn not to tread so softly among friends? A kodiak bear with the tread of a cat. Jesus!"

Lloyd laughed at the expression of love; it made him happy. "You look good, Dutch. Working a desk and losing weight! A fucking miracle."

Dutch gave Lloyd a warm, two-handed handshake. "It's no miracle, kid. I quit smoking and lost weight too. What have we got?"

"A gunsel. Works with a partner. He's got a pad on Saticoy. I figured we'd drive over and check if his car is around. If he's at home, we'll call for a couple of back-ups units, if he's gone, we'll wait him out and take him ourselves. You like it?"

"I like it. I brought my Ithaca pump. What's the joker's name?"

"Richard Douglas Wilson, white male, age thirty-four. Two-time loser with a Quentin jacket."

"Sounds like a charming fellow."

"Yeah, a Renaissance low lifer."

"You'll tell me about it in the car?"

"Yeah, let's go."

Richard Douglas Wilson was not at home. Having checked every street space, driveway and parking lot on the 11800 block of Saticoy Street for a '79 Firebird, Lloyd made a circuit of number 11879; a rundown, two-story apartment house. The mailbox designated Wilson as living in Number 14. Lloyd found the apartment at the rear of the building. A screen-covered, sliding glass window was wide open. He looked inside, then walked back to Dutch, who was parked across the street in the shadow of a freeway off-ramp.

"No car, no Wilson, Dutch," Lloyd said. "I looked in his window—brand new stereo, new TV, new clothes, *new money*."

Dutch laughed. "You happy, Lloyd?"

"Yeah, I am. Are you?"

"If you are, kid."

The two policemen settled in to wait. Dutch had brought a thermos of coffee, and when twilight stifled the heat and smog, he poured two cups. Handing one to Lloyd, he broke the long, comfortable silence. "I ran into Janice the other day. I had to testify for an old snitch of mine in Santa Monica. He took a fall for a burglary one, so I went down to rap sadness to the D.A. about how the poor bastard was strung out and would he talk to the judge about diverting him to a drug program. Anyway, I stop at a coffee shop, and there's Janice. She's got this fag with her, he's showing her fabrics out of this binder, really giving her the hard sell. Anyway, the fag sashays off and Janice invites me to sit down. We talk. She says the shop is doing well, it's acquiring a reputation, the girls are fine. She says that you spend too much time working, but that it's an old complaint and she can't change you. She looks

70

sort of disgusted, so I come to your aid. I say, 'Genius writes its own rules, sweetie. Lloyd loves you. Lloyd will change in time.' Janice screams at me, 'Lloyd is incapable of it, and his fucking love isn't enough!' That was it, Lloyd. She wouldn't talk about it any more. I tried to change the subject, but Janice keeps taking these cryptic little digs at you. Finally, she jumps up and kisses me on the cheek and says, 'I'm sorry, Dutch. I'm just being a bitch,' and runs out the door."

Dutch's voice trailed off as he searched for words to end his story. "I just thought I'd tell you," he said. "I don't believe partners should keep secrets from each other."

Lloyd sipped his coffee, his mind quietly turbulent, as it always was when he felt cracks appearing in his major dreams. "So what's the upshot, partner?" he asked.

"The upshot?"

"The riddle, you dumb fucking krauthead! The undercurrents! Haven't I taught you better than that? What was Janice *really* trying to tell you?"

Dutch swallowed his crushed pride and spat it out angrily. "I think she's wise to your womanizing, brainboy. I think she knows that the finest of L.A.'s finest is chasing cunt and shacking up with a bunch of sleazy bimbos who can't hold the remotest candle to the woman he married. That's what I think."

Lloyd went calm beneath his anger, and the cracks in his major dreams became fissures. He shook his head slowly, searching for mortar to fill them up. "You're wrong," he said, giving Dutch's shoulder a gentle squeeze. "I think Janice would let *me* know. And Dutch? The other women in my life aren't bimbos."

"Then what are they?"

"Just women. And I love them."

"You *love* them?"

Lloyd knew as he said the words that it was one of the proudest moments of his life. "Yes. I love all the women I

I sleep with, and I love my daughters and I love my wife."

After four hours of silent surveillance, Dutch had dozed off in the driver's seat, his head cradled into the half-opened front window. Lloyd remained alert, sipping coffee and keeping his eyes glued to the driveway of 11879 Saticoy Street. It was shortly after ten o'clock when he saw a late-model Firebird pull up in front of the building.

He nudged Dutch awake, placing a hand over his mouth. "Our friend is here, Dutch. He just pulled up, and he's still in the car. I think we should get out on my side and walk around and take him from the rear."

Dutch nodded and handed Lloyd his shotgun. Lloyd squeezed through the passenger door onto the sidewalk, keeping the shotgun pressed into his right leg. Dutch followed suit, slamming the door and throwing an arm around Lloyd, exclaiming, "God, am I smashed!" He went into an adept imitation of a weaving drunk, leaning against Lloyd and talking gibberish.

Lloyd kept his eyes on the black Firebird, waiting for the doors to open, wondering why Wilson was still inside. When they got to the end of the block, he handed Dutch the Ithaca pump and said, "You take the driver, I'll take the passenger." Dutch nodded and jacked a shell into the chamber. Lloyd whispered, "Now," and the men hunkered down and ran up behind the car, swooping down on it from opposite sides, Dutch jamming his shotgun into the driver's side window, whispering, "Police, don't move or you're dead"; Lloyd resting his .38 on the door jamb and saying to the woman passenger, "Freeze, sweetheart. Put your hands on the dashboard. We want your boyfriend, not you."

The woman stifled a scream and slowly complied with Lloyd's orders. The driver started to jabber, "Look man, you got this wrong, I ain't done nothin!"

Dutch tightened his finger on the trigger and rested the

barrel on the man's nose and said, "Put your hands behind your head. I'm gonna open this car door real slow. You get out *real* slow or you're gonna be *real* dead."

The man nodded and wrapped shaky hands around his neck. Dutch pulled the shotgun back and started to open the car door. As his hand hit the latch, the man kicked out with both legs. The door swung into Dutch's midsection, knocking him backwards, the shotgun exploding into the air as his finger reflexively yanked the trigger. The man jumped out of the car and stumbled into the street, then got up and started to run.

Lloyd relinquished his bead on the woman and fired a warning shot into the air, yelling, "Halt, halt!"

Dutch got to his feet and fired blindly. Lloyd saw the running figure starting to weave in anticipation of further volleys. He watched the rhythm of the man's swaying, then fired three times at shoulder level. The man buckled and fell to the pavement. Before Lloyd could approach cautiously, Dutch had run up and was slamming the man in the ribs with the butt of his shotgun. Lloyd ran over and pulled Dutch off, then cuffed the suspect's hands behind his back.

The man had been hit twice just below the collarbone. Clean, Lloyd noticed; two crisp exit wounds. He pulled the man roughly to his feet and said to Dutch, "Ambulance, back-up units." Looking around at the crowd that was starting to form on both sides of the street, he added: "And tell those people to back off onto the sidewalk."

Lloyd turned his attention to the suspect. "Richard Douglas Wilson, right?"

"I don't gotta tell you nothin'," the man answered.

"That's right, you don't. Okay, let's take care of the legalities. You have the right to remain silent. You have the right to have legal counsel present during questioning. If you cannot afford counsel, an attorney will be provided. You got anything to say, Wilson?"

"Yeah," the man said, twisting his wounded shoulder, "I say fuck your mother."

"A predictable response. Can't you guys come up with something original like 'Fuck your father'?"

"Fuck you, flatfoot."

"That's better; you're learning."

Dutch ran back over. "Ambulance and back-up are on their way."

"Good. Where's the girl?"

"She's still in the car."

"Good. Look after Mr. Wilson, will you? I want to talk to her."

Lloyd walked to the black Firebird. The young woman sat rigid in the passenger seat, her hands still clamped to the dashboard. She was crying, and her mascara had run all the way down to her chin. Lloyd knelt by the open door and placed a gentle hand on her shoulder. "Miss?"

The woman turned to face him, starting to weep openly. "I don't want to have a record!" she bawled. "I just met the guy. I'm not a bad person, I just wanted to get stoned and listen to some music!"

Lloyd smoothed an errant lock of her blonde hair. "What's your name?" he asked.

"Sarah."

"Sarah Bernhardt?"

"No."

"Sarah Vaughan?"

"No."

"Sarah Coventry?"

The woman laughed and wiped her sleeve across her face. "Sarah Smith," she said.

Lloyd took her hand. "Good. My name's Lloyd. Where do you live, Sarah?"

"In West L.A."

"I'll tell you what. You go over and wait in that crowd of

74

people. I've got a few things to do here, then I'll drive you home. Okay?"

"Okay...and I won't have a record?"

"No one will ever even know that you were here. Okay?"

"Okay."

Lloyd watched Sarah Smith compose herself and move into the crowd of rubberneckers on the sidewalk. He walked over to Dutch and Richard Douglas Wilson, who were leaning against the unmarked Matador. Lloyd motioned Dutch to leave, and as he departed, fixed Wilson with a hard look and disgusted shake of the head.

"No honor among thieves, Richard," he said. "None at all. Especially the punks over at Gangster Manor." Wilson's jaw trembled at the last words, and Lloyd continued. "I found a box of shells and a pantyhose wrapper there with your prints on them. But that wasn't how we nailed you. Somebody snitched you off. Somebody sent the Rampart dicks an anonymous letter making you for the Black Cat stick-up. The letter said you only knocked off fruit bars because you got turned out by some bad-ass jockers at Quentin, and you liked it. You love queers and you hate them too, because of what they made you."

"That's a fucking lie!" Wilson screamed. "I took down liquor stores, markets, even a fucking disco! I done — "

Lloyd cut him off with a chopped hand gesture and went in for the kill. "The letter said that you were drinking outside Gangster Manor after the heist, and you were bragging about all the cunt you scored. Your buddy said he was cracking up because he knew you liked to take it up the ass."

Richard Douglas Wilson's pale, sweat-streaked face went purple. He shrieked, "That scumbag motherfucker! I *saved* his ass from getting porked by every nigger on the yard! I carried that punk through Quentin, now he — "

Lloyd put a hand on Wilson's shoulder and said quietly, "Richard, you're looking at a dime *minimum* this time. Ten bullets. You think you can handle that? You're tough, you're a stand-up guy; I know that. I'm tough too. But you know what? I couldn't do a dime up there. They got niggers up there who'd eat me for breakfast. Turn your partner over, Richard. He snitched you off. I'll go..." Wilson was shaking his head frantically in denial. Lloyd started to shake his head in pure loathing. "You dumb asshole," he said. "Go by the old code, let some piece of shit rat on you, facing five to life and you look a gift horse in the mouth. You dumb motherfucker." He turned and started to walk away.

He had gotten only a few feet when Wilson called out, "Wait. Wait. Look——"

Lloyd stifled the huge grin that was lighting up his face and said, "I'll go to the D.A., I'll talk to the judge, I'll see to it that you go to the protective custody tank while you're waiting for your trial."

Richard Douglas Wilson weighed the pros and cons a last time, then capitulated. "His name is John Gustodas. 'Johnny The Greek.' He lives in Hollywood. Franklin and Argylle. The red brick building on the corner."

Lloyd squeezed Wilson's undamaged shoulder. "Good fellow. My partner will take down your statement at the hospital, and I'll be in touch." He craned his head to look for Dutch, and spotted him on the sidewalk talking to two uniformed officers. He whistled twice, and Dutch walked over, warily. "You tired, Dutchman?" Lloyd asked.

"A little. Why?"

"Wilson confessed. He snitched off his partner. The guy lives in Hollywood. I want to go home. You want to take down Wilson's statement, then call Hollywood dicks and give them the info on the guy?"

Dutch hesitated. "Sure, Lloyd," he said.

"Great. John 'Johnny The Greek' Gustodas. Franklin

and Argylle. Red brick apartment house on the corner. I'll write up *all* the reports, don't worry about that."

Lloyd heard the wail of an ambulance siren, and shook his head to combat the noise. "Fucking sirens ought to be outlawed," he said as the ambulance rounded the corner and ground to a halt. "There's your chariot. I gotta get out of here. I promised to take Janice out to dinner at eight. It's almost eleven now." The two policemen shook hands. "We did it again, partner," Lloyd said.

"Yeah. I'm sorry I barked at you, kid."

"You're on Janice's side. I don't blame you; she's better looking than I am."

Dutch laughed. "Talk to you tomorrow about Wilson's statement?"

"Right. I'll call you."

Lloyd found Sarah Smith with the remnants of the spectators, smoking a cigarette and shuffling her feet nervously on the pavement. "Hi, Sarah. How are you feeling?"

Sarah ground out the cigarette. "All right, I guess. What's going to happen to what's-his-name?"

Lloyd smiled at the sadness of the question. "He's going to prison for a long time. Don't you even remember his name?"

"I'm bad at names."

"Do you remember mine?"

"Floyd?"

"Close. Lloyd. Come on, I'll take you home."

They walked over to the unmarked Matador and got in. Lloyd scrutinized Sarah openly as she gave her address and fiddled with the contents of her purse. A good girl from a good family gone slightly loose, he decided. Twenty-eight or nine, the light blonde hair legit, the body beneath the black cotton pantsuit both slender and soft. A kind face trying to look tough. Probably a hard worker at her job.

Lloyd headed straight for the nearest westbound on-ramp, alternately savoring his anniversary triumph and picturing confrontations with Janice, who would doubtless give him one of her incredible slow burns—if not an outright battle for being so late. Feeling kindness well up in him for sparing Sarah Smith the harshness of the law, he tapped her shoulder and said, "It's going to be all right, you know."

Sarah dug into her purse looking for cigarettes and found only an empty pack. She muttered, "Shit" and threw it out the window, then sighed. "Yeah, maybe you're right. You really get off on being a cop, don't you?"

"It's my life. Where did you meet Wilson?"

"Is that his name? I met him at a country-western bar. Shit-kicker's paradise, but at least they treat women with respect. What did he do?"

"Held up a bar at gunpoint."

"Jesus! I figured he was just some kind of dope dealer."

Out of the mouths of babes, Lloyd thought. "I'm not lecturing you or anything like that," he said, "but you shouldn't hang out in dives. You could get hurt."

Sarah snorted. "Then where should I go to meet people?"

"You mean men?"

"Well...yeah."

"Try the continental approach. Drink coffee and read a book at some picturesque sidewalk café. Sooner or later some nice fellow will start a conversation with you about the book you're reading. You'll meet higher class people that way."

Sarah laughed wildly and clapped her hands, then poked Lloyd in the arm. When he took his eyes from the road and gave her a deadpan, her laughter became hysterical. "That's funny, that's so funny!" she squealed.

"It's not *that* funny."

"Yes, it is! You should be on TV!" Sarah's laughter

subsided. She looked at Lloyd quizzically. "Is that how you met your wife?"

"I didn't tell you I was married."

"I saw your ring."

"Very observant. But I met my wife in high school." Sarah Smith laughed until she ached. Lloyd laughed along in a more sedate cadence, then dug in his pocket for a handkerchief and reached over and dabbed at Sarah's tear-mottled face. She leaned into his hand, rubbing her nose along his knuckles.

"You ever wonder why you keep on doing things even when you know they don't work?" she asked.

Lloyd ran a finger under her chin and tilted her head upwards to face him. "It's because outside of the major dreams everything is always changing, and even though you keep doing the same things, you're looking for new answers."

"I believe that," Sarah said. "Get off at the next exit and turn right."

Five minutes later he pulled to the curb in front of an apartment building on Barrington. Sarah poked him in the arm and said, "Thanks."

"Good luck, Sarah. Try the book trick."

"Maybe I will. Thanks."

"Thank you."

"For what?"

"I don't know."

Sarah poked Lloyd's arm a last time and darted out of the car.

Janice Hopkins looked at the antique clock in her living room and felt her fearful slow burn leap ahead as the hour hand struck ten and she realized that this was her husband's "second major anniversary" and that she could not rationally fight with him over their missed dinner date, could not use that minor grievance to force confrontations on any of the disturbances that undercut their marriage, could do nothing but say, "Oh shit, Lloyd, where were you this time?", smile at his brilliant answer, and know how much he loved her. Tomorrow she would call her friend George, and he would come to the shop and they would commiserate at length about men.

"Oh God, George," she would say, "the life of a muse!"

And George would reply, "But you love him?"

"More than I know."

"Realizing that he's slightly off the deep end?"

"More than slightly, kiddo, what with his little phobias and all. But they just make him more human, more my baby."

And George would smile and talk of his lover, and they would laugh until the Waterford crystal rang and the bone china plates spun on their shelves.

Then George would take her hand and casually mention the brief affair they had had when George decided he needed to experience women to be more of one himself. It had lasted a week, when George accompanied her to San Francisco for a seminar on appraising antiques. In bed all he talked about was Lloyd. It disgusted her, but thrilled her too, and she went on to divulge the most intimate facts of her marriage.

When she realized that Lloyd would always be the unseen third party in bed with them, she broke it off. It was the only time she had cheated on her husband, and it was not for the standard reasons of neglect, abuse, or sexual boredom. It was to gain some kind of parity with him for the adventurous life he led. When Lloyd was frightened or angry and came to her with that look of his and she unhooked her bra and gave him her breasts, he was hers utterly. But when he read reports, or talked with Dutch Peltz and his other cop friends in the living room and she saw the wheels turning behind the pale grey eyes, she knew he was going to places that she never could. Her other parities — the success of the boutique, the book on Tiffany mirrors she had co-authored, her business acumen — all these satisfied only at the level of logic. Because Lloyd could fly and she couldn't; even after seventeen years of marriage, Janice Rice Hopkins did not possess a syllabus to explain why this was so. And inexplicably, her husband's capacity for flight began to frighten her.

Against the sum total of over twenty years of intimacy, Janice collated the recent evidences of Lloyd's strange behavior: his hour-long sojourns in front of the mirror, casting his eyes in circles as though trawling for flying insects; the increasingly long stints spent at his parents' house, talking to his mother, who had not uttered or comprehended a sound in nineteen years; the insanely sardonic set to his face when he talked to his brother on the telephone about their parents' care.

But the stories that he told the girls were the most disturbing: cop tales that Janice suspected to be half parable and half confession, lurid travelogues on the darkest Los Angeles streets, populated by hookers, junkies, and other sundry low-lifes and cops who were often as raunchy and brutal as the people they threw in jail. A year ago Janice had told Lloyd not to tell her the stories. He had agreed with a silent nod of his head and a cold look in his eyes, and took his parable/confessions to the girls, bringing them into adolescence with detailed accounts of sleaze and horror. Anne would shrug the stories off — she was fourteen and boy crazy; Caroline, thirteen and with a real talent for ballet, would brood over them and bring home true detective magazines and ask her father to discourse on the various articles inside. And Penny would listen and listen and listen, with pale grey eyes shining right through her father and her father's story to some distant termination point. When Lloyd concluded his parable, Penny would kiss him sternly on the cheek and go upstairs and knit the cashmere and madras plaid quilts that had already earned her feature coverage in five Sunday supplements.

Janice shivered. Was Penny's innocence blasted beyond redemption already? A master artisan and fledgling entrepreneur at twelve? She shivered again and looked at the clock. An hour of fearful speculation had passed, and Lloyd was still not home. Suddenly she realized that she missed him and wanted him beyond the limits of normal desire in a twenty-year-old love affair. She walked upstairs and undressed in the dark bedroom, lighting the scented candle that was Lloyd's signal to wake her up and love her. Crawling into bed, a last dark thought crossed her mind, like predator birds blackening a calm sky: As the girls grew older they looked more and more like Lloyd, especially in their eyes.

She heard Lloyd enter the house an hour later, his ritualistic sounds in the entrance hall: Lloyd sighing and yawning, unhooking his gunbelt and placing it on the telephone stand, the familiar shuffling noises he made as he slowly walked upstairs. Tensing herself for the moment when he would open the door and see her in amber light, Janice ran a teasing hand between her legs.

But the bedroom door didn't open; she heard Lloyd tiptoe past it and walk down the hall to Penny's room, then rap his knuckles lightly on her door and whisper, "Penguin? You want to hear a story?" The door creaked open a second later, and Janice heard father and child giggle in gleeful conspiracy.

She gave her husband half an hour, angrily chain-smoking. When her last remnants of ardor had fled and she started to cough from the half-dozen cigarettes, Janice threw on a robe and walked down the hall to listen.

Penny's bedroom door was ajar, and through it Janice could see her husband and youngest daughter sitting on the edge of the bed, holding hands. Lloyd was speaking very softly, in an awe-tinged storyteller's voice: "...after clearing the Haverhill/Jenkins homicide, I got assigned to a robbery deployment, a loan-out to the West L.A. squadroom. There had been a series of nighttime burglaries of doctor's offices, all in large buildings in the Westwood area. Cash and saleable drugs were the burglar's meat; in shortly over a month he'd ripped off over five grand in cash and a shitload of pharmaceutical speed and heavyweight downers. The West L.A. dicks had his M.O. figured out this way: The bastard used to hide out in the building until nightfall, then hit his mark, then break into a second floor office and jump out the window into the parking lot. There was evidence to point to this—chipped cement on the window ledges. The dicks figured him for a gymnast, a bullshit cat burglar type who could jump two stories without getting hurt. The commander of the squad was setting up parking lot surveillances to catch him. When the burglar hit an office building on Wilshire that two teams of detectives were staking out, it blew their thesis to hell and I was called in."

Lloyd paused. Penny nuzzled her head into his shoulder and said, "Tell me how you got the scumbag, Daddy."

Lloyd brought his storyteller's voice down to its lowest register: "Sweetheart, nobody jumps two stories repeatedly without getting hurt. I formed my own thesis: The burglar brazenly walked out of the buildings, waving to the security guards in the foyer as if everything were hunky-dory. Only one thing troubled me. Where was he carrying the dope he ripped off? I went back and checked with the guards on duty the nights of the robberies. Yes, both known and unknown men in business suits had walked out of the building in the early evening hours, but none were carrying bags or packages. The guards assumed them to be businessmen with offices in the building and didn't check them out. I heard that same statement six times before it all came together in my mind: The burglar dressed in drag, probably in the protective coloring of a nurse's uniform, carrying a large purse or shoulderbag. I checked with the guards again and, bingo! An unknown woman seen wearing a nurse's uniform and carrying a large shoulderbag was seen leaving the burglarized buildings at almost the exact time on all six burglary nights. The guards couldn't describe her, but said she was 'ugly,' 'a dog,' and so forth."

Penny fidgeted when Lloyd took in a deep breath and sighed. She took her head from his shoulder and poked him sharply in the arm. "Don't be a tease, Daddy!"

Lloyd laughed and said, "Alright. I ran a computer cross-check on vice offenders and registered sex offenders with burglary convictions. Double bingo! Arthur Christiansen, a.k.a. "Misty Christie", a.k.a. "Arlene the Queen" Christiansen. Specialties: giving cut-rate blow jobs to drunks who thought he was a woman and full-drag B & Es. I staked out his pad for thirty-six hours straight, determining that he was dealing uppers and Percodan—I heard his customers comment on the righteous quality of his stuff. This was solid corroboration, but I wanted to catch him-her in the act. The following afternoon old Arthur-Arlene left the pad with a giant quilted shoulderbag and drove to Westwood and walked into a big office building two blocks from the U.C.L.A. campus. Four hours later, an hour after dark, a very ugly creature in a nurse's uniform walks out, carrying the same shoulderbag. I whip out my badge, yell 'Police Officer!' and rush Arthur-Arlene, who screams, 'Chauvinist!' and swings on me. The blows are ineffectual and I'm reaching for my handcuffs when Arthur-Arlene's falsies pop out of his blouse. I get him handcuffed and flag down a black-and-white. Arthur-Arlene is screaming 'sisterhood is powerful' and 'police brutality,' and a crowd of U.C.L.A. students start shouting obscenities at me. I barely managed to get into the black-and-white. The scene was almost L.A.'s first transvestite police riot."

Penny laughed hysterically, collapsing on the bed and pounding the covers with her fists. She burrowed her head into the pillow to wipe away her tears, then giggled, "More, Daddy, more. One more before you go to bed."

Lloyd reached over and ruffled Penny's hair. "Funny or serious?"

"Serious," Penny said. "Give me some dark stuff to sate my ghoulish curiosity. If you don't make it good, I'll stay up all night thinking of Arthur-Arlene's falsies."

Lloyd traced circles on the bedspread. "How about a knight story?"

Penny's face grew somber. She took her father's hand and scooted down the bed so that Lloyd could rest his head in her lap. When father and daughter were comfortable, Lloyd stared up at the tartan quilt suspended from the ceiling and said, "The knight was caught in a dilemma. He had two anniversaries in one day—one personal, one professional. The professional one took precedence and in the course of it he shot a man, wounding him. About an hour later, after the man was in custody, the knight started to shake like he always did after he fired his gun. All those delayed reaction questions hit him: What if his shots rendered the asshole for good? What if next time he gloms the wrong info and takes out the wrong guy? What if he starts seeing red all the time and his discretion goes haywire? It's a shitstorm out there. You know that, don't you, Penguin?"

"Yes," Penny whispered.

"You know that you've got to develop claws to fight it?"

"Sharp ones, Daddy."

"You know the weird thing about the knight? The more complicated his doubts and questions become, the stronger his resolve gets. It just gets weird sometimes. What would you do if things got really weird?"

Penny played with her father's hair. "Sharpen my claws," she said, digging her fingers into Lloyd's scalp.

Lloyd grimaced in mock pain. "Sometimes the knight wishes he weren't such a fucking Protestant. If he were a Catholic he'd be able to get formal absolution."

"I'll always absolve you, Daddy," Penny said as Lloyd got to his feet. "Like the song said, 'I'm easy.' "

Lloyd looked down at his daughter. "I love you," he said.

"I love you too. One question before you go: You think I'd be a good Robbery/Homicide dick?"

Lloyd laughed. "No, but you'd be a great Robbery/Homicide dickless."

Janice watched Penny squeal in delight, and suddenly she was violated at the womb. She walked back to the bedroom she shared with her husband and flung off her robe, preparing to do *her* battle in the nude. Lloyd walked through the door moments later, smelling the scented candle and whispering, "Jan? You ardent this late, sweetheart? It's after midnight."

As he reached for the light switch, Janice threw her overflowing ashtray at the opposite wall and hissed, "You sick, selfish, son-of-a-bitch, can't you see what you're doing to that little girl? You call spilling out that violence being a father?" Frozen in the ugliness of the moment, Lloyd pushed the light switch, illuminating Janice, shivering in the nude. "Do you, Lloyd, goddamn you?"

Lloyd moved toward his wife, arms extended in a supplicating gesture, hoping that physical contact would quell the storm.

"No!" Janice said as she backed away, "Not this time! This time I want a promise from you, an oath that you will not tell our children those ugly stories!"

Lloyd reached a long arm out and caught Janice's wrist. She twisted it free and knocked down the nightstand between them.

"Don't, Lloyd. Don't want me and don't placate me and don't touch me until you promise."

He ran a hand through his hair and started to tremble. Fighting an impulse to punch the wall, he bent over and picked up the nightstand. "Penny is a subtle child, Jan, possibly a genius," he said. "What should I do? Tell her about the three. . . ."

Janice hurled her favorite porcelain lamp at the closet and shrieked, "She's just a little girl! A twelve-year-old little girl! Can't you understand that?"

Lloyd tripped across the bed and grabbed her around the waist, burying his head in her stomach, whispering, "She has to know, she had to know it, or she'll die. She has to know."

Janice raised her arms and molded her hands into fists. She started to bring them down, clublike, onto Lloyd's back but hesitated as a thousand instances of his erratic passion washed over her, combining to form an epigram whose words she was too terrified to speak.

She lowered her hands to her husband's face and gently pushed him away. "I want to see if the girls are all right," she said. "I'll have to tell them we were fighting. Then I think I want to sleep alone."

Lloyd got to his feet. "I'm sorry I was so late tonight."

Janice nodded dumbly and felt her sense of things confirmed. Then she put on a robe and went down the hall to check on her daughters.

Lloyd knew that he wouldn't be able to sleep. After saying good night to the girls, he prowled around downstairs looking for something to do. There was nothing to do but think of Janice and how he could not have her without giving up something dear to him and essential to his daughters. There was no place to go but backward in time.

Lloyd put on his gunbelt and drove to the old neighborhood.

He found it waiting for him in the pre-dawn stillness, as familiar as the sigh of an old lover. Lloyd drove down Sunset, feeling overwhelmed by the rightness of his usurping of innocence via parable. Let them learn it slowly, he thought, not the way I did. Let them learn the beast by story — not repeated example. Let that be the new hallmark of my Irish Protestant irregulars.

With this surge of affirmation, Lloyd floored the gas pedal, watching night-bound Sunset Boulevard explode in peripheral flashes of neon, sucking him into the middle of a swirling jetstream. He looked at the speedometer: one hundred thirty-five miles per hour. It wasn't enough. He bore down on the wheel with his whole being, and the neon turned to burning white. Then he closed his eyes and decelerated until the car hit an upgrade and the laws of nature forced it to a gliding stop.

Lloyd opened his eyes to discover them flooded with tears, wondering for an awkwardly long moment where on earth he was. Finally, a thousand memories clicked in and he realized that chance had left him at the corner of Sunset and Silverlake — the heart of the old neighborhood. Propelled by a subservient fate, he went walking.

Terraced hillsides drew Lloyd into a fusion of past, present, and future.

He sprinted up the Vendome steps, noting with satisfaction that the earth on both sides of the cement stanchions was as soft as ever. The Silverlake hills were formed by God to nurture — let the poor Mexicans live hearty here and thrive; let the old people complain about the steepness yet never move away. Let the earthquake the scientific creeps predicted come...Silverlake, the defiant traditionalist anomaly, would sustain its havoc and stand proud while L.A. proper burst like an eggshell.

At the top of the hill, Lloyd let his imagination telescope in on the few houses still burning lights. He imagined great loneliness and sensed that the light burners were importuning him for love. He breathed in their love and exhaled it with every ounce of his own, then turned west to stare through the hillside that separated him from the very old house where his crazy brother tended their parents. Lloyd shuddered as discord entered his reverie. The one person he hated guarding his two beloved creators. His one conscious compromise. Unavoidable, but . . .

Lloyd recalled how it happened. It was the spring of 1971. He was working Hollywood Patrol and driving over to Silverlake twice a week to visit his parents while Tom was away at work. His father had settled into a quiet, oblivious state in his old age, spending whole days in his back yard shack, tinkering with the dozens of television sets and radios that eclipsed almost every square inch of its floor space; and his mother, then eight years mute, stared and dreamed in her silence, having to be steered to the kitchen thrice daily lest she forget to eat.

Tom lived with them, as he had all his life, waiting for them to die and leave him the house that had already been placed in his name. He cooked for his parents and cashed their Social Security checks and read to them from the lurid picture histories of Nazi Germany that lined the bookshelves of his bedroom. It was Morgan Hopkins's express wish to Lloyd that he and his wife live out their days in the old house on Griffith Park Boulevard. Lloyd reassured his father many times, "You'll always have the house, Dad. Let Tom pay the taxes, don't even worry about it. He's a sorry excuse for a man, but he makes money, and he's good at looking after you and Mother. Leave the house to him; I don't care. Just be happy and don't worry."

There was a silent agreement between Lloyd and his brother, then thirty-six and a phone sales entrepreneur operating at the edge of the law. Tom was to live at home and feed and care for their parents, and Lloyd was to look the other way at the cache of automatic weapons buried in the back yard of the Hopkins homestead. Lloyd laughed at the inequity of the bargain — Tom, craven beyond words, would never have the guts to use the weaponry, which would be rusted past redemption within a matter of months anyway.

But one day in April of '71, Lloyd got a phone call informing him that there was now a gaping hole at the periphery of his major dreams. An old buddy from the Academy who worked Rampart Patrol had cruised by the Hopkins home, noticing a "For Sale" sign on the front lawn. Puzzled, since he had heard Lloyd often mention that his parents would rather die than give up the house, he called Lloyd at Hollywood Station to voice his puzzlement. Lloyd took the words in with a silent rage that had the locker room wobbling surreally before his eyes. Still wearing his uniform, he got his car from the parking lot and drove out to Tom's office in Glendale.

The "office" was a converted basement with four dozen small desks jammed together along the walls, and Lloyd walked into it oblivious to the salesmen shouting the panacea of aluminum siding and home bible-study classes into telephones.

Tom's desk was off by itself near the front of the room, next to a large urn filled with Benzedrine-laced coffee. Lloyd swung his lead-filled billy club into the urn, puncturing it and sending geysers of hot brown liquid into the air. Tom walked out of the men's room, saw the rage in his brother's eyes and the club, and backed into the wall. Lloyd advanced, and was arcing the club in a perfect roundhouse aimed at Tom's head when the terror in the pale grey eyes that so resembled his own halted him. He threw the billy down and ran to the first row of desks, startled phone salesman darting out of his way, running for cover at the back of the basement.

Lloyd began jerking the telephone cords out of their wall mountings and hurling the phones across the room. One row; two rows; three rows. When the salesmen had all deserted the office, and the floor was littered with broken glass, scattered order forms, and inoperative telephones, he walked up to his quaking older brother and said, "You will take the house off the market today and never leave Mother and Dad alone."

Tom nodded mutely and fainted into a puddle of his dope-saturated coffee.

Lloyd deepened his gaze into the dark hillside. That was over ten years ago. His mother and father were still alive in their separate solitudes; Tom was still their custodian. It was his one unsatisfying holding action, but there was nothing he could do about it. He recalled his last conversation with Tom. He was visiting his parents and found Tom in the back yard, burying shotguns under cover of night.

"Talk to me," Lloyd said.

"About what, Lloydy?" Tom asked.

"Say something real. Insult me. Ask me a question. I won't hurt you."

Tom backed a few steps away. "Are you going to kill me when Mom and Dad are gone?"

Lloyd was thunderstruck. "Why on earth would I want to kill you?"

Tom retreated again. "Because of what happened on Christmas when you were eight."

Lloyd felt himself embraced by monsters, over thirty years dead in the wake of the strong man he had become. His eyes strayed to his father's radio shack, and he had to will himself to return to the present, the force of the horrific memory was so compelling. "You're crazy, Tom. You've always been crazy. I don't like you, but I would never kill you."

Lloyd watched dawn creep up on the eastern horizon, outlining the L.A. skyline with strands of gold. Suddenly he was lonely and wanted to be with a woman. He sat down on the steps and considered his options. There was Sybil, but she had probably gone back to her husband — she was considering it the last time they talked. There was Colleen, but she was probably on her mid-week sales run to Santa Barbara. Leah? Meg? It was over with them, to resurrect it in the fierceness of early morning need would only cause pain later. There was only the uncertainty of Sarah Smith.

Lloyd knocked on her door forty-five minutes later. She opened it bleary-eyed, dressed in a denim bathrobe. When her eyes focused in on him she started to laugh.

"I'm not that funny looking, am I?" Lloyd asked.

Sarah shook her head. "What's the matter, your wife kick you out?"

"Sort of. She found out that I'm really a vampire in disguise. I prowl the lonely dawn streets of Los Angeles looking for beautiful young women to give me transfusions. Take me to your wisest muse."

Sarah giggled. "I'm not beautiful."

"Yes you are. Do you have to go to work today?"

Sarah said, "Yeah, but I can call in sick. I've never been with a vampire."

Lloyd took her hand as she motioned him inside. "Then allow me to introduce myself," he said.

PART THREE
CONVERGENCE

CHAPTER FIVE

Lloyd was seated in his office at Parker Center, his hands playing over papers on his desk, alternately forming steeples and hanging men. It was January 3, 1983, and from his sixth story cubicle he could see dark storm clouds barrelling northward. He hoped for a pulverizing rain storm. He felt warm and protective when foul weather raged.

The relative solitude of the office, situated between typewriter storage and Xeroxing rooms, was pleasing, but Lloyd's primary reason for acquiring it was its proximity to the dispatcher's office three doors down. Sooner or later, all homicides within the L.A.P.D.'s jurisdiction were reported over their phone lines, either by investigating officers requesting assistance or concerned parties screaming for help. Lloyd had rigged a special line to his own phone, and whenever an incoming call hit the switchboard a red light on his answering machine went on and he could pick up the receiver and listen in, often making him the first L.A.P.D. detective to gain crucial information on a murder. It was a sure-fire antidote to burdensome caseloads, dreary report writing, and court appearances; so when Lloyd saw the light on his machine blink, his heart gave a little lurch and he picked up the receiver to listen.

"Los Angeles Police Department, Robbery-Homicide Division," the woman at the switchboard said.

"Is this where you report a murder?" a man stammered in return.

"Yes, sir," the woman answered. "Are you in Los Angeles?"

"I'm in Hollyweird. Man, you wouldn't believe what I just seen..." Lloyd came alive with curiousity—the man sounded like he had witnessed a stoned visitation.

"Do you wish to report a homicide, sir?" The woman was brusque, even a little bullying.

"Man, I don't know if it was the real thing or a fuckin' hallucination. I've been doin' dust and reds for three days now."

"Where *are* you, sir?"

"I ain't *nowhere*. But you send the cops to the Aloha Apartments on Leland and Las Palmas. Room 406. There's something inside out of a fuckin' Peckinpah movie. I don't know, man, but either I gotta quit usin' dust or you got some heavy shit on your hands." The caller went into a coughing attack, then whispered, "Fuckin' Holly-weird, man; fuckin' weird," and slammed down his receiver.

Lloyd could almost feel the switchboard operator's befuddlement—she didn't know if the caller was for real or not. Muttering "Goddamned creep," she let her end of the line go dead. Lloyd jumped to his feet and threw on his sports jacket. *He* knew. He ran to his car and tore out for Hollywood.

The Aloha Regency was a four story, moss-hung, Spanish-style apartment house painted a bright electric blue. Lloyd walked through the unkempt entrance foyer to the elevator, quickly grasping the building as a once grand Hollywood address gone to despair. He knew that the inhabitants of the Aloha Regency would be an uneasy melange of illegal aliens, boozehounds, and welfare families. The sadness in the threadbare carpeted hallways was almost palpable.

He got into the elevator and pressed 4, then unholstered

his .38, feeling his skin start to tingle as he sensed the nearness of death. The elevator jerked to a halt and Lloyd got out. He scanned the hallway, noting that the doors on the even-numbered side leading up to 406 bore jimmy marks. After 406 the jimmy marks stopped. The wood on the door jambs was freshly splintered with no evidence of warping, which meant that the doors had probably been tried as recently as this morning. Feeling a thesis forming already, Lloyd pointed his .38 straight at the door of 406 and kicked it in.

Holding his gun in front of him as a directional finder, he walked into a small rectangular living room lined with bookshelves and tall potted plants. There was a desk wedged diagonally into one corner and three beanbag chairs on the floor, arranged in a semi-circle opened toward the front picture window. Lloyd walked through the room, savoring its feel. Slowly he swiveled to face the kitchenette off to the left. Freshly scrubbed tile and linoleum; dishes piled neatly by the sink. Which left the bedroom — separated from the rest of the apartment by a bright green door bearing a Rod Stewart poster.

Lloyd looked down at the floor and felt his stomach start to churn. In front of the crack below the door was a pile of dead cockroaches, melded together in a pool of congealed blood. He kicked in the door, murmuring, "Rabbit down the hole," closing his eyes until he assimilated the overwhelming stench of decomposing flesh. When he felt his tremors go internal and knew he wouldn't retch, he opened his eyes and said very softly, "Oh God, please no."

There was a nude woman hanging by one leg from a ceiling beam directly over a quilt-covered bed. Her stomach had been ripped open from pelvis to ribcage and her intestines were spilled out onto her upended torso, splaying out to cover her blood-matted face. Lloyd memorized the scene: the woman's free hanging leg swollen and purple and twisted out at a right angle, caked

97

blood on her breasts, a bluish-white tint on what he could see of her unbloodied flesh, the bed coverlet drenched with so much blood that it crusted and peeled in layers, blood on the floor and walls and dresser and mirror, all framing the dead woman in a perfect symmetry of devastation.

Lloyd went into the living room and found the telephone. He called Dutch Peltz at the Hollywood Station, saying only, "6819 Leland, Apartment 406. Homicide, ambulance, Medical Examiner. I'll call you later and tell you about it."

Dutch said, "Okay, Lloyd," and hung up.

Lloyd walked through the apartment a second time, willing his mind blank so that things could come to him, moving his eyes over the living room until he noticed a leather purse lying next to a cactus plant. He reached down and grabbed it, then dumped its contents onto the floor. Make-up kit, Excedrin, loose change. He opened a hand-tooled wallet. The woman had been Julia Lynn Niemeyer. The photo and statistics on her driver's license made him ache: pretty, 5'5", 120 pounds. D.O.B. 2-2-54, making her a month short of twenty-nine.

Lloyd dropped the wallet and examined the book-shelves. Romances and popular novels predominated. He noticed that the books on the top shelves were covered with dust, while the books on the bottom shelf were clean.

He squatted down to examine them more closely. The bottom shelf contained volumes of poetry, from Shakespeare to Byron to feminist poets in soft cover. Lloyd pulled out three books at random and leafed through them, feeling his respect for Julia Lynn Niemeyer grow — she had been reading good stuff in the days before her death. He finished flipping through the classics and picked up an outsized paperback entitled *Rage In The Womb — An Anthology of Feminist Prose.* Opening to the "Contents," he went numb when he saw dark brown stains on the inside cover. Flipping forward, he found pages stuck together with congealed blood and bloody smatterings growing fainter as he worked toward the end of the book. When he reached the glossy finished back cover, he gasped. Perfectly outlined in white were two bloody partial fingerprints — an index and pinky; enough to run a make on.

Lloyd whooped and wrapped the book in his handkerchief and carefully placed it on one of the beanbag chairs. On impulse, he walked back over to the bookshelf and ran a hand in the narrow space between the bottom shelf and the floor. He came away with a handful of vending machine dispensed sex tabloids — *The L.A. Nite-Line, L.A. Grope,* and *L.A. Swinger.*

He carried them over to the chair and sat down and read, saddened by the lurid fantasy letters and desperate liaison ads. "Attractive divorcee, 40, seeks well-hung white men for afternoon love. Send erect photo and letter to P.O. Box 5816, Gardena, 90808, Calif."; "Good looking gay guy, 24, into giving head, seeks hunky young high school guys with no mustache. Call anytime — 709–6404"; "Mr. Big Dick's my name, and fucking's my game! I give good lovin' to much acclaim! Let's get together for a swingin' nite, my dick is hard if your pussy's tight! — Send spread photo to P.O. Box 6969, L.A. 90069, Calif."

Lloyd was about to put the tabloids down and send up a mercy plea for the entire human race when his eyes caught an advertisement circled in red. "Your fantasy or mine? Let's get together and rap. Any and all sexually liberated people are invited to write to me at P.O. Box 7512, Hollywood, 90036, Calif. (I'm an attractive woman in her late 20s.)" He put the paper down and dug through the other two. The identical ad was featured in both.

He stuck the papers into his jacket pocket, walked back into the bedroom, and opened the windows. Julia Lynn Niemeyer swayed from the draft, turning on her one-legged axis, the ceiling beam creaking against her weight.

Lloyd held her arms gently. "Oh, sweetheart," he whispered, "oh, baby, what were you looking for? Did you fight? Did you scream?"

Almost as if in answer, the woman's cold left arm was caught by a gust of wind and flopped out of Lloyd's grasp. He grabbed it and held the hand tightly, his eyes moving to the large blue veins at the crook of the elbow. He gasped. A pair of needle marks were outlined clearly against the middle of the largest vein. He checked the other arm — nothing — then scraped away patches of dried blood from the ankles and backs of the knees. No other tracks; the woman had been professionally sedated at the time of her desecration.

Lloyd heard footsteps in the hallway, and seconds later a plainclothes cop and two patrolmen in uniform burst into the apartment. He walked into the living room to greet them, pointing a thumb over his shoulder and saying, "In there, guys." He was staring out the window at the black sky when he heard their first exclamations of horror, followed by the sound of retching.

The plainclothes cop was the first to recover, walking up to Lloyd and blurting out bluff-hearty, "Wow! That's some stiff! You're Lloyd Hopkins, aren't you? I'm Lundquist, Hollywood Dicks."

Lloyd turned to face the tall, prematurely grey young man, ignoring his outstretched hand. He scrutinized him openly and decided he was stupid and inexperienced.

Lundquist fidgeted under Lloyd's stare. "I think we got a botched-up burglary, Sergeant," he said. "I saw B. & E. marks on the door here. I think we should start our investigation by hauling in burglars know to use viol — "

Lloyd shook his head, silencing the younger detective. "Wrong. Those jimmy marks are fresh. The edges would have rounded off from moisture if the attempted burglaries coincided with the murder. That woman has been dead for at least two days. No, the burglar was the guy who called in to report the body. Now listen, the woman's purse is on that chair over there. Positive I.D. There's also a paperback book with two bloodstained partial prints. Get them to the lab and have the technicians call me at home when they have something conclusive one way or the other. I want you to search the premises, then seal it — no reporters, no TV assholes. You got that?"

Lundquist nodded.

"Good. Now, I want you to call the M.E. and S.I.D., and have them bring in a fingerprint team and dust this place from top to bottom. I want a complete forensic work-up. Tell the M.E. to call me at home with the autopsy report. Who's the top dog at Hollywood Dicks?"

"Lieutenant Perkins."

"Good. I'll call him. Tell him I'm handling this case for Robbery-Homicide."

"Right, Sergeant."

Lloyd walked back into the bedroom. The two patrolmen were staring at the corpse and cracking jokes. "I had a girlfriend once who looked like that," the older cop said. "Bloody Mary. I could only get together with her for two weeks outta the month, her period lasted so long."

"That's nothing," the younger cop said, "I knew an attendant at the morgue who fell in love with a corpse. He wouldn't let the Coroner slice her — said it took the R out of romance."

The other cop laughed and lit a cigarette with shaking hands. "My wife takes the R out of romance every night, also the O and the M."

Lloyd cleared his throat; he knew that the men were joking to keep their horror at bay, but he was offended anyway, and didn't want Julia Lynn Niemeyer to hear such things. He rummaged through the bedroom closet until he found a terrycloth robe, then walked into the kitchen and found a serrated-edged steak knife. When he re-entered the bedroom and stood up on the blood-spattered bed, the younger cop said, "You'd better leave her like that for the Coroner, Sergeant."

Lloyd said, "Shut the fuck up," and cut through the nylon cord that bound Julia Lynn Niemeyer at the ankle. He gathered her dangling limbs and violated torso into his arms and stepped off the bed, cradling her head into his shoulder. Tears filled his eyes. "Sleep, darling," he said. "Know that I'll find your killer." Lloyd lowered her to the floor and covered her with the robe. The three cops stared at him in disbelief.

"Seal the premises." Lloyd said.

Three days later, Lloyd was stationed at the main Hollywood Post Office with his eyes glued to the wall containing P.O. boxes 7500 through 7550, armed with the knowledge that Julia Lynn Niemeyer had placed her tabloid advertisements in the company of a tall, blonde woman of about forty. Office personnel at both the *L.A. Night-Line* and *L.A. Swinger* had positively identified the dead woman from her driver's license photograph, and distinctly remembered her female companion.

Lloyd fidgeted, keeping his anger and impatience at bay by recapitulating all the known physical evidence on the killing. Fact: Julia Lynn Neimeyer was killed by a massive dose of heroin, and was mutilated after her death. Fact: The Coroner had placed the time of her murder as seventy-two hours before the discovery of her body. Fact: No one at the Aloha Regency had heard signs of a struggle or knew much about the victim, who lived on money from a trust fund set up by her parents, who had died in a car accident in 1978. This information had been supplied by the woman's uncle, who had read of the killing in the San Francisco newspapers and who went on to describe Julia Niemeyer as a "very deep, very quiet, very intelligent girl who didn't let people get close to her."

The killing had made the newspapers in a big way, and

similarities to the Tate-LaBianca slayings of 1969 had been graphically pointed out. This caused a torrent of unsolicited information to flood the switchboards of the Los Angeles Police Department, and Lloyd had assigned three officers to interview all callers who didn't sound like outright cranks. The bloodstained fingerprints on the paperback book — the one *hard* piece of physical evidence — had been scrutinized by fingerprint experts, then computer fed and teletyped to every police agency in the continental United States, with astoundingly negative results: The partial index and pinky prints could not be attributed to anyone, anywhere, meaning that the killer had never been arrested, never been a member of the armed services or civil service, never been bonded, and had never applied for a driver's license in thirty-seven of the fifty United States.

Lloyd felt his thesis take on the form of what he called the "Black Dahlia Syndrome," a reference to the famous unsolved 1947 mutilation murder. He was certain that Julia Lynn Niemeyer had been killed by an intelligent middle-aged man who had never killed before, a man with a low sex drive who had somehow come in contact with Julia Niemeyer, whose persona somehow triggered his long dormant psychoses, and eventually led him to plan her murder carefully. He knew also that the man was physically strong and capable of maneuvering on a broad-based societal level: a solid citizen type who could also score heroin.

Lloyd was impressed with both killer and the challenge his capture presented. He surveyed the post office crowd at random, then shifted his gaze back to Box 7512. He felt his impatience grow. If the "tall blonde woman" didn't show by lunchtime, he would smash the box open and rip it off by the hinges.

She showed an hour later. Lloyd sensed that it was she as soon as she walked through the broad glass doors and nervously made for the aisles of boxes. A tall, strong-featured woman whose manner was like a barely controlled scream, he could almost feel her body tension as she looked fearfully in all directions, inserted her key and withdrew a handful of mail, then ran back outside.

Lloyd came up behind her as she was opening the door of a double-parked Pinto Hatchback. She turned around as she heard his footsteps, her hand flying to her mouth when she saw the badge he was holding up at eye level. Transfixed by the badge, the woman flopped against the car and let the handful of mail drop to the street.

Lloyd bent down and picked it up. "Police officer," he said quietly.

"Oh, Jesus," she said. "Vice?"

Lloyd said, "No, Homicide. It's about Julia Niemeyer."

An angry flush came over the woman's face. "Jesus," she said, "that's a relief. I was going to call you. I suppose you want to talk?"

Lloyd smiled; the woman had a certain panache. "We can't talk here," he said, "and I don't want to subject you to a police station. Do you mind driving somewhere?"

"No," the woman said, adding "Officer" with the thinnest edge of contempt.

Lloyd told her to drive south to Hancock Park. En route he learned that she was Joanie Pratt, age 42, former dancer, singer, actress, waitress, Playboy Club Bunny, model, and kept woman.

"What are you doing *now*?" he asked as she pulled into the Hancock Park parking lot.

"It's illegal," Joanie Pratt said, smiling.

"I don't care," Lloyd said, smiling back.

"Okay, I deal Quaaludes and fuck for selected older guys who don't want to get involved."

Lloyd laughed and pointed to a collection of plaster dinosaurs standing on a grassy knoll a few yards from the Tar Pits. "Let's go talk," he said.

When they were seated on the grass, Lloyd bored in, describing Julia Niemeyer's corpse in hideously graphic detail. Joanie Pratt turned white, then red and started to sob. Lloyd made no move to comfort her. When her tears subsided, he said softly, "I want this animal. I know about the ads you and Julia placed in the sex papers. I don't care if the two of you have fucked half of L.A. or the kangaroos in the San Diego Zoo or each other. I don't give a fuck if you deal dope, snort dope, shoot dope, or turn little kids on to dope. I want to know everything that you know about Julia Niemeyer: her love life, her sex life, and why she put those ads in those papers. Have you got that?"

Joanie nodded mutely. Lloyd dug a handkerchief out of his coat pocket and handed it to her. She wiped her face and said, "All right, it's like this. I was in the Hollywood Library about three months ago, returning some books. I notice this good-looking chick standing in line next to me, checking out all these scholarly books on sex — Kraft-Ebbing, Kinsey, *The Hite Report*. I crack a joke to the girl, who turns out to be Julia. Anyway, we go outside and smoke a cigarette and talk — about sex. Julia tells me she's researching sexuality — that she wants to write a book about it. I share my racy past with her, and tell her I've got this gig going — floating swingers' parties. It's kind of a scam — I know some heavyweight real estate people, and I score dope for them in exchange for letting me sublet these really primo houses when the owners are out of town. Then I place ads in the sex papers — high, *high* line sex parties. Two hundred dollars a couple — to keep the riffraff out. I provide good food and dope, music and a light show. Anyway, Julia — she's obsessed with sex, but she doesn't fuck — she's just a sex scholar . . ."

Joanie paused, and lit a cigarette. When Lloyd nervously blurted out, "Go on," she said, "Anyway, Julia wants to interview the people at my parties. I tell her 'fuck no! These people are paying *goood* money to come, and they don't want to be hassled by some sex-obsessed interviewer.' So Julia says, 'Look. I've got lots of money. I'll pay for people to come to the parties, and I'll interview them there, as their price for admission. That way, I can watch them have sex.' Anyway, that's why Julia placed those ads. People contacted her, and she offered to pay their way to the parties if they consented to interviews."

Lloyd was riveted, staring into Joanie Pratt's pale blue eyes until she started to wave a hand in front of his face. "Come back to earth there, Sergeant. You look like you just took a trip to Mars."

Lloyd felt vague instincts clicking into place. He brushed Joanie's hand away. "Go on."

"Okay, Mars Man. Anyway, Julia conducted her interviews and watched people fuck until she was blue in the face. She wrote out tons of notes and had the first draft of her book completed when her pad was burglarized and her manuscript and all her notes and files were stolen. She tol —"

"What!" Lloyd screamed.

Joanie leaped back, startled. "Whoa there, Sarge. Let me finish. This was about a month ago. The pad was ransacked. Her stereo and TV and a thousand dollars in cash were stolen. She..."

Lloyd interrupted. "Did she report it to the police?"

Joanie shook her head. "No, I told her not to. I told her she could always rewrite her book from memory and do some more interviews. I didn't want any cops nosing around us. Cops are notorious moralists, and they might have gotten wind of my scam. But listen. About a week before she died, Julia told me she had the feeling she was being followed. There was this man that she used to see in all these odd places — on the street, in restaurants, in the market. He never stared at her or anything like that, but she had this feeling he was stalking her."

Lloyd went cold all over. "Did she recognize the man from the parties?"

"She said she couldn't be sure."

Lloyd was silent for a long moment. "Do you have any of the letters Julia received?"

Joanie shook her head. "No, just the ones I picked up today."

Lloyd stuck out his hand, and Joanie withdrew the letters from her purse. He stared at her, tapping the collection of envelopes against his leg. "When are you having your next party?"

Joanie lowered her eyes. "Tonight."

Lloyd said, "Good. I'm going to attend. You're going to be my date."

The party was in a three story A-frame nestled at the end of a cul-de-sac on the Valley side of the Hollywood Hills. Lloyd wore cuffed chino pants, penny loafers, a striped polo shirt, and a crew-neck sweater over his .38 snubnose, prompting Joanie Pratt to exclaim, "Jesus, Sarge! This is a swing party, not a high school sock hop! Where's my corsage?"

"It's in my pants," he said.

Joanie laughed, then ran hooded eyes over his body. "Nice. You gonna fuck tonight? You'll get offers."

"No, I'm saving it for the senior prom. You want to show me around?"

They walked through the house. All the furniture in the living room and dining room had been moved up against the walls, and the carpets had been rolled up and wadded ceiling high next to a row of low tables where cold cuts, hors d'oeuvres, and canned cocktails in bowls of ice were arrayed. Joanie said, "Buffet and dance floor. There's a primo stereo system with a hook-up to speakers all over the house." She pointed to lighting fixtures hung from the ceiling. "The stereo is hooked up to the lights, so the music and the lights work together. It's wild." She took his hand and led him upstairs. The two upper floors contained bedrooms and dens on either side of a winding hallway. Red lights blinked on and off above the open doors, and Lloyd could see that inside the entire floor space of each room was covered by mattresses with pink silk sheets.

Joanie poked him in the ribs. "I hire these wetbacks from the slave market on Skid Row. They do all the heavy lifting. I give them ten bucks before the party, then twenty bucks and a bottle of tequila when they move all the furniture back. What's the matter, Sarge? You're scowling."

"I don't know," Lloyd said, "but it's funny. I'm here looking for a killer, this whole 'party' is probably against the law, and I think I'm happier than I've been in a long time."

The celebrants started to arrive half an hour later. Lloyd briefed Joanie on what he wanted—she was to circulate, and point out any people she recognized as having been interviewed by or having seemed interested in Julia Niemeyer. She was to report to him all men who even *mentioned* Julia or her recent demise. She was also to report anything that seemed darkly incongruous, anything that violated her self-described party ethos of "Good music, good dope, good fucking"; *no one* was to know that he was a police officer.

Lloyd stationed himself behind the two burly bouncers scrutinizing incoming guests and collecting their invitations. The partygoers, coupled off to insure an even ratio of partners, seemed to him to be the very microcosm of jaded money—the finest clothes in the latest styles over unfit, tension-ridden bodies, the men middle-aged and afraid of it, the women looking hard, competitive, and brassy in the worst camped-out faggot manner. As the bouncers locked and bolted the door behind the last arrivals, Lloyd felt that he had just viewed a perfect impressionist representation of hell. His left knee was twitching in reaction to it, and when he walked back to the buffet he knew that he would need every ounce of the love in his Irish Protestant ethos to keep from hating them.

He decided to play the jocular stud. As Joanie Pratt brushed by him, he whispered to her, "Make it look like we're together."

Joanie closed her eyes. Lloyd bent in slow motion to kiss her, his hands reaching out and grasping her waist and lifting her so that her feet dangled inches above the floor. Their lips and tongues met and played in perfect unison. Whistling and good natured jibes drowned out Lloyd's furious heartbeat, and when he broke the kiss and lowered Joanie to the floor he felt he had conquered the jaded assembly with love.

"That's all, folks," he said with a mock humble twang, patting Joanie on the shoulder. "You folks all have a good time. I have to go upstairs and rest." Wild applause greeted this irony, and he ran for the staircase.

Lloyd found a bedroom at the far end of the third story hallway. He locked himself in, feeling proud of his performance, yet ashamed of its ease and dumbfounded by the fact that he was starting to like the revelers downstairs. He sat down on the pink sheeted mattress and dug out the letters that Joanie had given him — the last correspondence delivered to P.O. Box 7512. He had planned to go over them later, aided by Joanie, but now he needed work to keep his almost heart-stricken ambivalence at bay.

The first two envelopes contained underground junk mail, form letters advertising king-size electric dildos and bondage attire. The third envelope was hand-printed. Lloyd looked more closely and noticed that the letters in the address were perfectly squared off, obviously formed by pen and ruler. His mind clicked, and he held the envelope gently by the edges and slit it open with a deft thrust of his fingernail. It contained a poem, block ruler printed in maroon ink. Lloyd tilted the page sideways. Something about the ink bothered him. Letting the paper wobble in front of his eyes, he realized that the maroon ink was starting to flake, revealing a brighter shade underneath. He deliberately smudged a stanza, then smelled his finger and felt his mind click a second time: The poem was written in blood.

Lloyd willed his mind to be still, using his method of deep breathing and forcing himself to concentrate on the vertical lines in the plaid quilt Penny had loomed for him two Christmases ago. When he had been blank for solid minutes, he began to read the blood-formed words:

> I took you from
>   your grief;
> I stole you like
>   a thief;
> I rent my heart
>   to give you
>   mercy;
> You begged me to end
>   your strife
> And I gave you life.
> Your body was the
>   ellipsis,
> Your heart my
>   wife
> Your whorish studies
>   my burden;
> Your death, my
>   life.
> I read your words,
>   hell bound;
> Sorrowed to the
>   core by the dirt

you found —
You grieved me more
Than all the rest —
You were the smartest,
The kindest, the worst
    and best —
And I faltered at the
    moment I put you
    to rest.

Tribute in anonymous
    transit,
Live life enclosed
    in a cancer
        cell,
Only the love in my
    knife grants it;
Reprieve from the gates
    of this blood-drenched
        hell.

Lloyd read the poem three more times, memorizing it, letting the permutations of the words enter him and regulate his heartbeat and the flow of his blood and the thrust of his brainwaves. He walked over and sought his image in the mirror that completely covered the back wall. He couldn't decide if he was an Irish Protestant knight or a gargoyle, and he didn't care; he had been placed in the vortex of divinely evil compulsions and he knew, at long last, precisely why he had been granted genius.

As the poem engulfed him further it began to assume musical dimensions, cadences of the corny signature tunes of all the old TV programs that Tom had made him . . . .

The cadences grew, and "Live life enclosed in a cancer cell" became an improvisation on the big band theme song of "Texaco Star Theatre," and suddenly Milton Berle was there next to him, rotating a cigar against his woodchuck teeth. Lloyd screamed and fell to his knees, his hands cupped to his ears.

There was a screeching, and the music stopped. Lloyd tightened his grip on his ears. "Tell me a story rabbit down the hole," he whimpered beatifically until he heard the crackle of static coming from a large speaker mounted on the bedroom wall. His dry sobs trailed into relieved laughter. It was the radio.

Rational thoughts of combat entered Lloyd's mind. He could trash the central source of the music by yanking a few wires and twisting a few dials; let the revelers fuck *sans* accompaniment, the whole scene was illegal anyway.

Carefully placing the poem back in its envelope and securing it in his pocket, Lloyd walked downstairs, his hands clamped against his sides, twisted into his pants legs. He ignored the couples who were fornicating in standing positions in bedroom doorways and concentrated on the shimmering crimson lights that bathed the hallway. The lights were the reality, the benign antithesis of the music, and if he could let them guide him to the stereo system, he would be safe.

The first floor was a massive swirl of nude bodies moving with the music, heeding and heedless of the beat, rhythmic and abandoned limbs flung wildly into the air, brushing flesh, lingering in the briefest of caresses before being yanked back in seizure-like movements. Lloyd threaded his way through the swirl, feeling arms and hands twist and prod and pluck at him. He saw the stereo system at the opposite end of the living room, Joanie Pratt standing beside it, scrutinizing a stack of record albums. Fully clothed, she looked like a fixed beacon light in a world of insane noise.

"Joanie!"

The alarm in his own voice startled him, jolting him away from the music, into bodies that retreated as he cut a path through them. He crashed through the kitchen, down strobe-lighted hallways and out into a pitch black yard that was enveloped by shuddering silence. Falling to his knees, he let the silent night air and the scent of eucalyptus embrace him.

"Sarge?"

Joanie Pratt knelt by his side. She stroked his back and said, "Jesus, are you o.k.? The look on your face on that dance floor...I've never seen anything like it." Lloyd forced himself to laugh. "Don't worry about it. I can't stand loud noise or music. It's old stuff." Joanie pointed a finger at her head and twirled it. "You've got a few loose up there. You know that?"

"Don't talk to me that way."

"I'm sorry. Wife and kids?"

Lloyd nodded and got to his feet. Helping Joanie up, he said, "Seventeen years. Three daughters."

"Is it good?"

"Things are changing. My daughters are wonderful. I tell them stories, and my wife hates me for it."

"Why? What kind of stories?"

"Never mind. When I was eight years old my mother told *me* stories, and it saved my life."

"What kind of..."

Lloyd shook his head. "No, let's change the subject. Did you hear anything at the party? Did anyone mention Julia? Did you notice anything unusual?"

"No, no, and no. Julia used a phony name when she interviewed people, and that was a bad photo of her on the news. I don't think anyone even made the connection."

Lloyd considered this. "I buy it," he said. "My instinct tells me that the killer wouldn't come to a party like this; he'd consider it ugly. I want to cover all the angles, though. One of those letters you gave me contained a poem. It was written by the killer; I'm sure of that. The poem made a vague reference to other victims, so I'm certain that he's killed more than one woman." When Joanie responded with a blank face, he went on. "What I need from you is a list of your regular partygoers."

Joanie was already frantically shaking her head. Lloyd grabbed her shoulders and said softly, "Do you want this animal to kill again? What's more important, saving innocent lives or the anonymity of a bunch of horny assholes?"

Hysterical giggling from inside the house framed Joanie's answer. "It's not much of a choice, Sarge. Let's go over to my place; I've got a Rolodex file on all my regulars."

"What about your party?"

"The hell with it. I'll have the bouncers lock up. Your car or mine?"

"Mine. Is this an invitation?"

"No, it's a proposition."

Afterwards, too full of each other to sleep, Lloyd played with Joanie's breasts, cupping and pushing and probing them into different shapes and running soft fingers around the edges of the nipples.

Joanie laughed and said *sotto voce*, "Do-wah, wah-wah, do-rann-rann." Lloyd asked her what the strange sounds meant and she said, "I forgot; you never listen to music.

"Okay. I came out here from Saint Paul, Minnesota in 1958. I was eighteen. I had it all figured out — I was gonna be the first female rock and roll star. I was blonde, I had tits, and I thought I could sing. I get off the bus at Fountain and Vine and walk north. I see the Capitol Records Tower north of the Boulevard, and I figure it's gotta be a message, so I hotfoot it up there, lugging this cardboard suitcase, wearing a crinoline party dress and high heels on the coldest day of the year.

"Anyway, I sit down in the waiting room, eyeballing all these gold records they've got on the walls. I'm thinking,

'Some day' . . . Anyway, this guy come up to me and says, 'I'm Pluto Maroon. I'm an agent. Capitol Records is not your gig. Let's splitsville.' I go, 'Huh?' and we splitsville— Pluto says a buddy-roo of his is making a movie-roo in Venice. We drive out there in this Cadillac soul wagon. Pluto's buddy is Orson Welles. No shit, Sarge; Orson fucking Welles. He's making *Touch of Evil*. Venice is doubling as this sleazy Mexican border town.

"Right off the bat I can tell that Orson baby is condescending to Pluto—that he digs him strictly as a sycophant, kind of an amusing picaresque buffoon. Anyway, Orson tells Pluto to dig him up some extras, locals who'd be willing to hang around all day for a few scoots and a jug. So Pluto and I go walking down Ocean Front Walk. What a revelation! Innocent Joanie from St. Paul hobnobbing with beatniks, junkies, and geniuses!

"Anyway, we go by this beatnik book store. A guy who looks like a werewolf is behind the counter. Pluto says, 'You wanna dig Orson Welles and make a five-spot?' The guy says, 'Crazy,' and we splitsville on down the boardwalk, picking up this incredible low life entourage on the way.

"Anyway, the werewolf zeroes in on me. 'I'm Marty Mason,' he says, 'I'm a singer.' I think, 'Wowie zowie!' and I say, 'I'm Joanie Pratt—I'm a singer, too.' Marty says, 'Sing "do-wah, wah-wah, do-rann-rann" ten times.' I do it, and he says, 'I'm playing a gig in San Berdoo tonight. Wanna be my backup?' I said, 'What do I have to do?' Marty says, 'Sing "do-wah, wah-wah, do-rann-rann".'

"So that was it. I did it. I sang 'do-wah, wah-wah, do-rann-rann' for ten years. I married Marty, and he became Marty 'Monster' Mason and cut the "Monster Stomp," capitalizing on his werewolf resemblance, and we were *biggg* time for a couple of years, then Marty got strung out and we got divorced, and now I'm sort of a business woman and Marty is on Methadone Maintenance and working as a fry cook at a Burger King in the Valley, and it's still 'do-wah, wah-wah, do-rann-rann.'"

Joanie sighed, lit a cigarette and blew smoke rings at Lloyd, who was tracing patterns on her thighs and thinking that he had just heard existentialism in a nutshell. Wanting Joanie's interpretation, he asked, "What does it mean?"

She said, "Whenever things are up in the air, or scary, or about to maybe get good, I sing 'do-wah, wah-wah, do-rann-rann', and they seem to fall into place; or at least they're not so scary."

Lloyd felt a little piece of his heart work its way loose and drift back to Venice in the winter of '58. "Can I sleep with you again?" he asked.

Joanie took his hand and kissed it. "Anytime, Sarge."

Lloyd got up and dressed, then picked up the Rolodex file and cradled it to his chest. "I'll be very discreet about this," he said. "I'll have smart, competent officers do whatever questioning has to be done."

"I trust you," Joanie said.

Lloyd bent over and kissed her cheek. "I've memorized your phone number. I'll call you."

Joanie leaned into the kiss. "Take care, Sarge."

It was dawn. Lloyd drove downtown to Parker Center, feeling spellbound with purpose. He took the elevator to the fourth floor computer room. There was a lone operator on duty. The man looked up from his science-fiction novel as he saw Lloyd approach, wondering if there was a chance to banter with the big detective the other cops called "The Brain." When he saw the look on Lloyd's face, he decided against it.

Lloyd said brusquely, "Good morning. I want printouts on every unsolved female homicide in Los Angeles County over the past fifteen years. I'll be up in my office. Ring extension 1179 when you have the information."

Lloyd about-faced and walked the two flights of stairs

up to his office. The cubicle was dark and quiet and peaceful, and he flopped into his chair and fell asleep immediately.

CHAPTER SIX

It was the poet's eleventh complete reading of the manuscript, his eleventh journey into his most recent beloved's shameful passion, his third since he consummated their love.

His hands shook as he turned the pages, and he knew that he would have to return to the repulsively fascinating third chapter, the words that tore and bit at him, that made him feel his organs and their functions, that made him sweat and tingle and drop things and laugh when nothing was funny.

The chapter was entitled "Straight Men — Gay Fantasies," and it reminded him of his early poetry writing days, the days before he became so obsessed with form, when stanzas didn't have to rhyme, when he trusted the thematic unity of his subconscious. In this chapter his beloved had gotten a disparate sampling of normal men to admit things like, "I would really like to take it up the ass just once. Just do it — and fuck the consequences, then go home and make love to my wife and wonder if it felt any different to her," and "I'm thirty-four now, and I've screwed every woman who'd let me for seventeen years and I still haven't quite found the nitty gritty excitement that I thought I would. I drive down Santa Monica Boulevard sometimes and see the male hustlers and everything goes slightly haywire and I think and think and...(here Interviewee sighs disgustedly)...and then I think that a new woman will do it, and I think of coming here to these parties and before you know it I'm turning off Santa Monica and thinking of my wife and kids and then...oh, shit!"

He put the looseleaf binder down, feeling the little body flushes that had ruled his life since his consummation with Julia. She had been dead for two weeks and they were continuing unabated, undaunted by the courage he had shown in writing her anonymous tribute etched in his own blood, undaunted by his first sexual transit since . . . .

He had read the third chapter beside Julia's body, savoring her nearness, wanting the completeness of her flesh and her words. The men who had told Julia their stories were so blighted in their dishonesty that he wanted to retch. Yet...he read the man's account of driving down Santa Monica Boulevard over and over, looking up only to watch Julia sway on her external axis. She was more *of* him than any of the first twenty-one, more even than Linda, who had moved him so deeply. She had given him *words* to keep — tangible love gifts that would grow in him. Yet...Santa Monica Boulevard...yet...the poor wretch so devastated by societal mores that he couldn't . . . .

He walked into the living room. *Rage In The Womb.* A lesbian poet wrote of her lover's "multiunioned folds of wetness." Visions of muscular torsos, broad shoulders, and flat, hard backsides entered him, given to him by Julia, telling him to seek a further union with her by showing courage where the cowardly wretch had failed. He balked inside, searching frantically for *words.* He tried anagrams of Julia and Kathy, five letters each. It didn't work. Julia wanted more than the others. He walked back to the bedroom to view her corpse a last time. She sent him visions of sullen young men in macho poses. He obeyed. He drove to Santa Monica Boulevard.

He found them a few blocks west of LaBrea, standing in

front of taco stands, porno book stores, and bars, outlined in neon tendrils that gave them the added enticements of halos, auras, and wispy appendages. The idea of looking for a specific image or body crossed his mind, but he killed the thought. It would give him time to retreat, and he wanted to impress Julia with his unquestioning compliance.

He pulled to the curb and rolled down the window, beckoning to the young man leaning against a newsrack with one hip thrust toward the street.

The young man walked over and leaned in through the window. "It's thirty; head only, pitch or catch," he said, getting an inward wave of the arm as his answer.

They drove around the corner and parked. He clenched his body until he thought his muscles would contract and suffocate him, then whispered, "Kathy," and let the young man unbutton his pants and lower his head into his lap. His contractions continued until he exploded, seeing colors when he came. He tossed a handful of cash at the young man, who vanished out the door. He was still seeing colors, and he saw them on his drive home and in his restive, but altogether wonderful, dreams that night.

His post-consummation ritual of sending flowers took up the following morning. Driving away from the florist's, he noticed that his usual valedictory feeling was missing. He spent the afternoon developing film and setting up shooting assignments for the following week, thoughts of Julia rendering his workday pursuits a treadmill of ugly boredom.

He read her manuscript again, staying up all night, seeing colors and feeling the weight of the young man's head. Then the terror began. He could feel foreign bodies within his body. Tiny melanomas and carcinomas that moved audibly through his bloodstream. Julia wanted more. She wanted written tribute; words to match her words. He severed an artery in his right forearm with a paring knife, then squeezed the gash until it yielded enough blood to fill completely the bottom of a small developing tray. After cauterizing the wound he took a pen quill and ruler and meticulously printed out his tribute. He slept well that night.

In the morning he mailed his poem to the post office address he had seen on the front page of Julia's manuscript. His feeling of normalcy solidified. But at night the terror returned. The carcinomas were inside him again. He started dropping things. He saw the colors, this time even more vividly. The Santa Monica Boulevard phantasmagoria flashed continually before his eyes. He knew that he had to do *something* or go insane.

The poet had now possessed the manuscript for the two weeks since Julia's death. He began to look on it as an evil talisman. The third chapter was particularly evil, inimical to the control that had been the hallmark of his life. That night he burned the manuscript in his kitchen sink. He doused the charred words with tap water and felt new purpose grip him. There was only one way to obliterate all memory of his twenty-second lover.

He had to find a new woman.

CHAPTER SEVEN

It had been seventeen days since the discovery of Julia Niemeyer's body, and Lloyd wondered for the first time if his Irish Protestant ethos had the juice to carry him through what was turning into the most vexing episode of his life, a crusade that portended some deep, massive loss of control.

For perhaps the thousandth time since securing the printouts, he recapitulated all the known physical evidence pertaining to Julia Niemeyer's murder and unsolved homicides of women in Los Angeles County: the blood that formed the words of the poem was O+. Julia Niemeyer's blood was AB. There were no fingerprints on the envelope or single piece of paper. Interviews with residents of the Aloha Regency Apartments had yielded nothing; no one knew much about the dead woman; no one knew her to have visitors; no one recalled any strange occurrences in the building near the time of her death. The surrounding area had been thoroughly searched for the double-bladed knife believed to have been used for the mutilations — nothing even closely resembling it had been found. Lloyd's vague hope that Julia's killer had been connected to her through the swing parties proved futile. Experienced detectives had interviewed all the people in Joanie Pratt's Rolodex and had come away with nothing but new insights into lust and sad knowledge of adultery. Two officers had been assigned to check bookshops specializing in poetry and feminist literature for weird male requests for "Rage in the Womb" and generally strange male behavior. All investigatory avenues were covered.

And the unsolved homicides: The twenty-three Los Angeles County police agencies whose feed-ins composed the central computer file listed 410 of them going back to January 1968. Discounting 143 vehicular homicides, this left 267 unsolved murders. Of these 267, 79 were of women between the ages of twenty and forty, what Lloyd considered to be his killer's perimeters of attraction — he was certain the monster liked them young.

He looked at the map of Los Angeles County adorning the back wall of his office. There were 79 pins stuck into it, denoting the locations where 79 young women met violent death. Lloyd scrutinized the territory represented and let his intimate knowledge of L.A. and its environs work in concert with his instincts. The pinpoints covered the whole of Los Angeles County, from the San Gabriel and San Fernando Valleys to the far-flung beach communities that formed her southern and western perimeters. Hundreds and hundreds of square miles. Yet of the seventy-nine, forty-eight were situated in what police referred to as "white trash" suburbs — low income, high crime areas where alcoholism and drug addiction were epidemic. Statistics and his own policeman's instinct told Lloyd that the bulk of these deaths were related to booze, dope, and infidelity. Which left thirty-one murders of young women, spread throughout middle, upper middle class, and wealthy L.A. County suburbs and municipalities; murders unsolved by nine police agencies.

Lloyd had groaned when he had taken his last available direct action of querying those agencies for Xeroxes of their complete case files, realizing that it might take them as long as two weeks to respond. He felt powerless and beset by forces far beyond his bailiwick, imagining a city of the dead co-existing with Los Angeles in another time warp, a city where beautiful women beseeched him with terrified eyes to find their killer.

Lloyd's feelings of powerlessness had peaked three days before, and he had personally telephoned the top interagency liaison officers at the nine departments, demanding that the files be delivered to Parker Center within forty-eight hours. The responses of the nine officers had varied, but in the end they had acquiesced to Lloyd Hopkins's reputation as a hot-shot homicide dick and had promised the paperwork in seventy-two hours tops.

Lloyd looked at his watch, a Rolex chronometer marked in the twenty-four hour military time method. Seventy hours and counting down. Adding two hours for bureaucratic delay, the paperwork should arrive by noon. He bolted from his office and ran down six flights of stairs to street level. Four hours of pounding pavement with no destination in mind and a willfully shut off brain would put him at his optimal mental capabilities — which he was certain that he would need to devour the thirty-one homicide files.

Four hours later, his mind clear from a dozen brisk circuits of the Civic Center area, Lloyd returned to Parker Center and jogged up to his office. He could see that the door to his cubicle was open and that someone had turned on the light. A lieutenant in uniform passed him in the hallway and hastily explained, "Your paperwork arrived, Lloyd. It's in your office."

Lloyd nodded and peered in his doorway. His desk and both his chairs were covered with thick manila folders filled with papers still reeking of the photostatic process. He counted them, then moved his chairs, wastebasket, and filing cabinet out into the hallway, arraying the files on the floor in a circle and sitting down in the middle of them.

Each folder was marked on the front with the victim's last name, first name, and date of death. Lloyd divided them first into region, then into year, never looking at the photographs that he knew were clipped to the first page. Starting with Fullmer, Elaine D; D.O.D. 3/9/68, Pasadena P.D., and ending with Deverson, Linda Holly; D.O.D. 6/14/82, Santa Monica P.D., he selected all the paperwork outside the L.A.P.D. and placed it to one side. This accounted for eighteen files. He looked at the thirteen L.A.P.D. files. Their front markings were slightly more detailed than those of the other departments; each victim's age and race were listed immediately below her name. Of the thirteen murdered women, seven were listed as black and Hispanic. Lloyd put these folders aside and double-checked his first instincts, letting his mind go blank for a full minute before returning to conscious thought. He decided he was right; his killer preferred white women. This left six L.A.P.D. files and eighteen from other agencies, twenty-four in total. Averting his eyes from the front page photos, Lloyd scanned the interagency files for mention of race. Eight of the victims were listed as being non-Caucasian.

Which left sixteen folders.

Lloyd decided to make a collage of photographs before reading the complete files. Again willing a blank mind, he slipped the snapshots out of their folders face down in chronological order. "Talk to me," he said aloud, turning the photographs over.

When six of the snapshots smiled up at him he felt his mind begin to lurch forward convulsively, grasping at the horrific knowledge that he was assimilating. He flipped over the remaining photos and felt the logic of terror grip him like a blood-spattered vice.

The dead women were all of a kind, almost kinlike in the Anglo-Saxon planes of their faces; all posessed demure, feminine hairstyles; all were wholesome-looking in the spirit of more traditional times. Lloyd whispered the single word that summed up his constituency of the dead, "Innocent, innocent, innocent." He surveyed the photographs a dozen more times, picking up details—strands of pearls and high school rings on chains, the absence of make-up, shoulders and necks clad in sweaters and anachronistic formal wear. That the women had been killed by one monster for the destruction of the innocence they heralded so splendidly was beyond question.

With trembling hands Lloyd read through the folders, partaking of death's communion served up by strangulation, gunshot, decapitation, forced ingestion of caustic fluids, bludgeoning, gas, drug overdose, poisoning, and suicide. Disparate methods that would eliminate police awareness of mass murder. The one common denominator: no clues. No physical evidence. Women chosen for slaughter because of the way they looked. Julia Niemeyer killed sixteen times over, and how many more in different places? Innocence was the epidemic of youth.

Lloyd read through the folders again, coming out of his trance with the realization that he had been sitting on the floor for three hours and that he was drenched in sweat. As he got to his feet and stretched his painfully cramped legs, he felt the *big* horror overtake him: The killer's genius was unfathomable. There were no clues. The Niemeyer trail was dead cold. The other trails were colder. There was *nothing* he could do.

There was *always* something he could do.

Lloyd got a roll of masking tape from his desk and began taping the photographs along the walls of his office. When the smiling faces of dead women stared down at him from all directions he said to himself, *"Finis. Morte. Cold City. Muerto. Dead."*

Then he closed his eyes and read the vital statistics page in each folder, forcing himself to think only *region*. This accomplished, he got out his notebook and pen and wrote:

> Central Los Angeles:
> 1. Elaine Marburg, D.O.D. 11/24/69
> 2. Patricia Petrelli, D.O.D. 5/20/75
> 3. Karlen La Pelley, D.O.D. 2/14/71
> 4. Caroline Werner, D.O.D. 11/9/79
> 5. Cynthia Gilroy, D.O.D. 12/5/71
>
> Valley and Foothill Communities:
> 1. Elaine Fullmer, D.O.D. 3/9/68
> 2. Jeanette Willkie, D.O.D. 4/15/73
> 3. Mary Wardell, D.O.D. 1/6/74
>
> Hollywood - West Hollywood:
> 1. Laurette Powell, D.O.D. 6/10/78
> 2. Carla Castleberry, D.O.D. 6/10/80

3. Trudy Miller, D.O.D. 12/12/68
4. Angela Stimka, D.O.D. 6/10/77
5. Marcia Renwick, D.O.D. 6/10/81

Bev Hills - Santa Monica - Beach Communities:
1. Monica Martin, D.O.D. 9/21/74
2. Jennifer Szabo, D.O.D. 9/3/72
3. Linda Deverson, D.O.D. 6/14/82

Willing himself to think only *modus operandi*, Lloyd read through the Vital Statistics page a second time, coming away with three bludgeonings, two dismemberments, one horseback riding accident that was seriously considered as a homicide, two deaths by gunshot, two stabbings, four suicides attributed to different means, one poisoning, and one drug overdose-gassing that was labeled "murder-suicide?" by a baffled records clerk.

Turning to *chronology*, Lloyd read over the dates of death that he had written next to his list of victims, gaining his first make on the killer's methodology. With the exception of a twenty-five month hiatus between Patricia Petrelli, D.O.D. 5/20/75 and Angela Stimka, D.O.D. 6/10/77, and a seventeen-month gap between Laurette Powell, D.O.D. 6/10/78 and Caroline Werner, D.O.D. 11/9/79, his killer performed his executions at intervals of between six months to fifteen months which, Lloyd concluded, was why he was able to elude capture for so long. The murders were undoubtedly brilliantly executed and based on intimate knowledge gleaned from long-term surveillance. And, he reasoned further, those longer hiatuses probably contained victims that could be attributed to lost files and computer errors — every police agency was susceptible to a large paperwork margin of error.

Lloyd closed his eyes and imagined time warps within time warps within time warps; wondering how far back the killings went — all police departments in Los Angeles County threw out their unsolved files after fifteen years, giving him *zero* access to information predating January, 1968.

It was then that his mind pulsated into perfect focus, and as he whispered "The forest for the trees," Lloyd looked at his list of Hollywood — West Hollywood homicides and felt his skin start to tingle. Four "suicide" killings had taken place on the identical date of June 10th; in 1977, '78, '80 and '81. It was the one indicator that pointed to obsessive, pathological behavior out of his killer's ice-water restraint norm.

Lloyd grabbed the four folders and read them from cover to cover, once, then twice. When he finished, he turned off the light in his cubicle and sat back and *flew* with what he had learned.

On Thursday evening, June 10th, 1977, residents of the apartment building at 1167 Larrabee Avenue, West Hollywood, smelled gas coming from the upstairs unit rented by Angela Marie Stimka, a twenty-seven year old cocktail waitress. Said residents summoned a deputy sheriff who lived in the building, and the deputy kicked in Angela Stimka's door, turned off the wall heater from which the gas was emanating and discovered Angela Stimka, dead and bloated on her bedroom floor. He carried her body outside and called the West Hollywood Sheriff's substation, and within minutes a team of detectives had combed the apartment and had come up with a suicide note that cited the breakup of a long-term love affair as Angela Stimka's reason for wanting to die. Handwriting experts examined Angela Stimka's diary *and* the suicide note, and decided that both were written by the same person. The death was labeled a suicide, and the case was closed.

On June 10th of the following year, a sheriff's patrol car was summoned to a small house on Westbourne Drive in

West Hollywood. Neighbors had complained of uncharacteristically loud stereo noise coming from the dwelling, and one old lady told the deputies that she was certain that something was "drastically wrong." When no one answered the officers' persistent knocking, they climbed in through a half opened window and discovered the owner of the house, thirty-one year old Laurette Powell, dead in a large wicker chair, the arms of the chair, her bathrobe, and the floor in front of her soaked with blood that had exploded out of the artery-deep gashes on both of her wrists. An empty prescription bottle of Nembutal lay on a nightstand a few feet away, and a razor-sharp kitchen cleaver was resting in the dead woman's lap. There was no suicide note, but homicide detectives, noting the hesitation marks on both wrists and the fact that Laurette Powell was a long time holder of several Nembutal prescriptions, quickly classified her death as a suicide. Case closed.

Lloyd's wheel turned silently. He knew that the Westbourne Drive and Larrabee Avenue addresses were a scant two blocks apart, and that the Tropicana Motel gun-in-mouth "suicide" of Carla Castleberry on 6/10/80 was less than a half mile from the first two crime scenes. He shook his head in disgust; any cop with half a brain and ten cents worth of experience should know that women *never* kill themselves with guns — the statistics on female gunshot suicides were nonexistant.

The fourth "suicide," Marcia Renwick, 818 North Sycamore, was the non sequitur, Lloyd surmised; the most recent June 10th murder, four miles east of the first three, in the L.A.P.D.'s Hollywood Division. Occurring a full year after the Carla Castleberry homicide, the Renwick pill overdose had the feel of an unimaginative impulse killing.

Lloyd turned his attention to the file of the most recent victim before Julia Niemeyer. He winced as he read the Coroner's report on Linda Deverson, D.O.D. 6/14/82; chopped to pieces with a two-edged fire axe. Blinding memories of Julia swaying from her bedroom ceiling beam combined with his new knowledge to convince him that somehow, for some god-awful, hellish reason, his killer's insanity was peaking.

Lloyd lowered his head and sent up a prayer to his seldom-sought lip-service God. "Please let me get him. Please let me get him before he hurts anyone else."

Thoughts of God were paramount in Lloyd's mind as he walked down the hall and knocked on the door of his immediate superior, Lieutenant Fred Gaffaney. Knowing that the lieutenant was a hard-ass, born-again Christian who held grandstanding, maverick cops in pious contempt, he decided to invoke the diety heavily in his plea for investigatory power. Gaffaney grudgingly had given him a free rein on his caseload, with the implicit proviso that he not beg favors; since he was about to plead for men, money, and media play, he wanted to pitch the lieutenant from a standpoint of mutual religiosity.

"Enter!" Gaffaney called out in answer to the knock.

Lloyd walked in the open door and sat down in a folding chair in front of the lieutenant's desk. Gaffaney looked up from the papers he was shuffling and fingered his cross-and-flag lapel pin.

"Yes, Sergeant?"

Lloyd cleared his throat and tried to affect a humble look. "Sir, as you know, I've been working full time on the Niemeyer killing."

"Yes. And?"

"And, sir, it's a stone cold washout."

"Then stick with it. I have faith in you."

"Thank you, sir. It's funny that you mentioned faith." Lloyd waited for Gaffaney to tell him to continue. When all he got was a silent deadpan, he went on. "This case has been a testing of my own faith, sir. I've never been much of a believer in God, but the way that I've been stumbling into evidence has me questioning my beliefs. I — "

The lieutenant cut him off with a chopped hand gesture. "I go to church on Sunday and to prayer meetings three times a week. I put God out of my mind when I clip on my holster. You want something. Tell me what it is, and we'll discuss it."

Lloyd went red and forced a stammer. "Sir, I . . . I . . ."

Gaffaney leaned back in his chair and ran his hands over his iron grey crew-cut. "Hopkins, you haven't called a superior officer 'Sir' since you were a rookie. You're the most notorious pussy hound in Robbery-Homicide, and you don't give a rat's ass about God. What do you *want*?"

Lloyd laughed. "Shall I cut the shit?"

"Please do."

"All right. In the course of my investigation into the Niemeyer killing I've come across solid, instinctive evidence that points to at least sixteen other murders of young women, dating back fifteen years. The M.O.s varied, but the victims were all of a certain physical type. I've gotten complete case files on these homicides, and chronological consistencies and other factors have convinced me that all sixteen women were killed by the same man, the man who killed Julia Niemeyer. The last two killings have been particularly brutal. I think we're dealing with a brilliant psychopathic intellect, and unless we direct a massive effort toward his capture he'll kill with impunity until the day he dies. I want a dozen experienced homicide dicks full time; I want liasions set up with every department in the county; I want permission to recruit uniformed officers for the shit work, and authority to grant them unlimited overtime. I want a full-scale media blitz — I've got a feeling that this animal is close to exploding, and I want to push him a little. I — "

Gaffaney raised both hands in interruption. "Do you have any *hard* physical evidence," he asked, "any *witnesses*, any notations from detectives within the

L.A.P.D. or other department that lend credence to your mass murder theory?"

"No." Lloyd said.

"How many of these sixteen investigations are still open?"

"None."

"Are there any other officers within the L.A.P.D. who corroborate your hypothesis?"

"No."

"Other departments?"

"No."

Gaffaney slammed his desk top with two flattened palms, then fingered his lapel pin. "No. I won't trust you on this. It's too old, too vague, too costly, and too potentially embarrassing to the department. I trust you as a troubleshooter, as a very fine detective with a superb record —— "

"With the best fucking arrest record in the department!" Lloyd shouted.

Gaffaney shouted back, "I trust your record, but I don't trust you! You're a showboat glory-hound womanizer, and you've got a wild hair up your ass about murdered women!" Lowering his voice, he added, "If you really care about God, ask him for help with your personal life. God will answer your prayers, and you won't be so disturbed by things out of your control. Look at how you're shaking. Forget this thing, Hopkins. Spend some time with your family; I'm sure they'd appreciate it."

Lloyd got to his feet, trembling, and walked to the door. His peripheral vision throbbed with red. He turned to look at Gaffaney, who smiled and said, "If you go to the media, I'll crucify you. I'll have you back in uniform rousting piss bums on skid row."

Lloyd smiled back and felt a strangely serene bravado course through him. "I'm going to get this animal, and I'm going to stick your words up your ass," he said.

Lloyd packed the sixteen homicide files into the trunk of his car and drove to the Hollywood Station, hoping to catch Dutch Peltz before he went off duty. He was in luck; Dutch was changing back into civilian clothes in the senior officers' locker room, knotting his necktie and staring at himself abstractedly in a full-length wall mirror.

Lloyd walked over, clearing his throat. Without taking his eyes from the mirror, Dutch said, "Fred Gaffaney called me. He told me that he figured you'd be coming my way. I saved your ass; he was going to blow the whistle on you to one of his born-again high brass buddies, but I told him not to. He owes me favors, so he agreed. You're a sergeant, Lloyd. That means you can only act like an asshole with sergeants and below. Lieutenants and up are *verboten. Comprende,* brain-boy?"

Dutch turned around, and Lloyd saw that his abstracted look was glazed over with fear. "Did Gaffaney tell you all of it?" Lloyd asked.

Dutch nodded. "How sure are you?"

"All the way."

"Sixteen women?"

"At least that many."

"What are you going to do?"

"Flush him out, somehow. Probably by myself. The department will never authorize an investigation; it makes them look too inept. I was stupid to go to Gaffaney in the first place. If I go over his head and make a stink, I'll get yanked off the Niemeyer case and detached to some bumfuck robbery assignment. You know what this feels like, Dutchman?"

Dutch looked up at his huge genius-mentor, then turned away when he felt tears of pride welling in his eyes. "No, Lloyd."

"It feels like I was made for this one," Lloyd said, keeping eye contact with his own mirror image. "That I won't know what I am or what I can be until I get this bastard and find out why he's destroyed so much innocence."

Dutch put a hand on Lloyd's arm. "I'll help you," he said. "I can't give you any officers, but I'll help you myself, we can. . . ." Dutch stopped when he saw that Lloyd wasn't listening; that he was transfixed by the light in his own eyes or some distant vision of redemption.

Dutch withdrew his hand. Lloyd stirred, jerked his gaze from the mirror and said, "When I had two years on the job, I got assigned to the junior high school lecture circuit. Telling the kids picaresque cop stories and warning them about dope and accepting rides from strangers. I loved the assignment, because I love children. One day a teacher told me about a seventh grade girl — she was twelve — who used to give blow jobs for a pack of cigarettes. The teacher asked me if I'd talk to her.

"I looked her up one day after school. She was a pretty little girl. Blonde. She had a black eye. I asked her how she got it. She wouldn't tell me. I checked out her home situation. It was typical — alcoholic mother on welfare, father doing three-to-five at Quentin. No money, no hope, no chance. But the little girl liked to read. I took her down to a bookstore on Sixth and Western and introduced her to the owner. I gave the owner a hundred bucks and told him that the little girl had that much credit there. I did the same thing at a liquor store down the block — a hundred bucks buys a lot of cigarettes.

"The girl was grateful and wanted to please me. She told me she got the black eye because her braces cut some guy she was sucking off. Then she asked me if I want some head. Of course I say 'No' and give her a big lecture. But I keep seeing her. She lives on my beat, and I see her all the time, always smoking and carrying a book. She looks happy.

"One day she stops me when I'm out cruising in my black-

and-white alone. She says, 'I really like you and I really want to give you head.' I say 'No,' and she starts to cry. I can't bear that, so I grab her and hold her and tell her to study like a demon so she can learn how to tell stories herself."

Lloyd's voice faltered. He wiped his lips and tried to remember the point he wanted to make. "Oh yeah," he said finally. "I forgot to mention that the little girl is twenty-seven now, and she's got a Masters in English. She's going to have a good life. But...but there's this guy out there who wants to kill her. And your daughters and mine...and he's very smart...but I'm not going to let him hurt anyone else. I swear that to you. I swear it."

When he saw that Lloyd's pale grey eyes were shrouded with a sadness that he could never express with words, Dutch said, "Get him."

Lloyd said, "I will," and walked away, knowing that his old friend had given him a carte blanche absolution for whatever he had to do, whatever rules he had to break.

CHAPTER EIGHT

The following morning, after a restive night of assimilating the data in the sixteen files, Lloyd drove to the downtown public library, figuring out the shit work logistics in his mind en route, sorting minor details and bureaucratic cover your ass stratagems to one side so that he could come to his first day of legwork in an absolutely silent mental state.

With the car windows rolled up and the squawk box of his two-way radio disconnected to reinforce the silence, Lloyd pushed aside all the extraneous details regarding his investigation. He was covered up drum-tight with Fred Gaffaney and the higher echelon Robbery-Homicide brass, having called the two detectives working under him on the Niemeyer case, learning that their bookstore canvass of the downtown/central L.A. area had thus far yielded nothing solid, telling them to pursue their instincts full-time and on their own autonomy and to report to Gaffaney twice weekly, letting the Jesus freak that they both despised know that Sergeant Hopkins was working hard in the dark solitude that was the stalking ground of genius. Gaffaney would accept this as part of their silent agreement, and if he complained about Lloyd's absence at Parker Center, Dutch Peltz would intercede and kibosh his complaints with every ounce of his prestige. He was covered.

As for the investigation itself, there were no physical facts that Lloyd didn't already know from his first run-through of the files. *Stunning* silence underlined this; Janice and the girls had slept over at the Ocean Park apartment of her friend George, and Lloyd had had a big silent house in which to do his reading. In a desire to juxtapose the destruction of innocence via murder to his own efforts to diminish it through storytelling, he had gone over the hellish manila folders in Penny's bedroom, hoping that his youngest daughter's aura would give him the clarity to forge facts out of elliptical psychic labyrinths. No new facts emerged, but his psychological character study of the killer gained an added dimension infused with a coldly subtle verisimilitude.

Although he had no access to information on unsolved homicides before 1968, Lloyd was certain that the murders did not date back much further. He based this on his strongest character assessment/feeling — the killer was a homosexual. His whole genealogy of death was an attempt to hide the fact from himself. *He did not yet know.* The homicides prior to Linda Deverson and Julia Niemeyer, though often brutal, bespoke an effete satisfaction with a job well done and an almost refined love of anonymity. *He did not have an inkling of what he was.* Linda and Julia, hideously butchered, were the dividing points, the division irrevocable and based on the terror of an emergent sexuality so shamefully compelling that it had to be drowned in blood.

Lloyd traced instinctual links back in time. His killer had to live in Los Angeles. His killer was tremendously strong, capable of severing limbs with a single swipe of an axe. His killer was undoubtedly physically attractive and capable of maneuvering with grace in the gay world. He wanted it desperately, yet to submit to the vulnerability inherent in sexual interaction would destroy his urge to kill. Sexuality burgeons in adolesence. Assuming that the killer was still in an ascendent sexual curve and assuming that the murders began in or around January, 1968, he allotted the monster a five-year trauma incubation period and placed him as coming of age in the early to middle 60s, making him now in his late thirties — forty at the oldest.

Exiting the freeway at Sixth and Figueroa, Lloyd whispered, "June 10th, June 10th, June 10th." He parked illegally on the wrong side of the street and stuck an "Official Police Vehicle" sign under his windshield wiper. Running up the library steps, the epiphany slammed him like an axe handle between the eyes: the monster killed because he wanted to love.

Lloyd's microfilm time travel consumed four hours and traversed every June 10th from 1960 to 1982. Starting with the Los Angeles *Times* and ending with the Los Angeles *Herald-Express* and its offshoot newspaper the L.A. *Examiner,* he sifted through headlines, feature articles, and clipped accounts detailing everything from major league baseball to foreign insurrections to previews of summer beach wear to primary election results. Nothing in the parade of information caught his eyes as being a potential contributing factor to murderous passion and nothing caused his mental gears to snap forward and expand on his thesis at any level. June 10th was his one crucial clue to the killer — but Los Angeles newspapers treated it like just another day.

Although Lloyd had expected the negative results, he was still disappointed and was glad that he had saved the film for the four "suicide" years of 1977, '78, '80, and '81 for last.

His disappointment grew. The deaths of Angela Stimka, Laurette Powell, Carla Castleberry, and Marcia Renwick were relegated to quarter-column obscurity. "Tragic" was the adjective both papers used to describe all four "suicides"; "Funeral arrangements pending" and the names and addresses of the next of kin took up the bulk of the print space.

Lloyd rolled up the microfilm, placed it on the librarian's desk and walked outside into the sunlight. Sidewalk glare and eyestrain from his hours of squinting combined to send a pounding up his neck into his head. Willing the pain down to a murmur, he considered his options. Interview the next of kin? No, sad denials would be the common denominator. Visit the death scenes? Look for indicators, chase hunches? "Legwork!" Lloyd shouted out loud. He ran for his car, and the headache disappeared altogether.

Lloyd drove to West Hollywood and scouted the first three June 10th killing grounds.

Angela Stimka, D.O.D. 6/10/77, had lived in a mauve-colored ten-unit apartment house, 'fifties-building boom-ugly, an obviously jerry-built structure whose one claim to prestige was its proximity to the gay bars on Santa Monica and the cross-sexual nightlife on the Sunset Strip.

Lloyd sat in his car and wrote down a description of the block, his eyes perking only once — when he noticed an "Illegal Nighttime Parking" sign across the street from the

1167 Larrabee address. His gears clicked twice. He was in the heart of the gay ghetto. His killer had *probably* chosen the Stimka woman for the location of her dwelling as well as for her physicality, somehow wanting to run a gauntlet of subconscious denial by choosing a victim in a largely homosexual neighborhood; and the West Hollywood Sheriff's were demons on parking enforcement.

Lloyd smiled and drove two blocks to the small wood-framed house on Westbourne Drive where Laurette Powell had died of Nembutal ingestion and "self-inflicted" knife wounds. Another "Illegal Nighttime Parking" sign, another click, this one very soft.

The Tropicana Motel yielded a whole series of clicks, resounding gear-mashings that went off in Lloyd's mind like gunshots that tore ceaselessly at innocent bodies. Carla Castleberry, D.O.D. 6/10/80, the means of death a .38 slug through the roof of the mouth and up into the brain. Women never blew their brains out. Classic homosexual symbolism, perpetrated in a sleazy "Boy's Town" motel room.

Lloyd scanned the sidewalk in front of the Tropicana. Crushed amyl nitrate poppers on the ground, fruit hustler junkies holding up the walls of the coffee shop. His thesis exploded in his mind. When its symbiotic thrust dawned through the noise of the explosion, he was terrified. He ignored his terror and ran for a pay phone, dialing seven familiar digits with shaking hands. When an equally familiar voice came on the line, sighing, "Hollywood Station, Captain Peltz speaking," Lloyd whispered, "Dutch, I know why he kills."

An hour later, Lloyd sat in Dutch Peltz's office, sifting through negative information that had him slamming his best friend's desk top in frustration. Dutch stood by the door, watching Lloyd read through the teletypes that had just come in from both the L.A.P.D. and Sheriff's central computers. He wanted to stroke his son's hair or smooth his shirtfront, anything to ease the anguish that had Lloyd's features contorted in rage. Feeling meek in the wake of that rage, Dutch said, "It's going to be alright, kid."

Lloyd screamed, "No, it's not! He was assaulted, I'm certain of that, and it happened on a June 10th when he was a juvenile! Juvenile sex-offense records are never shredded! If it's not on the computer, then it didn't happen in L.A. County or it was never fucking reported! There's nothing on these fucking juvie vice printouts except fruit shakedown and backseat blow jobs, and you don't become a fucking mass murder because you let some old man suck your cock in Griffith Park!"

Lloyd picked up a quartz bookend and hurled it across the room. It landed on the floor next to the window that overlooked the station parking lot. Dutch peered out at the nightwatch officers revving up their black-and-whites, wondering how he could love them all so much, yet not at all when compared to Lloyd. He placed the bookend back on his desk and ruffled Lloyd's hair.

"Feel better, kid?"

Lloyd gave Dutch a reflex smile that felt like a wince. "Better. I'm beginning to know this animal, and that's a start."

"What about the printout on the parking tickets? What about F.I. cards on the dates of the killings?"

"Negative. No parking tickets *at all* on the applicable dates and streets, and the only Sheriff's F.I. cards were filled out on women—hookers working the Strip. It was a long shot at best, and *our* department wasn't computerizing F.I.s when the Renwick woman was killed. I'm going to have to start from scratch again, send out sub-rosa queries to old-time juvie dicks, see if I can get some feedback on old assault cases that never made the files."

Dutch shook his head. "If this guy got molested or

porked or whatever around twenty years ago, like you figure, most of the dicks who might know something would be retired by now."

"I know. You send out the feelers, will you? Pull some tails, call in some favors. I want to keep moving out on the street; that's where it feels right."

Dutch took a chair across from Lloyd, trying to gauge the light in his eyes. "O.K., kid. Remember my party Thursday night, and get some rest."

"I can't. I've got a date tonight. Janice and the girls are probably hanging out with their fag buddy, anyway. I want to keep moving."

Lloyd's eye's flickered; Dutch's eyes bored in. "Anything you feel like telling me, kid?"

Lloyd said, "Yeah. I love you. Now let me get out of here before you get sentimental about it."

On the street, without his paperwork to refer to and with three hours to kill before meeting Joanie Pratt, Lloyd recalled that his subordinates had yet to canvass the Hollywood area bookstores.

He drove to a pay phone and leafed through the yellow pages, finding listings for one poetry bookshop and one specializing in feminist literature:

New Guard Poetry on La Brea near Fountain and the Feminist Bibliophile on Yucca and Highland.

Deciding on a circuit that would allow him to hit both stores and then head toward Joanie's house in the Hollywood Hills, Lloyd drove first to New Guard Poetry, where a bored, scholarly looking man in incongruous farmer overalls told him that no, there had been no suspicious browsers or sales of feminist prose collections to strongly built men in their middle to late thirties, for the simple reason that he did not stock feminist poetry—it was aberrantly anti-classicist. Most of his customers were academics of long standing who preferred to order from his catalog, and *that* was *that*.

Lloyd thanked the man and swung his unmarked Matador north, pulling up in front of the Feminist Bibliophile at precisely six o'clock, hoping that the small, converted-house bookstore would still be open. He trotted up the steps just as he heard the door being bolted from inside, and when he saw the lights in the windows going off he rapped on the door jamb and called out, "Police. Open up, please."

The door swung open a moment later, and the woman who opened it stood silhouetted against the light in a challenging attitude. Lloyd's body gave a slight shudder as he felt the pride in her pose, and before she could voice any challenge out loud he said, "I'm Detective-Sergeant Hopkins, L.A.P.D. Could I talk to you for a moment?"

The woman remained silent. The silence was unnerving, so to keep himself from doing an embarrased little foot-dance, Lloyd memorized her physicality, maintaining a probing eye contact that the woman returned without flinching. A rigid angularity trying to hold reign over a soft, strong body, he decided; thirty-four to thirty-six, the slight traces of make-up a concession to awareness of her age; the brown eyes, pale skin, and chestnut hair somehow denoting breeding; the severe tweed suit a coat of armor. Smart, contentious, and unhappy. An aesthete afraid of passion.

"Are you with the Intelligence Division?"

Lloyd gawked at both the non sequitur and the force in the woman's voice. Recovering, he shifted his feet and said, "No, why?"

The woman smiled mirthlessly and spat out her challenge: "The L.A.P.D. has a long history of trying to infiltrate causes they deem subversive, and my poetry has been published in feminist periodicals that have been highly critical of your department. This bookshop carries a list of titles that includes many volumes that explode myths surrounding the macho mentality."

The woman stopped when she saw that the big cop was beaming broadly. Aware that a parity of discomfiture had been achieved, Lloyd said, "If I wanted to infiltrate a feminist bookstore, I would have come in drag. May I come in, Miss —— "

"My name is Kathleen McCarthy," the woman said. "I prefer Ms., and I won't let you in until you tell me what this is all about."

It was the question Lloyd was hoping for. "I'm the most honored homicide detective on the west coast," he said softly. "I'm investigating the murders of close to twenty women. I discovered one of the bodies. I won't insult you by describing how it was mutilated. I found a blood-stained book at the crime scene, *Rage In The Womb*. I'm certain that the killer is interested in poetry — maybe feminist poetry in particular. That's why I came here."

Kathleen McCarthy had gone pale, and her challenging posture had slumped, then tensed up again as she grabbed the door jamb for support. Lloyd moved in, showing her his badge and I.D. card. "Call the Hollywood Station," he said. "Ask for Captain Peltz. He'll verify what I've told you."

Kathleen McCarthy motioned Lloyd inside, then left him alone in a large room filled with bookshelves. When he heard the sound of a phone being dialed he slipped off his wedding band and examined the books that covered the four walls and spilled over onto chairs, tables, and revolving metal bookracks. His respect for the strident poet grew — she had placed her own published works in preeminent spots throughout the room, alongside volumes by Lessing, Plath, Millett and other feminist ikons. An out-front ego, Lloyd decided. He started to like the woman.

"I apologize for judging you before I heard you out."

Lloyd turned around at the words. Kathleen McCarthy was not chagrined by her apology. He started to *feel* her, and threw out a line calculated to secure *her* respect. "I can understand your feelings. The Intelligence Division is overzealous, maybe even paranoid."

Kathleen smiled. "May I quote you on that?"

Lloyd smiled back. "No."

An embarrassed silence followed. Sensing the mutality of the attraction deepen, Lloyd pointed to a book strewn couch and said, "Could we sit down? I'll tell you about it."

In a low voice and with a deliberately cold deadpan stare, Lloyd told Kathleen McCarthy how he had discovered Julia Lynn Niemeyer's body and how a blood smeared copy of *Rage In The Womb,* along with the poem sent to Julia's post office box, had convinced him that his assumed one-time killer was in reality a mass murderer. Ending with a recounting of his chronological work-up and the psychological profile he had deduced, he said, "He's brilliant beyond words, and going completely out of control. Poetry is a fixation with him. I think that he *wants* subconsciously to lose control, and that he may view poetry as his means to that end. I need your feedback on *Rage In The Womb,* and I need to know if any strange men — specifically men in their thirties — have been coming here to your store, buying feminist works, acting furtive or angry or in any way out of the ordinary."

Lloyd sat back and savored Kathleen's reaction of cold, hard, muscle-constricting rage. When she was silent for a full minute, he knew that she was mustering her thoughts into a severe brevity, and that when she spoke her response would be a perfect model of control, devoid of rhetoric or expressions of shock.

He was right. "*Rage In The Womb* is an angry book," Kathleen said softly. "A polemic, a broadside against many things, violence on women in specific. I haven't stocked it in years, and when I did, I doubt if I ever sold a copy to a man. Beyond that, the only male customers that I get are men who come in with their girlfriends and college students—young men in their late teens and twenties. I can't remember when I've had a single man in his thirties in the store. I own the store, and run it by myself, so I *see* all my customers. I——"

Lloyd cut Kathleen off with a wave of his hand. "What about mail orders? Do you do a catalog business?"

"No, I don't have the facilities for mailings. All my business is done here in the shop."

Lloyd muttered "Shit," and punched the arm of the couch. Kathleen said, "I'm sorry, but listen...I have a lot of friends in bookselling. Feminist literature, poetry, and otherwise. Private dealers you've probably overlooked. I'll call around. I'll be persistent. I want to help."

"Thank you," Lloyd said. "I could use your help." Feigning a yawn, he added, "Do you have any coffee? I'm running on empty."

Kathleen said, "One moment," and departed into the back room. Lloyd heard the sounds of cups and saucers being readied, followed by the electric crackle of a radio and the blare of some kind of symphony or concerto. When the music picked up tempo, he called out, "Would you turn that off, please?" Kathleen called back, "Alright, but talk to me."

The music diminuendoed, then died altogether. Lloyd, relieved, blurted out, "What shall I talk about, police work?"

Kathleen came into the living room a moment later, bearing a tray with coffee cups and an assortment of cookies. "Talk about something nice," she said, clearing books from a low end table. "Talk about something dear to you." Scrutinizing Lloyd openly, she added, "You look pale. Are you feeling sick?"

Lloyd said, "No, I feel fine. Loud noise bothers me; that's why I asked you to turn off the radio." Kathleen handed him a cup of coffee. "That wasn't noise. That was music." Lloyd ignored the statement. "The things that are dear to me are hard to describe," he said. "I like poking around in sewers, seeing what I can do about justice, then getting the hell out and going someplace where it's gentle and warm."

Kathleen sipped coffee. "Are you talking about being with women?"

"Yes. Does that offend you?"

"No. Why should it?"

"This bookstore. Your poetry. 1983. Pick a reason."

"You should read my diaries before you judge me. I'm a good poet, but I'm a better diarist. Are you going to catch this killer?"

"Yes. Your reaction to my being here impresses me. I'd like to read your diaries, feel your intimate thoughts. How far do they date back?"

Kathleen flinched at the word "intimate." "A long time," she said, "since my days with the Marshall Clarion. I..." Kathleen stopped and stared. The big policeman was laughing and shaking his head delightedly. "What *is* wrong?" she asked.

"Nothing, except that we went to the same high school. I had you *all* wrong, Kathleen. I figured you for East Coast Irish money, and you turn out to be a mick from the old neighborhood. Lloyd Hopkins, Marshall High Class of '59 and cop of Irish Protestant grandparents meets Kathleen McCarthy, one-time Silverlake resident and Marshall High graduate, Class of..."

Kathleen's features brightened with her own delight. "Class of '64," she finished. "God, how funny. Do you remember the rotunda court?" Lloyd nodded. "And Mr. Juknavarian and his stories about Armenia?" Lloyd nodded again. "And Mrs. Cuthbertson and her stuffed dog? Remember, she called it her muse?" Lloyd doubled over, consumed with laughter. Kathleen continued, throwing nostalgia out between her own gleeful squeals. "And the Pachucos versus the Surfers, and Mr. Amster and those T-shirts he had made up? 'Amsters Hamsters'? When I was in tenth grade someone tied a dead rat to his car antenna and put a note under the wipers. The note said, 'Amster's Hamsters bite the big weenie!'"

Lloyd's laughter crescendoed into a coughing fit that had him in fear of spewing coffee and half-digested cookies all over the room. "No more, no more, please, or I'll die," he managed to get out between body-wracking coughs. "I don't want to die this way."

"How *do* you want to die?" Kathleen asked playfully.

As he wiped his tear-stained face, Lloyd sensed a probing intent behind the question. "I don't know," he said, "either very old or very romantically. You?"

"Very old and wise. Autumnal serenity long gone into deep winter, with my words carefully prepared for posterity."

Lloyd shook his head. "Jesus, I don't believe this conversation. Where did you live in Silverlake?"

"Tracy and Micheltorena. You?"

"Griffith Park and St. Elmo. I used to play 'chicken' on Micheltorena when I was a kid. *Rebel Without A Cause* had just come out and chicken was *in*. Being too young to drive, we had to play it on sleds with little rubber wheels attached. We started at the top of the hill above Sunset, at two-thirty every morning that summer; '55 I think it was. The object of the game was to sled all the way across Sunset against the light. At that time of the morning there was just enough traffic out to make it slightly risky. I did it once a night, all summer long. I never dragged my feet or hit the hand brakes. I never turned down a dare."

Kathleen sipped her coffee, wondering how bluntly she should phrase her next question. To hell with it, she decided and asked, "What were you trying to prove?"

"That's a provocative question, Kathleen," Lloyd said.

"You're a provocative man. But I believe in parity. You can ask me anything you like, and I'll answer."

Lloyd's face lit up at the possibilities for exploration. "I was trying to follow the rabbit down the hole," he said. "I was trying to light a fire under the world's ass. I wanted to be considered a tough guy so that Ginny Skakel would give me a hand job. I wanted to breathe pure white light. Good answer?"

Kathleen smiled and gave Lloyd a sedate round of applause. "Good answer, Sergeant. Why did you quit?"

"Two boys got killed. They were riding on one sled. A '53 Packard Caribbean smashed them to pieces. One of the boys was decapitated. My mother asked me to quit. She told me that there were safer ways to express courage. She told me stories to take the edge off my grief."

"Your *grief*? You mean you wanted to continue playing that insane game?"

Lloyd savored Kathleen's incredulous look and said, "Of course. Teenage romanticism dies hard. Turnabout, Kathleen?"

"Of course."

"Good. Are you a romantic?"

"Yes... In all the deepest essentials... I...."

Lloyd cut her off. "Good. May I see you tomorrow night?"

"What did you have in mind? Dinner?"

"Not really."

"A concert?"

"Very amusing. Actually, I thought we might be-bop around L.A. and check out urban romanticism."

"Is that a pass?"

"Absolutely not. I think we should do something that neither of us has ever done before, and that rules out *that*. You in?"

Kathleen took Lloyd's outstretched hand. "I'm in. Here at seven o'clock?"

Lloyd brought the hand to his lips and kissed it. "I'll be here," he said, walking out the door before anything could happen to defuse the power of the moment.

147

When Lloyd wasn't home by six o'clock, Janice went about preparing for her evening, feeling relief on all fronts. She was relieved that Lloyd's absences were becoming more frequent and predictable, relieved that the girls were so engrossed in their hobbies and social life that they didn't seem to mind their missing father, relieved that her own loving detachment seemed to be growing to the point where some time soon she would be able to tell her husband, "You have been the love of my life, but it is over. I cannot get through to you. I cannot stand any more of your obsessive behavior. It is over."

As Janice dressed for her night of dancing she recalled the episode that had first given her the impetus to consider leaving her husband forever. It was two weeks ago. Lloyd had been gone for three days. She missed him and wanted him physically, and was even ready to make concessions about his stories. She had gone to bed nude and had left her bedside candle buring, hoping to be awakened by Lloyd's hands on her breasts. When she finally did awaken, it was to the sight of Lloyd hovering above her in the nude, gently spreading her legs. She held back a scream as he entered her, her eyes transfixed by his hellishly contorted features. When he came and his limbs contracted spastically, she held him very tight and knew that she had finally been given the power to forge a new life.

Janice dressed in a silver lamé pantsuit, an outfit that would brilliantly reflect the swirling lights at Studio One. She felt little twinges of slavish loyalty, and reflexively defined her husband in coldly clinical terms: He is a disturbed, driven man. An anachronistic man. He is incapable of change, a man who never listened.

Janice rounded up her daughters and drove them over to George's apartment in Ocean Park. His lover Rob would look after them while she and George discoed the night away. He would tell them kind, gentle stories and cook them up a big vegetarian feast.

Studio One was crowded, bursting to the rafters with stylish men undulating toward and away from each other under the benevolent distortions of stereo-synched strobe lights. Janice and George tooted some coke in the parking lot and imagined their entrance as one of the grandest, most closely scrutinized promenades in history. The only woman on the dance floor, Janice knew that she was the most desired body under the lights—desired not in lust but in desperate yearning for transference—tall, regal, tanned, and graceful, every man there wanted to *be* her.

When she returned home late that night, Lloyd was waiting in bed for her. He was especially tender, and she returned his caresses with great sorrow. Her mind ran disconnected images together to keep her from succumbing to his love. She thought of many things, but never came close to guessing that he had made love to another woman just two hours earlier; a woman who considered herself "something of a businesswoman" and who once sang unintelligible rock and roll lyrics; and that with her, as well as now with his wife, his thoughts were of an Irish girl from the old neighborhood.

That night Kathleen wrote in her diary:

Today I met a man; a man whom I think fate put in my path for a reason. To me he represents a paradox and possibilities that I cannot begin to access; such is his incongruous force. Enormous physically, fiercely bright—yet of all things, a man content to go through life as a policeman! I know that he wants me (when we met I noticed him wearing a wedding band. Later, as his attraction to me grew more obvious, I saw that he

149

had slipped it off—a roundabout and very endearing subterfuge). I think that he has a rapacious ego and will—ones to match his size and self-proclaimed brilliance. And I sense—I know—that he wants to change me, that he sees in me a kindred soul, one to touch deeply but also one to manipulate. I must watch my dialogue and my actions with this man. For the benefit of my growth, there must be a give and take. But I must keep my purest inner soul apart from him; my heart must remain inviolate.

CHAPTER NINE

Lloyd spent the morning at Parker Center, putting in a ritual appearance to appease Lieutenant Gaffaney and any other superior officers who might have noted his prolonged absence. Dutch Peltz called early; he had already initiated informal inquiries on old homosexual assault cases, delegating two desk officers the job of phoning the entire list of retired Juvenile detectives in the L.A.P.D.'s "private" retired personnel file. Dutch would be telephoning current Juvenile dicks with over twenty years on the job himself, and would call back as soon as he had gleaned a solid pile of information for evaluation. With Kathleen McCarthy checking out the bookstore angle, there was nothing Lloyd could do but chase paper—read the suicide files over and over again until something previously missed or overlooked or misunderstood jumped out at him.

It took two hours and digestion of thousands of words to make a connection, and when the number 408 appeared in the same context in two different files, Lloyd didn't know if it was a lead or a mere coincidence.

The body of Angela Stimka was discovered by her neighbor, L.A. County Deputy Sheriff Delbert Haines, badge #408, *other* neighbors having summoned the off-duty deputy when they smelled gas coming from the woman's apartment. A year to the day later, officers T. Rains, #408, and W. Vandervort, #691, were called to the scene of the Laurette Powell "suicide." Rains, Haines—a stupid spelling blunder; the identical badge numbers obviously denoted the same deputy.

Lloyd read over the file of the third West Hollywood "suicide"—Carla Castleberry, D.O.D. 6/10/80, the Tropicana Motel on Santa Monica Boulevard. Entirely different officers had filed this death report, and the names of residents of the motel who were interviewed at the scene—Duane Tucker, Lawrence Craigie, and Janet Mandarano—did not appear at all in any of the other files.

Lloyd picked up his phone and dialed the West Hollywood Sheriff's Substation. A bored voice answered. "Sheriff's. May I help you?"

Lloyd was brusque. "This is Detective Sergeant Hopkins, L.A.P.D. Do you have a Deputy Haines or Rains, badge 408, working out of your station?" The bored officer muttered, "Yessir, Big Whitey Haines. Day watch patrol."

"Is he on duty today?"

"Yessir."

"Good. Contact him on his radio. Tell him to meet me at the pizza joint on Fountain and La Cienega in one hour. It's urgent. You got that?"

"Yessir."

"Good. Do it now." Lloyd hung up. It was probably nothing—but at least it was movement.

Lloyd arrived at the restaurant early, ordering coffee and taking a booth with a view of the parking lot, the better to get a visual fix on Haines before their interview.

Five minutes later a sheriff's black-and-white pulled in and a uniformed deputy got out, squinting myopically against the sunlight. Lloyd sized the man up — big, blonde, a strong body going to flab. Middle thirties. Ridiculously sculpted hair, the sideburns too long for a fat face; the uniform encasing his musclebound upper torso and soft stomach like a sausage skin. Lloyd watched him don aviator sunglasses and hitch up his gunbelt. Not intelligent, but probably street-smart; play him easy.

The deputy walked directly to Lloyd's booth. "Sergeant?" he said, extending his hand.

Lloyd took the hand, squeezed it, and pointed across the table, waiting for the man to take off his sunglasses. When he sat down without removing them and picked nervously at an acne cluster on his chin, Lloyd thought: Speed. Play him hard.

Haines fidgeted under Lloyd's stare. "What can I do for you, sir?" he asked.

"How long have you been with the Sheriff's, Haines?"

"Nine years." Haines said.

"How long at the West Hollywood Station?"

"Eight years."

"You live on Larabee?"

"That's right."

"I'm surprised. West Hollywood is a faggot sewer."

Haines flinched. "I think a good cop should live on his beat."

Lloyd smiled. "So do I. What do your friends call you? Delbert? Del?"

Haines tried to smile, involuntarily biting his lip. "Whitey. Whwh-what do you — "

"What am I here for? I'll tell you in a moment. Does your beat include Westbourne Drive?"

"Y — yeah."

"Have you worked the same car plan your whole time at the station?"

"S — sure. Except for some loan out time to Vice. What's this all — "

Lloyd slammed the table top. Haines jolted backwards in his seat, reaching up and straightening his sunglasses with both hands. The muscles around his eyes twitched and tics started at the corners of his mouth. Lloyd smiled. "Ever work Narco?"

Haines went flush and whispered "No" hoarsely, a network of veins throbbing in his neck. Lloyd said, "Just checking. Basically, I'm here to question you about a stiff you found back in '78. A wrist slash job. A woman on Westbourne. You remember that?"

Haines's whole body went lax. Lloyd watched his muscles unclench into an almost stuporous posture of relief. "Yeah. My partner and I got an unknown trouble squeal from the desk. The old bag who lived next door called in about the stiff's record player blasting. We found this good lookin' babe all bl — "

Lloyd cut him off. "You found another suicide in your own building the year before, didn't you, Whitey?"

"Yeah," Haines said, "I sure did. I got wasted from the gas, they had to detox me at the hospital. I got a commendation and my picture on the honor board at the station."

Leaning back and stretching out his legs beneath the table, Lloyd said, "Both those women killed themselves on June 10th. Don't you think that's a strange coincidence?"

Haines shook his head. "Maybe. Maybe not. I don't know."

Lloyd laughed. "I don't know, either. That's all, Haines. You can go."

After Haines had left, Lloyd drank coffee and thought. A transparently stupid cop strung out on speed. No guilty knowledge of the two murder-suicides, but undoubtedly involved in so much penny-ante illegality that a questioning on old homicides was like being spared the guillotine — he never asked *why* the interview was taking place. Coincidence that he discovered both bodies? He lived *and* patrolled the same area. *Logically*, it fit.

But instinctively it was somehow out of kilter. Lloyd weighed the pros and cons of a daylight breaking and entering. The pros won. He drove to 1167 Larrabee Avenue.

The mauve-colored apartment building was perfectly still, the doors of the ten units closed, no activity on the walkway leading back to the carport. Lloyd scanned the mailboxes at the front of the building. Haines lived in apartment 5. Running his eyes over the numbers embossed on the first story doorways, he spotted his target — the rear apartment. No screen door, no heavy brass hardware indicating security locks.

Working a short bladed pen knife and a plastic credit card in unison, Lloyd snapped the locking mechanism and pushed the door open. Flicking on a wall light, he shut the door and surveyed the tasteless living room he had expected to find: cheap naugahyde couch and chairs, a formica coffee table, a ratty "deep-pile" carpet going threadbare. The walls boasted velveteen landscape prints and the built-in bookcases held no books — only a pile of skin magazines.

He walked into the kitchen. Mildew on the chipped linoleum floor, dirty dishes in the sink, a thick layer of grease on the cabinets and ceiling. The bathroom was dirtier still — shaving gear scattered on a sidebar near the sink, congealed shaving cream on the walls and mirror, a clothes hamper spilling soiled uniforms.

In the bedroom, Lloyd found his first indicators pointing to character traits other than aesthetic bankruptcy and sloth. Above the unkempt bed was a glass-fronted mahogany gunrack holding a half dozen shotguns — one of them an illegal double barreled sawed-off. Lifting the mattress, he discovered a Browning .9 millimeter automatic and a rusted bayonet with a tag affixed to its handle: *"Genuine Viet Cong Execution Sword! Guaranteed Authentic!"* The drawers beside the bed yielded a large plastic baggie filled with marijuana and a bottle of Dexedrine.

After going through the closets and dressers and finding nothing except dirty civilian clothes, Lloyd walked back into the living room, relieved that his instincts about Haines had been validated, yet still troubled that nothing more had *spoken* to him. With a blank mind, he sat down on the couch and let his eyes circuit the room, trawling for anything that would perk his mental juices. One circuit; two circuits; three. Floor to ceiling, along the walls and back again.

On his fourth circuit, Lloyd noted an inconsistency in the color and shape of the wainscoting at the juncture of the two walls directly over the couch. He stood up on a chair and examined the area. The paint had been thinned, and some sort of quarter-dollar size circular object had been stuck to the wood, then lightly painted over. He squinted, and felt himself go cold all over. There were tiny perforations in the object, which was the exact size of a high-powered condensor microphone. Running a finger along the bottom ridge of the wainscoting, Lloyd felt the wire. The living room was bugged.

Standing on his tiptoes, he traced the wire along the walls to the front door, down the door jamb and through a bored-out floor runner to a bush immediately adjacent to the steps of the apartment. Once outside, the wire was covered with a mauve-colored stucco spackling identical in hue to the whole building. Reaching behind the bush, Lloyd found the wire's terminus, an innocuous looking metal box attached to the wall at just about ground level. He grabbed at the box with both hands, and wrenched with all his strength. The cover snapped off. Lloyd crouched, then looked down the walkway for witnesses. None. He held the bush and metal cover to one side and looked at his prize.

The box contained a state-of-the-art tape recorder. The tape spool was not running, which meant that whoever was doing the bugging had to turn the machine on himself or, more likely, there was a triggering device at work, probably one that Whitey Haines unconsciously activated himself.

Lloyd looked at the door, a scant three paces from where he stood. It *had* to be the trigger.

He walked to the door, unlocked it from the inside, then closed it again, and walked back to the recorder. No movement of the spools. He repeated the procedure, this time opening the door from the outside, then closing it. Squatting by the bush, he admired the results. A red light was glowing, and the tape spools spun silently. Whitey Haines worked day watch. Whoever was interested in his activities knew this and wanted his evenings recorded — the front-door-opening-inward trigger was proof of that.

Lloyd locked the door. Take the recorder with him, or stake out the apartment and wait for the bugger to come and pick up the tape? Was any of this even *connected* to his case? Again scanning the walkway for witnesses, Lloyd tried to make up his mind. When curiosity prickled up his spine and bludgeoned all his other considerations to death, he cut the wire with his penknife, picked up the tape machine and ran for his car.

Back at Parker Center, Lloyd donned surgical thin rubber gloves and examined the tape recorder. The machine was identical to a prototype he had seen at an F.B.I. seminar on electronic surveillance equipment — a "deep dish" model that featured four separate twin spools stationed on either side of self-cleaning heads that snapped into place automatically as each eight-hour increment of tape was used up, making it possible to record for as long as thirty-two hours without coming near the machine.

Probing inside the recorder, Lloyd saw that the primary spools and the three auxiliary spools all held tape, and that the tape on the primary spool was half on the blank side and half on the recorded side, meaning that there was no more than approximately four hours of recorded material contained in the machine. Wanting to be certain of this, he checked the compartment that stored the finished spools. It was empty.

Lloyd removed the auxiliary tapes and placed them inside his top desk drawer, thinking that the small amount of "live" tape was a mixed blessing — there would probably be very little information to be gleaned from four hours of bugging time, but assuming that the bugger had a good fix on Whitey Haines's habits and some kind of shut-off device secreted inside his apartment to record only x number of hours per night, the absence of "live" tape would allow plenty of time to set up a stake-out to catch the bugger when he returned to put in fresh spools. Anyone clever enough to set up an electronic surveillance this complex would risk only a minimum number of tape pick-up forays.

Lloyd ran down the hall to the interrogation cubicle that bordered the sixth floor briefing room. He grabbed a battered reel-to-reel recorder from atop a cigarette-scarred table and carried it back to his office. "Be good", he said as he placed the "live" tape on the spindle. "No music, no loud noise. Just be good."

The tape spun, and the built-in speaker hissed, then crackled with static. There was the sound of a door being locked, then a baritone grunt followed by a noise Lloyd recognized immediately—the thud of a gunbelt dropped on a couch or chair. Next came barely audible footsteps, then another grunt, this one octaves higher than the first. Lloyd smiled. There were at least two people in Haines's apartment.

Haines spoke. "You gotta feed me more, Bird; cut the coke with some of the bennies I glom from the narco guys, raise your prices, find some new fucking customers or some fucking thing. We got new fish coming in, and if I don't lay some bread on them, all my fuckin' juice ain't gonna keep you and your asshole buddies outta the queens' tank. You dig me, homeboy?"

A high-pitched male voice answered. "Whitney, you said you wouldn't raise my nut! I'm giving you six bills a month plus half the dope action, plus kickbacks from half the punks on the street! You said —— "

Lloyd heard a whirring sound dissolve into a sharp crack. There was silence, then Haines's voice. "You start that shit again and I'll hit you for real. You listen, Bird—Without me, you are shit. You are the king fucking dick of Boy's Town because I got you to lift weights and build up your puny body and because I get the fucking kiddy bulls to roust the pretty boy juvie's off your turf, and because I shoot you the dope and the protection that make you and your punk pals a class act. As long as I've got clout with Vice, you are safe. And that takes money. There's a transfer-happy new day watch commander, and if I don't grease his fucking palm I may end up busting nigger heads down in Compton. There's two new fish rotating into Vice, and I got no fucking idea if I can keep them off your tight little ass. *My* nut is two grand a month before I see a fucking dollar profit. *Your* nut is going up twenty percent as of today. You dig me, Bird?"

The high voiced man stammered, "Sh-sh-sure, Whitey." Haines chuckled, then spoke in a soft voice rich with insinuation. "I've always took good care of you. Keep your nose clean and I always will. You just gotta feed me more. Now c'mon in the back. I wanta feed you."

"I don't want to, Whitey."

"You got to, Birdy. It's part of your protection."

Lloyd listened as the sound of footsteps metamorphosed into a silence inhabited by pitiful monsters. The silence stretched into hours. It was broken by the sound of muted sobbing and the slamming of a door. Then the tape went dead.

Fruit hustler shakedowns, vice pay-offs, dope dealing and a corrupt, brutal cop unfit to wear a badge. But was it connected to mass murder? And *who* had bugged Whitey Haines's apartment, and *why*?

Lloyd made two quick phone calls, to the Internal Affairs Divisions of both the L.A.P.D. and Sheriff's Department. Using his reputation as a lever, he was able to get straight answers from the I.A.D. high brass. No, Deputy Delbert Haines, badge 408, was not under investigation by either Division. Disturbed, Lloyd ran down a mental list of probable parties interested in the affairs of Whitey Haines: rival dope rings, rival male prostitution combines, a fellow deputy with a grudge. All were possible, but none of the choices rang any bells. Some sort of homosexual tie-in to his killer? Unlikely. It violated his theory of the murderer having been chaste for years, and Haines had no guilty knowledge of the two June 10th suicides he had discovered.

Lloyd took the concealed tape recorder down to the third floor offices of the Scientific Identification Division and showed it to a data analyst who he knew was particularly enamored of bugging devices. The man whistled as Lloyd placed the machine on his desk, and reached over lovingly to touch it.

"Not yet, Artie," Lloyd said. "I want it run for latents." Artie whistled again, pushing back his chair and sending

"Ooh la la" eyes heavenward. "It's gorgeous, Lloyd. It's perfection."

"Run it down for me, Artie. Omit nothing."

The analyst smiled and cleared his throat. "The Watanabe A.F.Z. 999 Recorder. Retail price around seven thousand clams. Available at only the very best stereo showrooms. Used primarily by two rather diverse groups of people: music lovers interested in recording rock festivals or lengthy operas in one fell swoop, and police agencies interested in long term clandestine bugging. Every component of this machine is the finest that money can buy and Jap technology can produce. You are looking at absolute perfection."

Lloyd gave Artie a round of applause. "Bravo. One other question. Are there hidden serial numbers on the thing? Individual numbers or prototype numbers that can fix the date when the machine was sold?"

Artie shook his head. "The A.F.Z. 999 hit the market in the middle '70s. One prototype, no serial numbers, no different colors—just basic black. The Watanabe Corporation has a thing about tradition; they will not alter the design on these babies. I don't blame them. Who can improve on perfection?"

Lloyd looked down at the recorder. It was in perfect shape, not a scratch on it. "Shit," he said, "I was hoping to narrow down the list of possible buyers. Look, is this thing listed in one of S.I.D.'s Retailer Files?"

"Sure," Artie said. "Want me to compile a list?" Lloyd nodded. "Yeah. Do it now, will you? I'm going to take our baby down the hall and leave it for dusting. I'll be right back."

There was one fingerprint technician on duty at the S.I.D.'s Central Crime Lab. Lloyd handed him the tape recorder and said, "Latent prints, nationwide teletype. I want you to *personally* compare them to L.A.P.D. Homicide Bulletin 16222, Niemeyer, Julia L., 1/3/83, partial right index and pinky. Those prints were bloodstained; if you're in doubt about a match-up on the bulletin, roll the new prints in a blood sample, then recompare. You got that?"

The technician nodded assent, then asked, "Think we'll find prints?"

"It's doubtful, but we have to try. Be thorough; this is very important." The technician opened his mouth to offer assurances, but Lloyd was already running away.

"Eighteen retailers," Artie said as Lloyd burst through the door. "That's up to date, too. Didn't I tell you our baby was esoteric?" Lloyd took the printed list and put it in his pocket, looking reflexively at the clock above Artie's desk. 6:30 — too late to begin calling the stereo supply stores. Remembering his date with Kathleen McCarthy, he said, "I have to run. Take care, Artie. Some day I may tell you the whole story."

Kathleen McCarthy closed the store early and went back to her living quarters to write and prepare for her evening with the big policeman. Her business day had been frustrating. No sales, and an endless series of browsers who had wanted to discuss feminist issues while she was on the phone trying to secure information toward the capture of a psychopathic woman-killer. The irony was both profound and cheap, and Kathleen felt a vague diminishing of selfhood in its aftermath. She had hated the police for so long that even though she was doing her moral duty in aiding them, the price was a piece of her ego. Bolstering herself with logic, Kathleen grabbed the ego fragment and killed it with words. Dialectic at the expense of helping others. Pride. Your intractable Irish heart. The rhetoric fell short of its mark, and Kathleen smiled at the *real* irony — sex. You want the cop, and you don't even know his first name.

Kathleen walked into the bathroom and stripped before

the full length mirror. Strong flesh, satisfyingly lean; firm breasts, good legs. A tall, handsome woman. Thirty-six, yet looking...Kathleen's eyes clouded with tears, and she braced herself by maintaining eye contact with her image. It worked — the tears died, stillborn.

Throwing on a robe, Kathleen walked into her living room-study and arrayed pen, paper and thesaurus on her desk, then went through her prewriting ritual of letting random prose patterns and thoughts of her dream lover battle for primacy of her mind. As always, her dream lover won, and Kathleen plucked absently at the crotch of her robe and relinquished herself to the smell of the flowers that always came just when she most needed them, when her life was almost to some brink. Then, anonymously and in perfect psychic sync the flowers would be at her doorstep and she would be overwhelmed and wonder who, and look to the faces of strange men for signs of kinship or commiseration or *special* interest.

She knew that he had to be tall and intelligent and about her age — eighteen years of floral tribute without a clue to his identity! Except that he had to have come from the old neighborhood, had to have seen her on the way to school with her court...

Thoughts of her court gave Kathleen a hook. She took up her pen and wrote:

> Bring back the dead
> Give them head
> Remember the songs they sang
> And the words they said.
> From protracted adolesence
> To premature senescence
> I do penance with regret;
> For the epiphanies I never held
> And the joy I never met.

Sighing, Kathleen settled back in her chair. Sighing again, she got out her diary and wrote:

Good prose seems just about to burst out of me, so I'll do a little tease number and sit back and collate the present again, from approximately my nine thousandth "good prose breakout" plateau. Weird these days. Even good serviceable prose seems contrived. This diary (which will probably never be published!) seem much more real. I'm probably moving into a period where I'll just sit back and let things happen, figure them out as they happen, then shut whatever is happening out and sit down and grind out another book. The cop seems to be evidence of this. O.K., he's compelling and attractive, but even if he weren't I'd probably give his attentions a shot. Weirder yet: Is this "Let it flow" attitude undertaken out of the desire for edification or out of loneliness, horniness, and the desire to ultimately give up that awful part of me that wants to stand apart from the whole human race and exist through my words? Empirically speaking, who knows? My solitude has given me brilliant words, as have my abysmal relationships with men. Another (nine billionth?) meditation on the identity of *him*? Not today, today is strictly the realm of things possible. All of a sudden I'm tired of words. I hope the cop isn't too right wing. I hope he is capable of bending.

Kathleen placed her pen across her words, surprised that the combination of her dream lover and the policeman had inspired such somber sentiments. Smiling at the unpredictability of muses, she glanced at her watch. 6:30. As she showered for her date, she wondered where those first stanzas would take her and how she would react when her doorbell rang at seven o'clock.

The bell rang precisely at seven. When Kathleen opened the door, Lloyd was standing there, wearing beat-up cords and a pullover sweater. She saw a holstered revolver outlined on his left hip and cursed herself; her Harris tweed pantsuit was a definite overdress. To correct the mistake she said, "Hi, Sergeant" and grabbed at the gun bulge and pulled Lloyd inside. He let himself be led, and Kathleen cursed herself again when she saw him smile at the gesture.

Lloyd sat on the couch and spread out his long arms in a mock crucifixion pose. Kathleen stood over him selfconsciously. "I made those phone calls," she said. "To over a dozen bookdealers. Nothing. None of my friends recall seeing or talking with a man like the one you described. It was bizarre. I was helping the police to find an insane woman-killer, and women kept interrupting me to ask questions about the Equal Rights Amendment."

"Thank you," Lloyd said. "I didn't really expect anything. Right now I'm just fishing. Badge 1114, homicide fisherman on the job."

Kathleen sat down. "Are you supervising this investigation?" she asked.

Lloyd shook his head. "No, right now I *am* this investigation. None of my superiors would authorize me to detach officers to work under me, because the idea of mass murderers killing with impunity makes them afraid for their careers and the Department's prestige. I *have* supervised homicide investigations, duties normally assigned to Lieutenants and Captains, but I'm — "

"But you're that good." Kathleen said it as a matter-of-fact.

Lloyd smiled. "I'm better."

"Can you read minds, Sergeant?"

"Call me Lloyd."

"All right, Lloyd."

"The answer is sometimes."

"Do you know what I'm thinking?"

Lloyd draped his arm over Kathleen's tweed shoulders. She buckled, but didn't resist. "I've got an idea," he said. "How's this for starters? Who is this guy? Is he a right-wing loony, like most cops? Does he spend hours cracking jokes about niggers and discussing pussy with his policeman buddies? Does he like to hurt people? To *kill* people? Does he think there's a Jew-commie-nigger-homo conspiracy to take over the world? Does. . ."

Kathleen put a gentle restraining hand on Lloyd's knee and said, "*Touché.* In basic theme you were correct on all counts." She smiled against her will, slowly withdrawing her hand.

Lloyd felt his blood start to race to the tempo of their banter. "Do you want my answers?" he asked.

"No. You've already given me them."

"Any other questions?"

"Yes. Two. Do you cheat on your wife?"

Lloyd laughed and dug into his pants pocket for his wedding band. He slipped it onto his ring finger and said, "Yes."

Kathleen's face was expressionless. "Have you ever killed anyone?" she asked.

"Yes."

Kathleen grimaced. "I shouldn't have asked. No more talk of death and woman-killers, please. Shall we leave?"

Lloyd nodded and took her hand as she locked the door behind them.

They drove aimlessly, ending up cruising the terraced hills of the old neighborhood. Lloyd steered the unmarked Matador through the topography of their mutual past, wondering what Kathleen was thinking.

"My parents are dead now," she said finally. "They were both so old when I was born, and they doted on me because they knew they'd only have me for twenty years or so. My father told me he moved to Silverlake because the hills reminded him of Dublin."

She looked at Lloyd, who sensed that she wanted to end her games of will and be gentle. He pulled to the curb at Vendrome and Hyperion, hoping that the spectacular view would move her to divulge intimate things, things that would make him care for her. "Do you mind if we stop?" he asked.

"No," Kathleen said, "I like this place. I used to come here with my court. We read memorial poems for John Kennedy here on the night he was shot."

"Your court?"

"Yes. My court. The 'Kathy Kourt'—spelled with two Ks. I had my own little group of underlings in high school. We were all poets, and we all wore plaid skirts and cashmere sweaters, and we never dated, because there was not one boy at John Marshall High School worthy of us. We didn't date and we didn't neck. We were saving it for Mr. Right, who, we all figured, would make the scene when we were published poets of renown. We were unique. I was the smartest and the best-looking. I transferred from parochial school because the Mother Superior was always trying to get me to show her my breasts. I talked about it in hygiene class and attracted a following of lonely, bookish girls. They became my court. I gave them an identity. They became *women* because of me. Everyone left us alone; yet we had a following of equally lonely, bookish boys—'Kathy's Klowns' they were called, because we never even deigned to speak to them. We... We...."

Kathleen's voice rose to a wail, and she batted off Lloyd's tentative hand on her shoulder. "We... We... loved and cared for each other, and I know it sounds pathetic, but we were strong. Strong! Strong...."

Lloyd waited a full minute before asking, "What happened to your court?"

Kathleen sighed, knowing that her answer was an

anticlimax. "Oh, they drifted away. They found boyfriends. They decided not to save it for Mr. Right. They got prettier. They decided they didn't want to be poets. They...they just didn't need me anymore."

"And you?"

"I died, and my heart went underground and resurfaced looking for cheap kicks and true love. I slept with a lot of women, figuring I could find a new entourage that way. It didn't work. I screwed a lot of men — that got me the entourage, all right, but they were creeps. And I wrote and wrote and wrote and got published and bought a bookstore and here I am."

Lloyd was already shaking his head. "And what *really*," he said.

Kathleen spat out angrily, "And I am a damn good poet and a better diarist! And who the hell are you to question me? And? And? *And?*"

Lloyd touched her neck with gentle fingertips and said, "And you live in your head, and you're thirty-something, and you keep wondering if it's ever going to get better. Please say yes, Kathleen, or just shake your head." Kathleen shook her head. Lloyd said, "Good. That's why I'm here — because I want it to get better for you. Do you believe that?" Kathleen shook her head affirmatively and stared into her lap, clenching her hands. "I have a question for you," Lloyd said. "A rhetorical question. Did you know that the L.A.P.D. treats the undercarriage of all their unmarked cars with a special shock-proof, scrape-proof coating?"   •

Kathleen laughed politely at the non sequitur. "No," she said.

Lloyd reached over and secured the passenger safety harness around her shoulders. When she remained blank-faced he waggled his eyebrows and said, "Brace yourself," then hit the ignition and dropped into low gear, popping the emergency brake and flooring the gas pedal simultaneously, sending the car forward in an almost vertical wheel stand. Kathleen screamed. Lloyd waited until the car began its crashing downward momentum, then gently tapped the accelerator a half dozen times until the rear wheels caught friction and the car lurched ahead, straining to keep its front end airborne. Kathleen screamed again. Lloyd felt gravity fighting sheer engine power and winning. As the hood of the Matador swung down, he punched the gas pedal and the car nosed upward, holding its pattern until he saw an intersection coming up and hit the brakes, sending them into a tire squealing fishtail. The car was spinning out toward a row of trees when its front end finally smashed into the pavement. Lloyd and Kathleen bounced in their seats like spastic puppets. Dripping with nervous sweat, Lloyd rolled down his window and saw a group of Chicano teenagers giving him a wild ovation, stomping their feet and saluting the car with raised beer bottles.

He blew them a kiss and turned to Kathleen. She was crying, and he couldn't tell if in fear or joy. He unstrapped the harness and held her. He let her cry, and gradually felt the tears trail into laughter. When Kathleen finally raised her head from his chest, Lloyd saw the face of a delighted child. He kissed that face with the same tenderness as he kissed the faces of his daughters.

"Urban romanticism," Kathleen said. "Jesus. What next?"

Lloyd considered options and said, "I don't know. Let's stay mobile, though. All right?"

"Will you observe all traffic regulations?"

Lloyd said, "Scout's honor" and started up the car, waggling his eyebrows at Kathleen until she laughed and begged him to stop. The teenagers gave him another round of applause as he pulled out.

They cruised Sunset, the main artery of the old

168

neighborhood. Lloyd editorialized as he drove, pointing out immortal locations of his past:

"There's Myron's Used Cars. Myron was a genius chemist gone wrong. He got strung out on heroin and kicked out of his teaching post at U.S.C. He developed a corrosive solution that would eat off the serial numbers on engine blocks. He stole hundreds of cars, lowered the blocks into his vat of solution and set himself up as the used car king of Silverlake. He used to be a nice guy. He was a big rooter for the Marshall football team, and he lent all the star players cars for hot dates. Then one day when he was fucked up on smack he fell into his vat. The solution ate off both his legs up to the knee. Now he's a cripple and the single most misanthropic individual I've ever known."

Kathleen joined in the travelogue, pointing across the street and saying, "Cathcart Drugs. I used to steal stationery there for my court. Scented purple stationery. One day I got caught. Old man Cathcart grabbed me and dug into my purse. He found some poems I had written on the same kind of stationery. He held me and read the poems aloud to everyone in the store. Intimate poems. I was so ashamed."

Lloyd felt a sadness intrude on their evening. Sunset Boulevard was too loud and garishly neon. Without saying a word he turned the car north on Echo Park Bouelvard and drove past the Silverlake Reservoir. Soon they were in the shadow of the power plant, and he turned and looked at Kathleen for approval.

"Yes," she said, "it's perfect."

They walked uphill silently, holding hands. Dirt clods broke at their feet, and twice Lloyd had to pull Kathleen forward. When they reached the summit they sat in the dirt, heedless of their clothes, leaning into the wire fence that encircled the facility. Lloyd felt Kathleen pulling apart from him, regrouping against the momentum of her tears. To close the gap, he said, "I like you, Kathleen."

"I like you, too. And I like it here."

"It's quiet here."

"You love the quiet and you hate music. Where does your wife think you are?"

"I don't know. Lately she goes out dancing with this fag guy she knows. Her soul sister. They snort cocaine and go to a gay disco. *She* loves music, too."

"And it doesn't bother you?" Kathleen said.

"Well...more than anything else I just don't understand it. I understand why people rob banks and become thieves and get strung out on dope and sex and become cops and poets and killers, but I don't understand why people fart around in discos and listen to music when they could be goosing the world with an electric cattle prod. I can understand you and your court and your screwing all those dykes and creeps. I understand innocent little children and their love, and their trauma when they dicover how cold it can get, but I don't understand how they cannot want to fight it. I tell my daughters stories so they'll fight. My youngest, Penny, is a genius. She's a fighter. My two older girls I'm not so sure about. Janice, my wife, isn't a fighter. I don't think she was ever innocent. She was born practical and stable and stayed that way. I think...I think maybe...that's why I married her. I think...I *knew* I didn't have any more innocence, and I wasn't quite sure that I was a fighter. Then I found out I *was* and got scared of the price and married Janice."

Lloyd's voice had assumed an almost disembodied monotone. Kathleen thought briefly that he was a ventriloquist's pawn, and that whoever was pulling his strings was really trying to get to *her*; laying clues in the strange barrage of confession she had just heard. Two words—"killers" and "price" stuck out, and in her haste to make sense of the story Kathleen said, "And so you became a policeman to prove you were a fighter, and then you killed in the line of duty and you knew."

Lloyd shook his head. "No, I killed a man — an evil man — first. Then I became a cop and married Janice. I lose track of chronology sometimes. Sometimes...not often...when I try to figure out my past I hear noise...music...awful noise...and I have to stop."

Kathleen felt Lloyd wavering in and out of control, and knew that she had broken through to his essence. She said, "I want to tell you a story. It's a true romantic story."

Lloyd shifted his head onto her lap and said, "Tell me."

"All right. There was once a quiet, bookish girl who wrote poetry. She didn't believe in God or her parents or the other girls who followed her. She tried very hard to believe in herself. It was easy, for awhile. Then her followers left her. She was alone. But someone loved her. Some tender man sent her flowers. The first time there was an anonymous poem. A sad poem. The second time just the flowers. The dream lover continued to send the flowers, anonymously, for many years. Over eighteen years. Always when the lonely woman needed them most. The woman grew as a poet and diarist and kept the flowers dated and pressed in glass. She speculated on this man, but never tried to discover his identity. She took his anonymous tribute to her heart and decided that she would reciprocate his anonymity by keeping her diaries private until after her death. And so she lived and wrote and listened to music — a quiet mover. It almost makes you want to believe in God, doesn't it, Lloyd?"

Lloyd took his head from its soft tweed resting place, shaking it to bring the sad story into sharper focus. Then he stood up and helped Kathleen to her feet. "I think your dream lover is a very strange fighter," he said, "and I think he wants to own you, not inspire you. I think he doesn't know how strong you are. Come on, I'll take you home."

They stood in the doorway of Kathleen's bookstore-apartment, holding each other loosely. Kathleen burrowed into Lloyd's shoulder, and when she raised her head he thought that she wanted to be kissed. As he bent to her, Kathleen pushed him gently away. "No. Not yet. Please don't force it, Lloyd."

"All right."

"It's just that the whole thing is so unexpected. You're so special, and it just..."

"You're special, too."

"I know, but I've got *no* idea of who you are, of your natural habitat. The *little* things. Do you understand?"

Lloyd pondered this. "I think so. Look, would you like to go to a dinner party tomorrow night? Policemen and their wives? It'll probably be dull, but illuminating for you."

Kathleen smiled. His offer was a major capitulation; he was willing to be bored to please her. "Yes. Be here at seven." She moved backward into her dark front room and closed the door behind her. When she heard Lloyd's departing footsteps she turned on the lights and got out her diary. Her mind rambled with profundities until she muttered, "Oh, fuck it," and wrote:

> He is capable of bending. I am going to be his music.

Lloyd drove home. He pulled into the driveway to find Janice's car gone and all the lights in the house glowing brightly. He unlocked the door and walked inside, seeing the note immediately:

> Lloyd, darling:
> This is goodbye, for awhile at least. The girls and I have gone to San Francisco to stay with a friend of George's. It is for the best, I know that, because I

172

know that you and I have not communicated for a long, long time, and that our values are markedly different. Your behavior with the girls was the final straw. I have known almost since the beginning of our marriage of some deep disturbance in you — one you disguised (for the most part) very well. What I will not tolerate is your passing your disturbance on to them. Your stories are cancerous in their effect, and Anne, Caroline, and Penny must be free of them. A note on the girls — I am going to enroll them in a Montessori School in S.F., and I will have them call you at least once a week. George's roommate Rob will look after the shop in my absence. I will decide in the coming months whether or not I want a divorce. I care for you deeply, but I cannot live with you. I am withholding our address in S.F. until I am certain you will not try to do something rash. When I get settled, I'll call. Until then be well and don't worry.

Janice

Lloyd put down the note and walked through the empty house. Everything feminine had been cleared out. The girls' room had been picked clean of personal belongings; the bedroom that he shared with Janice now contained only his solitary aura and the navy blue cashmere quilt that Penny had crafted for his thirty-seventh birthday.

Lloyd drew the quilt around his shoulders and walked outside. He looked up at the sky and hoped for an annihilating rainstorm. When he realized that he couldn't will thunder and lightning, he fell to his knees and wept.

CHAPTER TEN

When the poet saw the empty metal box, he screamed. Cancer cells materialized out of the dawn sky and threw themselves at his eyes, hurling him onto the cold pavement. He wrapped his arms around his head and drew himself into a fetal ball to keep the tiny carcinogens from going for his throat, then rocked back and forth until he had blunted all his senses and his body started to cramp, then numb. When he felt self-asphyxiation coming on he breathed out, and familiar Larrabee Avenue came into focus. No cancer cells in the air. His beautiful tape machine was gone, but Officer Pig was still asleep and the early morning scene on Larrabee was normal. No police cars, no suspicious vehicles, no trench-coated figures huddled behind newspapers. He had changed the tape forty-eight hours ago, so the machine was mostly likely discovered that day, when it was empty or running, or yesterday, when it contained a minimum of recorded material. If he hadn't wanted to touch himself so badly he would never have risked the early pick-up, but he needed the stimulus of Officer Pig and his lackey, who had been doing things to each other on the couch for weeks now, things that Julia had written about in her evil manu —

He couldn't complete the thought; it was too shameful.

He got to his feet and looked in all directions. No one had seen him. He bit at the skin of his forearms. The blood that trickled out was red and healthy looking. He opened his mouth to speak, wanting to be sure that the cancer cells hadn't severed his vocal cords. The word that came out was "safe." He said it a dozen times, each time with a more awed inflection. Finally he shouted it and ran for his car.

Thirty minutes later he had scaled the bookstore roof, a silenced .32 automatic in his windbreaker pocket, smiling when he saw that his Sanyo 6000 was still hidden underneath an outsized sheaf of tarred-over pipe insulation. He grabbed the two spools of finished tape from the machine's storage compartment. Safe. Safe. Safe. Safe. He said the word over and over again on his drive home, and he was still saying it as he put the first spool on the old machine in the living room, then sat back to listen, his eyes moving over the rose branches and photographs on the walls.

The sound of a switch being flipped; the porch light going on; the trigger activating the tape. His original beloved muttering to herself, then deep silence. He smiled and touched his thighs. She was writing.

The silence stretched. One hour. Two. Three. Four. Then the sound of yawning and the switch being flipped again.

He got to his feet, stretched and changed spools. Again the porch light trigger — his punctual darling, 6:55, like clockwork.

He sat down, wondering if he should make himself explode now while he could hear footsteps, or wait and take a chance on his original beloved talking to herself. Then a doorbell rang. Her voice: "Hi, Sergeant." The scuffle of feet. Her voice again: "I made those phone calls. To over a dozen bookdealers. Nothing. None of my friends recall seeing or talking with a man like the one you described. It was bizarre. I was helping the police to find an insane woman-killer, and women kept — "

At the last words he began to tremble. His body went ice cold, then turned burning hot. He punched the stop button and fell to his knees. He clawed at his face until he drew blood, whimpering safe, safe, safe. He crawled to the window and looked out at the passing parade on Alvarado. He took hope with every identifiable evidence of business as usual: traffic noise, Mexican women with children in tow, junkies waiting to score in front of the Burrito stand. He started to say "safe," then hesitated and whispered "maybe." "Maybe" grew in his brain until he screamed it and stumbled back to the recorder.

He pushed the play button. His first beloved was saying something about women interrupting her. Then a man's voice: "Thank you. I didn't really expect anything. Right now I'm just fishing. Badge 1114, homicide fisherman on the job."

He forced himself to listen, gouging his genitals with both hands to keep from screaming. The horrific conversation continued, and words leaped out and made him gouge himself harder. "The idea of mass murderers killing with impunity makes them afraid...I *have* supervised homicide investigations...call me Lloyd."

When the door slammed and the tape spun in blessed silence he took his hands from between his legs. He could feel blood dripping down his thighs, and it reminded him of high school and poetry and the sanctity of his purpose. Mrs. Cuthbertson's eleventh grade honors English class. Logical fallacies: *post hoc, propter ergo hoc* — "After this, therefore because of this." Knowledge of crimes committed does *not* mean knowledge of the perpetrator. Policemen were not breaking down his door. "Lloyd," "Homicide fisherman badge 1114," had no idea that his original beloved's dwelling was bugged, and may have had nothing to do with the theft of his other tape recorder. "Lloyd" was "fishing" in shark-infested waters, and if he came near him he would eat the policeman alive. Conclusion: they had no idea who he was, and it was business as usual.

Tonight he would claim his twenty-third and most hurriedly courted beloved. No "maybe." It was a pure "yes," powerfully affirmed by his meditation tape and every one of his beloveds from Jane Wilhelm on up. Yes. Yes. The poet walked to the window and screamed it to the world at large.

CHAPTER ELEVEN

His sleepless night in the empty house had been the precursor to a day of total bureaucratic frustration, and each negative feedback tore at Lloyd like a neon sign heralding the end of all the gentle restraining influences in his life. Janice and the girls were gone, and until his genius killer was captured, he was powerless to get them back.

As the day wound down into early evening, Lloyd recounted his dwindling options, wondering what on God's earth he would do if they died out and left him with only his mind and his will.

It had taken him six hours to call the eighteen stereo supply stores and secure a list of fifty-five people who had purchased Watanabe A.F.Z. 999 recorders over the last eight years. Twenty-four of the buyers had been women, leaving thirty-one male suspects, and Lloyd knew from experience that telephone interviews would be futile — experienced detectives would have to size up the buyers in person and determine guilt or innocence from the suspects' response to questioning. And if the recorder had been purchased outside L.A. County...and if the whole Haines angle had nothing to do with the killings...and he would need manpower for interviewing...and if Dutch turned him down at the party tonight...

The negative feedback continued, undercut with memories of Penny and her quilts and Caroline and Anne squealing with delight at his stories. Dutch had gotten nothing positive from his queries to both retired and long-term active juvenile detectives and the "monicker" files on "Bird" and "Birdy" had yielded only the names of a dozen ghetto blacks. Useless—the high pitched voice in Whitey Haines's living room had obviously belonged to a white man.

But the greatest frustration had been the absence of a print make on the tape recorder. Lloyd had stalked the crime lab repeatedly, looking for the technician he had left the machine with, calling the man at home, only to find that his father had had a heart attack and that he had driven to San Bernardino, taking the recorder with him, intending to use the facilities of the San Bernardino Sheriff's Department for his dusting and comparison tests. "He said that you wanted him to do the tests *personally,* Sergeant," the technician's wife had said. "He'll call from San Bernardino in the morning with the results." Lloyd had hung up cursing semantics and his own authoritarian nature.

This left two last-ditch, one-man options: Interview the thirty-one buyers himself or cop some bennies and stake out Whitey Haines's apartment until the bugger showed up. Desperation tactics—and the only avenues he had left.

Lloyd got his car and headed west, toward Kathleen's bookstore-cottage. When he got off the freeway he realized he was bone weary and flesh hungry and pointed his Matador north, in the direction of Joanie Pratt's house in the Hollywood Hills. They could love and talk and maybe Joanie's body would smother his feeling of doomsday attrition coming from all sides.

Joanie jumped on Lloyd as he walked through the open front door, exclaiming, "Sarge, *wilkommen!* Romance on your mind? If so, the bedroom is immediately to your right." Lloyd laughed. Joanie's big carnal heart was the perfect spot to place his tenderness.

"Lead the way."

When they had loved and played and looked at the sunset from the bedroom balcony, Lloyd told Joanie that his wife and children were gone and that in the wake of his abandonment there was only himself and the killer. "I'm giving my investigation two more days," he said, "then I'm going public. I'm taking everything I have to Channel 7 News and flushing my career down the toilet. It hit me while we were lying in bed. If the leads I have now don't pan out I'm going to create such a fucking public stink that every police agency in L.A. County will *have* to go after this animal; if my reading of him is correct, the exposure will drive him to do something so rash that he'll blow it completely. I think he has an incredible ego that's screaming to be recognized, and when he screams it to the world I'll be there to get him."

Joanie shuddered, then put a comforting hand on Lloyd's shoulder. "You'll get him, Sarge. You'll give him the big one where it hurts the most."

Lloyd smiled at the imagery. "My options are narrowing down," he said. "It feels good." Remembering Kathleen, he added, "I've got to go."

"Hot date?" Joanie asked.

"Yeah. With a poetess."

"Do me a favor before you go?"

"Name it."

"I want a happy picture of the two of us."

"Who's going to take it?"

"Me. There's a ten-second delay on my Polaroid. Come on, get up."

"But I'm naked, Joanie!"

"So am I. Come on."

Joanie walked into the living room and came back with a camera affixed to a tripod. She pushed some buttons and ran to Lloyd's side. Blushing, he grabbed her around the waist and felt himself start to go hard. The flash cube popped. Joanie counted the seconds and pulled the film from the camera. The print was perfect: the nude Lloyd and Joanie, she smiling carnally, he blushing and semi-erect. Lloyd felt his tenderness explode as he looked at it. He took Joanie's face in his hands and said, "I love you."

Joanie said, "I love you too, Sarge. Now get dressed. We've both got dates tonight, and I'm late for mine."

Kathleen had spent her entire day in preparation for her evening; long hours in the women's departments of Brooks Brothers and Boshard-Doughty, searching for *the* romantic purist outfit that would speak eloquently of her past and flatter her in the present. It *took* hours, but she found it: pink Oxford cloth button down shirt, navy blue ankle socks and cordovan tassel loafers, a navy crew neck sweater and the *piece de resistance* — a knee length, pleated, red tartan skirt.

Feeling both sated and expectant, Kathleen drove home to savor waiting for her romantic conspirator. She had four hours to kill, and prescribed getting mildly stoned and listening to music as the way to do it. Since tonight she would be juxtaposed iconoclastically against a staid gathering of policemen and their wives, she put a carefully selected medley of flower child revolution on the turntable and sat back in her robe to smoke dope and listen, filled with the knowledge that tonight she would teach the big policeman — wow him with her poetry, read classic excerpts from her diary, and maybe let him kiss her breasts.

As the Colombian gold took her over, Kathleen found herself playing out a new fantasy. Lloyd was her dream lover. He was the one who had sent the flowers all those years; he had waited for the terrible impetus of searching for a killer to bring them together — a casual meeting wouldn't have been romantic enough for him. The genesis of his attraction had to be Silverlake — they had grown up a scant six blocks apart.

Kathleen felt her fantasy drift apart with the diminishing of her high. To fortify it, she smoked her last Thai stick. Within minutes she was at one with the music and Lloyd was nude in front of her, admitting his deepening love of almost two decades, breathless in his desire to have her. Regal in her magnanimity, Kathleen accepted, watching him grow bigger and harder until she, Lloyd, and the deep bass guitar of the Jefferson Airplane exploded at once and her hand jerked from between her legs and she looked reflexively at the clock and saw that it was ten of seven.

Kathleen walked to the bathroom and turned on the shower, then dropped her robe and let the stream of water run alternately hot and cold over her until she felt her sober self tenuously emerge. She dressed and appreciated her image in the full-length mirror: She was perfect, and pleased to note that dressing in such nostalgic garments caused her not a hint of remorse.

The bell rang at seven. Kathleen turned off the stereo and threw open the door. Seeing Lloyd standing there, huge and somehow graceful, jerked her back to her fantasy. When he smiled and said, "Jesus, are you stoned," she returned to the present, laughed guiltily and said, "I'm sorry. Weird thoughts. Do you like my outfit?"

Lloyd said, "You're beautiful. Traditional clothes become you. I didn't think you were a doper. Come on, let's get out of here."

Dutch Peltz and his wife Estelle lived in Glendale, in a ranch-style house adjoining a golf course. Lloyd and Kathleen drove there in tense silence, Lloyd thinking of desperation tactics and killers and Kathleen thinking of ways to regain the parity she had lost by appearing loaded.

Dutch greeted them in the doorway, bowing to Kathleen. Lloyd made the introductions.

"Dutch Peltz, Kathleen McCarthy."

Dutch took Kathleen's hand. "Miss McCarthy, a pleasure."

Kathleen returned the bow with a satirical flourish. "Should I call you by your rank, Mr. Peltz?"

"Please call me Arthur or Dutch, all my friends do." Turning to Lloyd, he said, "Circulate for awhile, kid. I'll show Kathleen around. We should talk before you leave."

Catching the edge in Dutch's voice, Lloyd said, "We need to talk sooner than that. I'm going to get a drink. Kathleen, if Dutch gets too boring, have him show you his boot trick."

Kathleen looked down at Dutch's feet. Although dressed in a business suit, he was wearing thick-soled black paratrooper boots. Dutch laughed and banged the back of his right heel on the floor. A long, double-bladed stiletto sprang out of the side of his boot. "My trademark," he said. "I was a commando in Korea." He nudged the knife point into the carpet, and the blade retracted.

Kathleen forced a grin. "Macho."

Dutch smiled. "*Touché.* Come on Kathleen, I'll show you around."

Dutch steered Kathleen toward the dining room buffet, where women were readying dishes of salad and standing over steaming hot trays of corned beef and cabbage, laughing and lauding the food and party preparations. Lloyd watched them depart, then walked into the living room, whistling when he saw that every inch of floor space was eclipsed by heavyweight high brass: Commanders, Inspectors, and up. He counted heads—seven Commanders, five Inspectors, and four Deputy Chiefs. The lowest ranking officer in the room was Lieutenant Fred Gaffaney, standing by the fireplace with two Inspectors wearing cross-and-flag lapel pins. Gaffaney looked over and caught Lloyd's eye, then turned quickly away. The two Inspectors followed suit, flinching when Lloyd stared straight at them. Something was *off.*

Lloyd found Dutch in the kitchen, regaling Kathleen and a Deputy Chief with one of his dialect anecdotes. When the

Chief walked away shaking his head and laughing, Lloyd said, "Have you been holding out on me, Dutchman? Something's got to be up; I've never seen this many heavy hitters in one place in my whole career."

Dutch swallowed. "I took the Commander's exam and passed high. I didn't tell you because I —— " He nodded toward Kathleen.

"No," Lloyd said, "she stays. Why didn't you tell me, Dutch?"

"You don't want Kathleen to hear this," Dutch said.

"I don't care. Tell me, goddamnit!"

Dutch spat it out. "I didn't tell you because with me on the Commander's list there would be no end to the favors you would have asked. I was going to tell you *if* I passed and *when* I got assigned. *Then* I got the word from Fred Gaffaney — They're going to offer me the command of Internal Affairs when Inspector Eisler retires. Gaffaney is on the Captain's list; he's almost certain to be my exec. Then *you* blew up at him, causing *me* to lose a great deal of face. I patched it up; old Dutch always looks out for his temperamental genius. Things are changing, Lloyd. The department has been taking a beating from the media — shootings of blacks, police brutality, those two cops busted for possession of coke. There's a shake-up coming. I.A.D. is filled with born-agains, and the Chief *himself* wants a crackdown on officers shacking up, fucking whores, chasing pussy, that kind of bullshit. I'm going to have to go along with it, and I don't want *you* to get hurt! I told Gaffaney that you'd apologize to him, and I *expected* you to show up with your wife, not one of your goddamned girlfriends!"

"Janice left me!" Lloyd screamed. "She took the girls with her, and I wouldn't apologize to that sanctimonious cocksucker to save my life!"

Lloyd looked around. Kathleen stood rigid against the wall, shock-stilled, her hands balled into fists. A group of officers and wives filled the dining room door. When he saw nothing but awe and self-righteous judgment in their eyes, Lloyd whispered, "I need five men, Dutch. For thirty-one suspect interviews. Just for a few days. It's the last favor I'll ever ask you for. I don't think I can get him by myself."

Dutch shook his head. "No, Lloyd."

Lloyd's whisper became a sob. "Please."

"No. Not now. Sit on it for awhile. Take a rest. You've been working too hard."

The crowd in the doorway had spilled over into the kitchen. Moving his eyes over the entire assembly, Lloyd said: "Two days, Dutch. Then I'm taking my act on TV. Watch for me on the six o'clock news."

Lloyd turned to walk away, then hesitated. He about-faced and swung his open right hand at Dutch's face. The crack of flesh on flesh died into a huge collective gasp. "Judas," Lloyd hissed.

Kathleen snuggled close to Lloyd in the car, abandoning herself to wanting his reckless courage. She was afraid of saying the wrong thing, so she stayed silent and tried not to speculate on what he was thinking.

"What do you hate?" Lloyd asked. "Be specific."

Kathleen thought for a moment. "I hate the Klondike Bar," she said. "That's a leather bar on Virgil and Santa Monica. A sadist hangout. The men who park their motorcycles in front frighten me. I know you wanted me to say something about killers, but I just don't feel that way."

"Don't apologize. It's a good answer."

Lloyd pulled a U-turn, throwing Kathleen off to the other side of the seat. Within minutes they were parked in front of the Klondike Bar, watching a group of short-haired, leather-jacketed men snort amyl nitrate, then throw rough arms around each other and walk inside.

"One other question," Lloyd said. "Do you want to

spend the rest of your life as a cut-rate Emily Dickinson or do you want to go for some pure white light?"

Kathleen swallowed. "Pure white light," she said.

Lloyd pointed to the neon sign above the swinging bar doors. A muscular Yukon adventurer, wearing nothing but a Mountie hat and jock strap, glared down at them. Lloyd reached into the glove compartment and handed Kathleen his off-duty .38. "Shoot it," he said.

Kathleen shut her eyes and fired blindly out the window until the gun was empty. The Yukon adventurer exploded with the last three shots, and suddenly Kathleen was breathing cordite and pure white light. Lloyd gunned the car and peeled rubber for two solid blocks, driving with one hand on the wheel and the other on the squealing Kathleen's tartan lap.

When they pulled up in front of her bookstore, he said, "Welcome to the heart of my Irish Protestant ethos."

Kathleen wiped tears of laughter from her eyes and said, "But I'm an Irish Catholic."

"No matter. You've got heart and love, and that's what matters."

"Will you stay?"

"No. I have to be alone and figure out what I have to do."

"But you'll come by soon?"

"Yes. In a couple of days."

"And you'll make love to me?"

"Yes."

Kathleen closed her eyes and Lloyd leaned over and kissed her alternately soft and hard, until her tears ran between their lips and she broke the embrace and ran from the car.

At home, Lloyd tried to think. Nothing happened. When plans, theories, and contingency strategies wouldn't coalesce in his mind he had a brief moment of panic. Then the classic simplicity hit him. His entire life had been the prelude to this breathless pause before flight. There was no turning back. His divine instinct for darkness would take him to the killer. The rabbit had gone down the hole and would never return to daylight.

PART FOUR
MOON DESCENDING

CHAPTER TWELVE

His intended was named Peggy Morton, and she was chosen for the challenge her consummation presented as much as for her persona.

Since Julia Niemeyer and her manuscript and his curbside assignation he had been feeling slippage on all fronts. His lean, strong body looked the same, but *felt* sluggish and flaccid; his normally clear blue eyes were evasive, clouded with fear when he stared at himself in the mirror. To combat these little crumblings the poet had resurrected several of his pre-Jane Wilhelm disciplines. Hours were spent practicing judo and karate and firing his handguns at the N.R.A. range, doing push-ups and chin-ups and sit-ups until he was one mindless ache. They worked only as a picayune holding action, and nightmares still gnawed at him. Fetching young men on the street seemed to be pantomiming obscene overtures; cloud formations twisted into bizarre patterns that spelled his name for all of Los Angeles to read.

Then his tape recorder was stolen and he gained a faceless nemesis: Sergeant Lloyd the homicide fisherman. In the eleven hours since first hearing the man's voice on the tape he had exploded four times, progressively more graphic Boy's Town fantasies driving him into a near stuporous state that would evaporate within minutes, leaving him ready to explode again, but afraid of the price. Looking at the memorabilia on his walls didn't help; only the voice excited him. Then he thought of Peggy Morton, who lived only a few blocks from a street filled with young men for hire, young men to match the shame-including voice on the tape, young men who shared the hideous lifestyle of "Officer Pig" and his lackey. He drove to West Hollywood and consummation.

Peggy Morton lived in a "security" building on Flores Avenue, two blocks south of the Sunset Strip. He had followed her home one morning from the all-night market on Santa Monica and Sweetzer, staying along the tree shrouded sidewalk, listening as she conjugated verbs in French. There was something very simple and wholesome about her; and in the traumatic aftermath of Julia he had seized on that simplicity as the basis for his ardor.

It had taken him a scant week to establish the pretty young redhaired woman as an extreme creature of habit: She left her cashier's job at Tower Records at precisely midnight, and her lover Phil, the night manager of the store, would walk her down to the market, where she would buy groceries, then walk her home. Phil would sleep over only on Tuesdays and Fridays.

"It's our deal, sweetie," he heard Peggy say a half dozen times. "I have to study my French. You promised you wouldn't press me."

The good natured, doltish Phil would protest briefly, then grab Peggy and her shopping bag in an exasperated embrace and walk away shaking his head. Peggy would then shake *her* head as if to say, "Men," and dig a bunch of keys out of her purse and unlock the first of the many doors that would take her up to her fourth floor apartment.

The apartment building fascinated and challenged him. Seven stories of glass and steel and concrete, advertised by signs in its entrance foyer as "a 24-hour total electronic security environment." He shook his head at the sadness of people needing such protection and rose to the challenge. He knew that there were four keys on Peggy's key ring, and that they were all necessary to gain access to her

190

apartment — he had heard Phil joke about it. He knew also that wall-mounted electronic movie cameras patrolled the foyer constantly. The first step had to be to obtain keys...

It was easily accomplished, but gained him only partial access. After three days of studying Peggy's routine, he knew that when she arrived at work at four o'clock she went first to the employees' "breakroom" at the back of the store. She would then leave her purse on a table next to the Coke machine and walk to the adjoining storeroom to check out the incoming supply of albums. He observed this through a sliding glass door for three days running. On the fourth day he made his move — and botched it when Peggy's returning footsteps forced him to run back into the store proper with only one key in his hand.

But it was the key to the front entrance foyer, and that night, dressed as a woman and carrying a bag of groceries as camouflage, he brazenly unlocked the door and walked straight to a bank of mailboxes that designated Peggy's apartment as 423. From there he circled the foyer and learned that a separate key was required for the elevator door. Undaunted, he noticed a door off to his left. It was unlocked. He opened it and walked down a dingy hallway to a laundry room filled with coin-operated washers and dryers. He scanned the room and noticed a wide ventilator shaft in the ceiling. Noise from the apartments above him caught his ears, and his wheels started to turn...

Again dressed as a woman, but this time wearing a tight cotton jumpsuit underneath the feminine garb, he parked across the street to wait for Peggy to return home. His tremors of expectation were so great that no thoughts of the homicide fisherman's voice crossed his mind.

Peggy showed at 12:35. She shifted her grocery bag and fumbled her new key into the lock and let herself in. He waited for half an hour, then walked over demurely and followed suit, partially shielding his face with his own shopping bag. He walked through the foyer to the laundry room and placed a hand-lettered "Out Of Order" sign on the door, then bolted it shut from the inside. Breathing shallowly, he stripped off his loose fitting gingham dress and emptied his work tools from the bag: screwdriver, chisel, ball peen hammer, hacksaw, and silencer-fitted .32 automatic. He stuck them into the compartments of an army surplus cartridge belt, then wrapped the belt around his waist and donned surgical gloves.

Bringing to mind his few fond memories of Peggy, he stood up on top of the washer directly beneath the ventilator shaft and peered into the darkness, then took a deep breath and placed his hands above his head in a diving position and leaped upward until his arms caught the corrugated metal walls of the shaft's interior. With a huge, lung-straining effort he hoisted himself up into the shaft, flattening out his arms, shoulders, and legs to gain a purchase that propelled him slowly up. Feeling like a worm doing penance in hell, he inched forward, a foot at a time, modulating his breathing in concert with his movement. The shaft was stifling hot and the metal stung his skin through his jumpsuit.

He reached the second floor connecting shaft, and found it wide enough to climb through. He moved along it, savoring the feeling of again being horizontal. The crawl space terminated at a metal plate covered with tiny holes. Cool air was pouring through them, and he squinted and saw that he was at ceiling level across the hallway from apartments 212 and 214. He rolled onto his back and removed the hammer and chisel from his cartridge belt, then twisted back on his stomach and wedged the chisel head into the edge of the plate and snapped it off with one sharp hammer blow. The plate dropped onto the blue carpeted hallway, and he crawled through the open hole and dropped to the floor in a handstand. He caught his breath and replaced the metal plate crookedly in the shaft, then walked down the hall, his eyes constantly trawling for hidden security devices. Seeing none, he walked through two connecting doorways and up two flights of concrete service stairs, feeling his heartbeat reach a new crescendo with each step he took.

The fourth floor cooridor was deserted. He walked to the door of apartment 423 and placed his ear to it. Silence. He took the .32 automatic from his belt and checked to see that the silencer was screwed tight to the barrel. Concentrating on the timbre of doltish Phil's voice, he rapped on the door and said, "Peg? It's me, babe."

There was a shuffling of feet within the apartment, followed by the fondly muttered words, "You crazy..." The door opened a moment later. When Peggy Morton saw the man in the black jumpsuit her hands flew to her mouth in surprise. She looked into his light blue eyes and saw longing. When she saw the gun in his hand she tried to scream, but nothing came out.

"Remember me," he said, and fired into her stomach.

There was a soft plop, and Peggy sank to her knees, her terrified mouth trying to form the word "No." He rested the gun barrel against her chest and squeezed the trigger. She pitched backward into her living room and expelled a soft "No" along with a mouthful of blood. He stepped inside and closed the door behind him. Peggy's eyelids were fluttering and she was gasping for breath. He bent down and opened her robe. She was naked underneath it. He placed the barrel to her heart and fired. Her body lurched and her head snapped upwards. Blood poured from her mouth and nostrils. Her eyelids fluttered a last time, then closed forever.

He walked into the bedroom and found an oversized shift dress that looked like it would fit him, then rummaged in the dresser until he found a brunette wig and a large straw hat. He put the outfit on and checked his getaway image in the mirror, deciding that he was beautiful.

A circuit of the kitchen yielded a large, double-strength shopping bag and a stack of newspapers. He carried them into the living room, then placed them on the floor beside the body of his most recent beloved. He removed Peggy's blood-soaked robe and got his hacksaw. He lowered the saw and closed his eyes and felt sharp sprays of blood cut the air. Within minutes tissue, bone, and viscera had been separated and the pale yellow carpet had turned dark crimson.

He walked to the balcony and looked out at the silent jetstream of cars on the Sunset Strip. He wondered briefly where all the people were going, then walked back to his twenty-third beloved and picked up her severed arms and legs. He carried them to the edge of the balcony and flung them to the world, watching as they disppeared, weighted down with his power.

Now only the head and torso remained. He let the torso lie and wrapped the head in newspaper and placed it in the supermarket bag. Sighing, he walked out the door of the apartment and through the silent security building and into the street. At curbside he slid out of Peggy Morton's dress and removed her wig and straw hat and dumped them in the gutter, knowing that he had met the equivalent of all of mankind's wars and had emerged the victor.

He took his trophy out of the shopping bag and walked along the sidewalk. At the corner he saw a beautiful, pristine white Cadillac. He placed Peggy Morton's head on the hood. It was a declaration of war. Warrior slogans passed through his mind. "To the victor belong the spoils" caught and stuck. He got his car and went looking for spartan revelry.

Benevolent voices propelled him down Santa Monica Boulevard. He drove slowly in the right lane, the tight rubber gloves numbing his hands on the wheel. There was little traffic, so the absence of street noise left him free to *listen*; to *hear* the thoughts of the young men lounging against stop signs and bus benches. Keeping eye contact was hard, and it would be even harder to make up his mind based on looks alone, so he stared straight ahead, throwing his encounter open to the voice of fate.

Near Plummer Park, crude hustler catcalls and importunings assailed him. He kept going; better *nothing* than someone nasty.

He crossed Fairfax, moving out of Boy's Town, frightened and relieved that his gauntlet was ending. Then he hit the red light at Crescent Heights and voices came down on him like shrapnel: "Good weed, Birdy. You carry dime bags for your johns and you'll clean up."

"I already cleaned up, what do you think I am, a fucking janitor?"

"It might not be a bad idea, beauty. Janitors get social security, jockers get the clap."

All three voices dissolved into laughter. He looked over. Two young blondes and the lackey. He gripped the wheel so hard that his numb hands came to life and twisted in spastic tremors, hitting the horn by accident. The voices stopped at the noise. He could feel their gazes zeroing in. The light turned greed; the color reminding him of tape slithering through bloody apertures. He stood his ground; to run now would be cowardice. Cancer cells started to crawl over his windshield, and then a soft voice was at his passenger window.

"You looking for company?"

It was the lackey. Staring at the green light, he ran through a mental litany of his twenty-three beloveds. Their images calmed him; they *wanted* him to do it.

"I *said*, 'You want some company?'"

He nodded in return. The cancer cells vanished at the act of courage. He forced himself to look over and open the door and smile The lackey smiled back, no recognition in his eyes. "The silent type, huh? Go ahead, stare. I know I'm gorgeous. I've got a pad down near La Cienega.

Five minutes and Larry the Bird flies you straight to heaven."

The five minutes stretched into twenty-three eternities; twenty-three female voices saying "Yes." He nodded each time and felt himself go warm all over.

They pulled into the motel parking lot, Larry leading the way up to his room and closing the door behind them, whispering, "It's fifty. In advance." The poet reached into his jumpsuit and extracted two twenties and a ten. He handed them to Larry, who put them in a cigar box on the nightstand and said, "What'll it be?"

"Greek," the man said.

Larry laughed. "You'll love it, doll. You ain't been fucked till you been fucked by Larry the Bird."

The man shook his head. "No. You've got it mixed up. I want to fuck you."

Larry breathed out angrily. "Buddy, *you* got it all wrong. I don't take it up the ass, I give it up the ass. I been rippin' off butthole since high school. I'm Larry Bir--"

The first shot caught Larry in the groin. He crashed into the dresser, then slid to the floor. The man stood over him and sang, "On, o' noble Marshall, roll right down that field; with your banner flying o'er us, we will never yield." Larry's eyes came alive. He opened his mouth, and the man stuck the silencer-fitted barrel into it and squeezed off six shots. The back of Larry's head and the dresser behind it exploded. He removed the spent clip and reloaded, then rolled the dead hustler onto his back and pulled off his pants and jockey shorts. He spread Larry's legs and wedged the gun barrel into his rectum and pulled the trigger seven times. The last two shots ricocheted off the spinal cord and tore through the jugular as they exited, sending crisscrossed geysers of blood into the cordite-reeking air.

The poet got to his feet, surprised to find that he could hold himself steady. He held both of his hands in front of his face and noticed that they were steady, too. He pulled off his rubber gloves and felt symbolic life return to his hands. He had now killed twenty-three times for love, and once for revenge. He was capable of bringing death to man and woman, lover and rapist. He knelt beside the corpse and reached his hands into a pile of dead viscera and immersed them in blood, then turned on all the lights in the room and wrote on the wall in bloody finger strokes: "I am not Kathy's Klown."

Now that he knew it himself, he pondered the proper means of spreading the news to the world. He found the telephone and dialed "Operator," requesting the number of the Homicide Division, Los Angeles Police Department. The operator gave it to him and he dialed, drumming bloody fingers on the nightstand as he listened to the dial tone. Finally, a gruff voice answered, "Robbery-Homicide, Officer Huttner speaking. May I help you?"

"Yes," the man said, going on to explain that a very kind Detective Sergeant had rescued his dog. His daughter wanted to send the nice policeman a Valentine. She forgot his name, but remembered his badge number — 1114. Would Officer Huttner get the word to the nice policeman?

Officer Huttner said "Shit" to himself and "Yes sir, what's the message?" into the mouthpiece.

The man said, "Let the war begin," then yanked the cord out of the wall and hurled the phone across the bloody motel room.

CHAPTER THIRTEEN

Lloyd drove to Parker Center at dawn, the possible ramifications of his outburst at the party banging in his head like cymbals gone mad. Whatever the upshot, from formal assault charges to departmental censure, he was going to be the object of an I.A.D. investigation that would result in his being immediately placed on a full-time specific assignment that would preclude investigating the killings. It was time to take his investigation underground, stay unavailable to the department in general and the I.A.D. witch hunters in particular, make his amends to Dutch later and get the killer, whatever the price to his career.

Lloyd ran the six flights of stairs up to his office. There was a note on his desk from the night officer downstairs: "Badge 1114. Let the war begin? Probably a crank — Huttner." I.A.D. psychological warfare, Lloyd decided; religious fanatics were never subtle.

Lloyd walked down the hall to the junior officers' lounge, hoping that there would be no night-watch dicks lingering there. He was going to be out on the street for a long stretch, and coffee alone wouldn't do it.

The lounge was deserted. Lloyd checked the undersides of the lunch tables, the classic "Long term surveillance" cops' hiding place. On his fourth try he was rewarded: a plastic baggie filled with Benzedrine tablets. He grabbed the whole bag. Thirty-one names on his stereo supply list *and* a one man stake-out of Whitey Haines's apartment. Better too much speed than too little.

The Parker Center corridors were coming alive with early arriving officers. Lloyd saw several unfamiliar men with crew-cuts and stern looks give him the eye, and immediately made them for I.A.D. detectives. Back in his office, he saw that the papers on his desk had been gone over. He was raising his fist to slam the desk when his phone rang.

"Lloyd Hopkins," he said into the mouthpiece. "Who's this?"

A distressed male voice answered. "Sergeant, this is Captain Magruder, West Hollywood Sheriff's. We've got two homicides out here, separate locations. We've got a set of prints, and I'm certain they match the ones in your teletype on the Niemeyer killing. Can you..."

Lloyd went cold. "I'll meet you at the station in twenty minutes," he said.

It took him twenty-five, running red lights and siren all the way. He found Magruder at the Information Desk, in uniform, poring over a stack of folders. Noting his name tag, Lloyd said, "Captain, I'm Lloyd Hopkins."

Magruder jumped back as if stung by a swarm of bees. "Thank God," he said, sticking out a trembling hand. "Let's go into my office."

They walked down a hallway crowded with uniformed officers talking in animated whispers. Magruder opened his office door and pointed Lloyd to a chair, then sat down behind his desk and said, "Two homicides. Both last night. One woman, one man. Murder scenes a mile apart. Both victims blown to hell with a .32 automatic. Identical spent casings at both scenes. The woman was dismembered, probably with a saw. Her arms and legs were found in the swimming pool of the adjoining apartment building. Her head was wrapped up in a newspaper and placed on the hood of a car directly outside her apartment house. A nice girl, twenty-eight years old. The second victim was a fruit hustler. Worked out of a motel a few blocks from here. The killer stuck the .32 in his mouth and up his ass and blew him to shit. The night manager, who lives directly below, didn't hear a thing. She called us when blood started dripping down through her ceiling."

Lloyd, stunned beyond thought at the news of the male victim, watched Magruder reach into his desk drawer and pull out a fifth of bourbon. He poured a large shot into a coffee cup and downed it in one gulp. "Jesus, Hopkins," he said. "Holy Jesus Christ."

Lloyd declined the bottle. "Where were the prints found?" he asked.

"The fruit hustler's motel room," Magruder said. "On the telephone and the nightstand and next to some writing in blood on the walls."

"No sexual assault?"

"No way to tell. The guy's rectum was obliterated. The M.E. told me he'd never seen ——"

Lloyd raised a hand in interruption. "Do the papers know about it yet?"

"I think so...but we haven't released any information. What have you got on the Niemeyer killing? Any leads you can give my men?"

"I've got nothing!" Lloyd screamed. Lowering his voice, he said, "Tell me about the fruit hustler."

"His name was Lawrence Craigie, A.K.A. Larry "The Bird," A.K.A. "Birdman." Middle thirties, blond, muscles. I think he used to hustle off the street down near Plummer Park."

Lloyd's mind exploded, then coalesced around an incredible series of connections: Craigie, the witness at the 6/10/80 suicide; the "Bird" in Whitey Haines's bugged apartment. It *all* connected.

"You *think*?" Lloyd shouted. "What about his rap sheet?"

Magruder stammered, "We...We've run a make on him. All we got was unpaid traffic warrants. "We ——"

"And this guy was a known male prostitute? With no record at *all*?"

"Well...maybe he paid a lawyer to get his misdemeanors wiped."

Lloyd shook his head. "What about your vice files? What do your vice officers say about him?"

Magruder poured himself another drink and knocked it back. "The Vice Squad doesn't come on duty until nightwatch," he said, "but I've already checked their files. There's nothing on Craigie."

Lloyd felt widening connections breathing down his neck. "The Tropicana Motel?" he asked.

"Yes." Magruder said. "How did you know?"

"Body removed? Premises sealed?"

"Yes."

"I'm going over. You've got officers stationed there?"

"Yes."

"Good. Call the motel and tell them I'm coming."

Lloyd stilled his mental tremors and ran out of Magruder's office. He drove the three blocks to the Tropicana Motel, expecting rare glimpses of hell and his own destiny.

He found an upholstered slaughterhouse, reeking of blood and shattered flesh. The young deputy who guarded the door contributed gory details: "You think this is bad, Sergeant? You shoulda been here earlier. The guy's brains were all over that dresser over there. The Coroner had to scoop them into a plastic bag. They couldn't even mark the outline of the stiff with chalk, they had to use tape. Jesus."

Lloyd walked over to the dresser. The light blue carpet next to it was still sopping wet with blood. In the middle of the dark red expanse was the metallic tape outline of a spread-eagled dead man. He ran his eyes over the rest of the room: a large bed with a purple velour coverlet, muscle boy statuettes, a cardboard box filled with chains, whips, and dildos.

Surveying the room again, Lloyd noticed that a large part of the wall above the bed had been covered with brown wrapping paper. He called to the deputy, "What's with this paper on the wall?"

The deputy said, "Oh, I forgot to tell you. There's some writing underneath. In blood. The dicks covered it up so the TV and newspaper guys wouldn't see it. They think maybe it's a clue."

Lloyd grabbed a corner of the wrapping paper and

pulled it free. "I Am Not Kathy's Klown" stared down at him in bold, blood-formed letters. For one brief second, his computer jammed, whirled, and screeched. Then all the fuses blew out and the words blurred and metamorphosed into noise, followed by perfect silence.

Kathleen McCarthy and her court — "We had a following of equally bookish, lonely boys. Kathy's Klown's they were called." Dead women who resembled wholesome early 'sixties high school girls. A dead fruit hustler and his perverse, corrupt cop buddy and . . . and . . .

Lloyd felt the young deputy tugging at his sleeve. His silence became pure Satanic noise. He grabbed the deputy by the shoulders and pushed him into the wall. "Tell me about Haines," he whispered.

The young officer quaked and stammered out, "Wh — What?"

"Deputy Haines," Lloyd repeated slowly. "Tell me about him."

"Whitey Haines? He's a loner. He sticks to himself. I've heard talk that he takes dope. Th — thats all I know."

Lloyd released the deputy's shoulders. "Don't look so scared, son," he said.

The deputy swallowed and straightened his tie. "I'm not scared," he said.

"Good. You keep quiet about our conversation."

"Yes . . . Sir."

The telephone rang. The deputy picked it up, then handed it to Lloyd. "Sergeant, this is Officer Nagler from S.I.D.," a frenzied voice blurted out. "I've been trying to get you for hours. The switchboard at the Center tol —"

Lloyd cut him off. "What *is* it, Nagler?"

"Sergeant, it's a match. The index and pinky on the Niemeyer teletype match perfectly with the index and pinky I got off the tape recorder."

Lloyd dropped the receiver and walked out onto the balcony. He looked down at the parking lot filled with rubber-necking ghouls and sad curiosity seekers, then shifted his gaze to the street scene. Everything he saw was as awesome as a baby's first glimpse of life out of the womb and into the breach.

CHAPTER FOURTEEN

Propelled by a whirlwind of interlocking fates, Lloyd drove to Kathleen McCarthy's house. There was a note on the front door: "Buying books — Will return at noon — U.P.S. leave packages on steps."

Lloyd snapped the lock on the door with a short, flat kick. The door burst open, and he closed it behind him and headed straight for the bedroom. He went through the dresser first; intimate apparel, scented candles, and a bag of marijuana were revealed. He checked the walk-in closet. Boxes of books and record albums covered every inch of rack and floor space. There was a shelf at the back, partially hidden by an ironing board and rolled up carpet. Lloyd ran a hand across it and hit smoothly finished wood that shifted at his touch. He reached up with both hands and pulled the object out. It was a large box of beautifully varnished oak with a brass hinged top. It was heavy; Lloyd strained as he lowered it first to his shoulders, then to the bedroom floor.

He pulled the box over to the bed and knelt beside it, wedging the ornamental gold lock off with his handcuff holder.

The box contained narrow, gold-bordered picture frames, arranged lengthwise on their edges. Lloyd pulled one out. Encased behind glass were shriveled red rose petals pressed on parchment. There was minute writing beneath the petals. He carried the frame over to a floor lamp and switched on the light and squinted to read it. Under the first petal on the left was written:

"12/13/68: Does he know that I broke up with Fritz? Does he hate me for my short interludes? Was he that tall man browsing through the Farmer's Market? Does he know how much I need him?"

Lloyd followed the floral tributes across the picture frame and across time: "11/24/69: O' dearest, can you read my mind? Do you know how I return your homage in my diary? How it is all for you? How I would forever eschew fame to continue the growth our anonymous rapport gives me?" "2/15/71: I write this in the nude, darling, as I know you pick the flowers you send me. Do you feel my telepathic poetry? It comes from my *body*."

Lloyd put the frame down, knowing something was wrong—he should be more moved by Kathleen's words. He stood very still, knowing that if he forced it, it would never come. He closed his eyes to increase the depth of the silence, and then...

Even as it hit him, he started to shake his head in denial. It couldn't be, it was too incredible.

Lloyd emptied the oak box onto the bed. One by one, he held the picture frames to the light and read the dates beneath the withered petals. The dates corresponded with the murder dates of the women in his computer printouts, either exact matches or with a variance factor of two days at the most. But there were more than sixteen rose petals—there were twenty-three, going back to the summer of 1964.

Lloyd recalled Kathleen's words at the power plant. "The first time there was a poem, the second time just the flowers. And they kept coming for over eighteen years." He went through the glass cases again. The oldest rose fragments were dated 6/10/64—over eighteen years ago. The next oldest were dated 8/29/67, over three years later.

What had the monster been doing during those three years? How many more had he killed, and *Why? Why? Why?*

Lloyd read over Kathleen's words and recalled the dead faces that matched them. Jeanette Willkie, D.O.D. 4/15/73, caustic poisoning; flowers dated 4/16/73, "Darling, have you kept yourself chaste for me? I have now been celibate four months for you." Mary Wardell, D.O.D. 1/6/74, strangled to death; flowers dated 1/8/74, "Thank you for my flowers, dearest. Did you see me last night by my window? I was nude for you." And on and on through Julia Niemeyer, D.O.D. 1/2/83, heroin overdose, butchered after death; flowers dated 1/3/83, "My tears stain this parchment, my love. I need you inside me so much."

Lloyd sat down on the bed, willing his raging mind silent. Innocent, romantic Kathleen, a mass murderer's obsessive love object. *"We had a following of equally lonely, bookish boys."*

Lloyd's mind jerked his body upright. Yearbooks—the *Marshall Baristonian*. He tore through drawers, shelves, closets and bookcases until he found them, wedged behind a disused TV set. 1962, 1963 and 1964; pastel naugahyde bound. He flipped through '62 and '63—no Kathleen, Kathy Kourt, or Kathy Klowns.

He was halfway through 1964 when he hit paydirt—Delbert "Whitey" Haines, caught for posterity giving the raspberry sign. On the same page was a skinny, acne-faced boy named Lawrence "Birdman" Craigie, wittily denoted as "Bad news for L.B.J.'s Great Society." Lloyd flipped through a dozen more pages of blasted innocence before he found the Kathy Kourt: four plain-pretty girls in tweed skirts and cardigan sweaters looking up in awe at a similarly attired, heartbreakingly young Kathleen McCarthy. When he saw what it all meant, Lloyd started to tremble. The dead women were all variations of the girls in Kathy's Kourt. The same wholesome features, the same fatuous innocence, the same incipient acceptance of defeat.

Lloyd's tremors became full-out body shudders. Whispering "rabbit down the hole," he dug the list of tape recorder purchasers from his pocket and turned to the index of the 1964 *Baristonian*. Seconds later the final connection sprung to life: Verplanck, Theodore J., member of the Marshall High School Class of 1964; Verplanck, Theodore, 1976 purchaser of a Watanabe A.F.Z. 999 recorder.

Lloyd studied the photograph of the genius killer as a smiling teenager. Intelligence formed the face; a terrible arrogance rendered the smile ice-cold. Theodore Verplanck had looked like a boy who had lived within himself, who had created his own world and armed it to the teeth with highly developed adolescent conceits. Shuddering, Lloyd pictured the coldness in the young eyes magnified by almost twenty years of murder. The thought filled him with awe.

Lloyd found the phone and dialed the California Department of Motor Vehicles Office in Sacramento, requesting a complete make on Theodore J. Verplanck. It took the switchboard operator five minutes to come back with the information: Theodore John Verplanck, D.O.B. 4/21/46, Los Angeles. Brown hair, blue eyes. 6', 155 lbs. No criminal record, no outstanding traffic warrants, no record of traffic violations. Two vehicles: 1978 Dodge Fiesta Van, P-O-E-T, 1980 Datsun 280Z, DLX-191. Address, res. and bus. — Teddy's Silverlake Camera, 1893 North Alvarado, L.A. 90048. (213) 663–2819.

Lloyd slammed down the receiver and finished writing the information in his notepad. His awe moved into a sense of irony: The poet-killer still lived in the old neighborhood. Taking a deep breath, he dialed 663–2819. After three rings, a recorded message came on. "Hi, this is

Teddy Verplanck, welcoming your call to Teddy's Silverlake Camera. I'm out right now, but if you'd like to talk about camera supplies, photo-finishing or my super-high-quality portrait photography and candid group shootings, leave a message at the beep. Bye!"

After hanging up, Lloyd sat down on the bed, savoring the killer's voice, then clearing his mind for the final decision: Take Verplanck himself or call Parker Center and request a back-up team. He wavered for long minutes, then dialed his private office number. If he let it ring long enough, someone would pick it up and he could get a fix on what trustworthy officers were available.

The phone was picked up on the first ring. Lloyd grimaced. Something was wrong; he hadn't plugged in his answering machine. An unfamiliar voice came on the line. "This is Lieutenant Whelan, Internal Affairs. Sergeant Hopkins, this message was recorded to inform you that you are suspended from duty pending an I.A.D. investigation. Your regular office line is open. Call in and an I.A.D. officer will arrange for your initial interview. You may have an attorney present and you will receive full pay until our investigation is settled."

Lloyd dropped the phone to the bed. So it ends, he thought. The final decision: They couldn't and wouldn't believe him, so they had to silence him. The final irony: They didn't love him the way he had loved them. The fulfillment of his Irish Protestant ethos would cost him his badge.

Noticing a small back yard through the bedroom window, Lloyd walked outside. Rows of daisies growing out of loosely packed dirt and a makeshift clothesline greeted him. He knelt down and plucked a daisy, then smelled it and ground it under his heel. Teddy Verplanck would probably not give up without a fight. He would have to kill him, which would mean never knowing *why*. Some sort of explanation from Whitey Haines had to be his first step, and if Verplanck took it into his mind to kill or flee while he was drumming a confession out of Haines he —

The sound of weeping interrupted Lloyd's thoughts. He walked back into the bedroom. Kathleen was standing over her bed, replacing the glass encased flowers in the oakwood box. She brushed tears out of her eyes as she worked, not even noticing his presence. Lloyd stared at her face; it was the most grief-stricken visage he had ever seen.

He walked to her side. Kathleen shrieked when his shadow eclipsed her. Her hands flew to her face and she started to back away; then recognition hit and she threw herself into Lloyd's arms. "There was a burglar," she whimpered. "He wanted to hurt my special things."

Lloyd held Kathleen tightly; it felt like grasping the loose ends of a trance. He rocked her head back and forth until she murmured, "My *Baristonians,*" and shook herself free of his embrace and reached for the yearbooks scattered on the floor. Her desperate ruffling of pages angered Lloyd, and he said, "You could have gotten duplicates. It wouldn't have been much trouble. But you're going to have to rid yourself of them. They're killing you. Can't you see that?"

Kathleen came all the way out of her trance. "What are you talking about?" she said, looking up at Lloyd. "Are. . . Are you the one who broke in and hurt my things? My flowers? Are you?" Lloyd reached for her hands, but she yanked them away. "Tell me, goddamnit!"

"Yes," Lloyd said.

Kathleen looked at her yearbooks, then back at Lloyd. "You animal," she hissed. "You want to hurt me through my precious things." She clenched her hands into fists and hurled them at him. Lloyd let the ineffectual blows glance off his chest and shoulders. When she saw that she was inflicting no damage, Kathleen grabbed a brick bookend and flung it at his head.

The edge caught Lloyd's neck. Kathleen gasped and

recoiled from the act. Lloyd wiped off a trickle of blood and held it up for her to see. "I'm proud of you," he said. "Do you want to be with me?"

Kathleen looked into his eyes and saw madness and power and harrowing need. Not knowing what to say, she took his hand. He cradled her to him and closed the door and turned off the light.

They undressed in the semidarkness. Kathleen kept her back to Lloyd. She pulled off her dress and stepped out of her pantyhose, afraid that another look at his eyes would prevent her from consummating this rite of passage. When they were nude they fell onto the bed and into each other's arms. They embraced fiercely, joined at odd places, her chin locked in his breastbone, his feet twisted into her ankles, her wrists bearing into his bloody neck. Soon they were coiled into one force and the pressure of their interlocking limbs forced them to separate as they began to go numb and lightheaded. In perfect synchronization they created a space between themselves, offering the most tentative of overtures to close that gap, a stroking of arms and shoulder blades and stomachs; caresses so light that soon they ceased to touch flesh and the space between them became the object of their love.

Lloyd began to see pure white light in the space, growing in and around and out of Kathleen. He drifted into the permutations of that light, and all the forms that came to him spoke of joy and kindness. He was still adrift when he felt Kathleen's hand between his legs, urging him to grow hard and fill the light-hallowed void between their bodies. Brief panic set in, but when she whispered, "Please, I *need* you," he followed her lead and violated the light and entered her and moved inside her until the light dissipated and they coiled and peaked together and he knew that it was blood he expelled; and then awful noise wrenched him from her, and she said very softly as he twisted into the bedcovers, "Hush, darling. Hush. It's just the stereo next door. It's not *here*. I'm *here*."

Lloyd dug into the pillows until he found silence. He felt Kathleen's hands stroking his back and turned around to face her. Her head was surrounded by floating amber halos. He reached up and stroked her hair, and the halos scattered into light. He watched them disappear and said, "I...I think I came blood."

Kathleen laughed. "No, it's just my period. Do you mind?"

Unconvinced, Lloyd said, "No," and shifted over to the middle of the bed. He took a quick inventory of his body, touching odd parts of himself, probing for wounds and disconnected tissue. Finding nothing but Kathleen's internal flow, he said, "I guess I'm all right. I think I am."

Kathleen laughed. "You *think* you are? Well, I'm wonderful. Because now I know that after all these years it was you. Eighteen long years, and now I know. Oh, darling!" She bent down and kissed his chest, running her fingers over his ribs, counting them.

When her hands dropped to his groin, Lloyd pushed her away. "I'm not your dream lover," he said, "but I know who he is. He's the murderer, Kathleen. I'm certain that he kills out of some twisted kind of love for you. He's killed twenty-odd women, going back to the middle 60s. Young women who looked like the girls in your court. He sends you flowers after each murder. I know it sounds incredible, but it's true."

Kathleen heard every word, nodding along in cadence. When Lloyd finished she reached over and switched on the lamp next to the bed. She saw that he was perfectly serious and therefore perfectly insane, terrified at violating his anonymity after close to two decades of courtship.

She decided to bring him out very slowly, as a mother would a brilliant but disturbed child. She put her head on his chest and pretended to need comfort while her mind ran in circles, looking for a wedge to break through his fear and give her access to his innermost heart. She thought of opposites: Yin-Yang, dark-light, truth-illusion. After a moment, she hit it: fantasy-reality. He must think that I believe his story, and so *I* must barter for his *real* story, the story that will let me break through fantasy and make our consummation real. He hates and fears music. If I am going to be his music, *I must find out why.*

Lloyd reached an arm over and drew Kathleen closer.

"Are you sad?" he asked. "Are you sad that it had to end this way? Are you frightened?"

Kathleen nuzzled into his chest. "No, I feel safe."

"Because of me?"

"Yes."

"That's because you have a real lover now."

He stroked her hair absently. "We have to talk about this," he said. "We have to get Marshall High circa '64 out of the way before we can be together. I need to get a handle on the killer before I take him. I need to learn all I can about him, to get this thing straight in my mind before I act. Do you understand?"

Kathleen nodded, shielding her eyes. "I understand," she said. "You want me to dig into my past for you. That way you can solve your puzzle and we can be lovers. Right?"

Lloyd smiled. "Right."

"But my past hurts, darling. It hurts to rehash it. Especially when you're such a puzzle yourself."

"I'll be less of a puzzle as we go on."

Angered at the condescension, Kathleen raised her head. "No, that's not true. I need to *know* you, don't you understand? No one knows you. But I *have* to."

"Look, sweetheart..."

Kathleen batted away his placating hand. "I need to know what happened to you," she said. "I need to know why you're afraid of music."

Lloyd began to tremble, and Kathleen saw his pale grey eyes turn inward and fill with terror. She took his hand. "Tell me," she said.

Lloyd's mind moved backward in time, collating moments of joy to counterbalance the horror story that only he and his mother and brother knew. He gained strength with each recollection, and when his mental time machine came to a halt in the spring of 1950 he knew that he had the courage to tell his story. Taking a deep breath, he began.

"In 1950, around my eighth birthday, my maternal grandfather came to Los Angeles to die. He was Irish; a Presbyterian minister. He was a widower with no family except my mother, and he wanted to be with her while the cancer ate him up. He moved in with us in April, and he brought everything he owned with him. Most of the stuff was junk; rock collections, religious knick-knacks, stuffed animal heads, that kind of thing; but he also brought a fabulous collection of antique furniture — desks, dressers, wardrobes — all made of rosewood so well varnished that you could see your reflection just as in a mirror. Grandfather was a bitter, hateful man; a rabid anti-Catholic. He was also a brilliant story-teller. He used to take my brother Tom and me upstairs and tell us stories of the Irish Revolution and how the noble Black and Tans wiped out the Catholic rabble. I liked the stories, but I was smart enough to know that Grandfather was twisted with hate and that I shouldn't take what he said completely to heart. But it was different with Tom. He was six years older than me and already twisted with hate himself. He took Grandfather seriously, and the stories gave his hatred a form; he started aping Grandfather's broadsides against Catholics and Jews.

"Tom was fourteen then, and he didn't have a friend in the world. He used to make me play with him. He was bigger than me, so I had to go along with it or he'd beat me up. Dad was an electrician. He was obsessed with television. It was new, and he thought it was God's greatest gift to mankind. He had a workshop in our back yard. It was crammed to the rafters with TV sets and radios. He spent hours and hours out there, mixing and matching tubes and running electrical relays. He never watched TV for enjoyment; he was obsessed with it as an electrician. Tom loved TV, though. He believed everything he saw on it, and everything he heard on the old radio serials. But he hated being alone while he watched and listened. He didn't have any friends, so he used to make me sit with him out in the workshop, watching *Hopalong Cassidy*, and *Martin Kane, Private Detective* and all the rest. I hated it; I wanted to be outside playing with my dog or reading. Sometimes I tried to escape, and Tom would tie me up and make me watch. He...He..."

Lloyd faltered, and Kathleen watched his eyes shift in and out of focus, as if uncertain of what time period they were viewing. She put a gentle hand on his knee and said, "Go on, *please*."

Lloyd drew in another breath of fond memories.

"Grandfather's condition got worse. He started coughing up blood. I couldn't stand seeing it, so I took to running away, ditching school and hiding out for days at a time. I was befriended by an old derelict who lived in a tent on a vacant lot near the Silverlake Power Plant. His name was Dave. He was shellshocked from the First World War, and the neighborhood merchants sort of looked after him, giving him stale bread and dented cans of beans and soup that they couldn't sell. Everyone thought Dave was retarded, but he wasn't; he slipped in and out of lucidity. I liked him; he was quiet, and he let me read in his tent when I ran away."

Lloyd hesitated, then plunged ahead, his voice taking on a resonance unlike anything Kathleen had ever heard.

"My parents decided to take Grandfather to Lake Arrowhead for Christmas. A last family outing before he died. On the day we were to leave I had a fight with Tom. He wanted me to watch television with him. I resisted, and he beat me up and tied me to a chair in Dad's work-shop. He even taped my mouth shut. When it came time to leave for the lake, Tom left me there. I could hear him in the back yard telling Mother and Dad that I had run away. They believed him and left, leaving me alone in the shack. There was no way I could move a muscle or make a sound. I was there for a day or so, cramped up in awful pain, when I heard someone trying to break into the shack. I was scared at first, but then the door opened, and it was Dave. But he didn't rescue me. He turned on every TV set and radio in the shack and put a knife to my throat and made me touch him and eat him. He burned me with tube testers and hooked up live wires and stuck them up my ass. Then he raped me and hit me and burned me again and again, with the TVs and radios going full blast the whole time. After two days of hurting me, he left. He never turned off the noise. It grew and grew and grew and grew...Finally my family came home. Mother came running into the shack. She took the tape off my mouth and untied me and held me and asked me what happened. But I couldn't talk. I had screamed silently for so long that my vocal cords had shredded. Mother made me write down what had happened. After I did it, she said, 'Tell no one of this. I will take care of everything.'

"Mother called a doctor. He came over and cleansed my wounds and sedated me. I woke up in my bed much later. I heard Tom screaming from his bedroom. I snuck over. Mother was lashing him with a brass studded belt. I heard Dad demanding to know what was happening and Mother telling him to shut up. I snuck downstairs. About an hour later, Mother left the house on foot. I followed her from a safe distance. She walked all the way up to the Silverlake Power Plant. She went straight up to Dave's tent. He was sitting on the ground reading a comic book. Mother took a gun from her purse and shot him six times in the head, then walked away. When I saw what she had done, I ran to her, and she held me and walked me back home. She took me to bed with her that night and gave me her breasts, and she taught me how to speak again when my voice returned and she nurtured me with many stories. After Grandfather died she would take me up to the attic and we would talk, surrounded by antiquity."

Rigid with pity and terror, tears streaming down her face, Kathleen breathed out: "And?"

"And," Lloyd said, "my mother gave me the Irish Protestant ethos and made me promise to protect innocence and seek courage. She told me stories and made me strong again. She's mute now, she had a stroke years ago and can't speak; so I talk to *her*. She can't respond, but I know she understands. And I seek courage and protect innocence. I killed a man in the Watts Riot. He was evil. I hunted him down and killed him. No one ever suspected Mother of killing Dave, no one ever suspected me of killing Richard Beller and if I have to kill him, no one will suspect me of ridding the world of Teddy Verplanck."

Kathleen went shock-still at the words "Teddy Verplanck." Caught in a benign web of her own memories, she said, "Teddy Verplanck? I knew him in high school. He was a weak, ineffectual boy. A very kind boy. He— "

Lloyd waved her quiet. "He's your dream lover. He was one of the Kathy Klowns back in high school; you just never knew it. Two of your other classmates are involved in the killings. A man named Delbert Haines and a man who was killed last night—Lawrence Craigie. I discovered a bugging device—a tape recorder, at Haines's apartment—that's what put me on to Verplanck. Now listen to me...Teddy has killed over twenty women. What I need from you is information on him. I need your insights, your..."

Kathleen leaped from the bed. "*You* are insane," she said softly. "After all these years you have to construct this policeman's fantasy to protect yourself? After all these years, you— "

"I'm not your dream lover, Kathleen. I'm a police officer. I have a duty to perform."

Kathleen shook her head frantically. "I'll *make* you prove it. I still have the poem from 1964. I'll make you copy it, then we'll compare handwritings."

She ran nude into the front room. Lloyd heard her murmuring to herself, and suddenly knew that she could never accept reality. He got up and pulled on his clothes, noting that in the aftermath of confession his sweat-drenched body was both relaxed and incandescently alive. Kathleen returned a moment later, holding a faded business card. She handed it to Lloyd. He read:

'6/10/64.

My love for you
     now etched in blood;
My tears caked in
     resolute passion;
Hatred spent on me
     will
     metamorphose into
          love
     Clandestinely you
          will be mine.'

Lloyd handed the card back. "Teddy, you poor, twisted bastard." He bent and kissed Kathleen's cheek. "I have to go," he said, "but I'll be back when this is settled."

Kathleen watched him walk out the door, closing it on her entire past and all her recent hopes for the future. She picked up the phone and dialed Information, securing two telephone numbers. She dialed the first one breathlessly, and when a male voice came on the line, said, "Captain Peltz?"

"Yes."

"Captain, this is Kathleen McCarthy. Remember me? I met you at your party last night?"

"Sure, Lloyd's friend. How are you, Miss McCarthy?"

"I . . . I . . . I think Lloyd is crazy, Captain. He told me he killed a man in the Watts Riot, and that his mother killed a man and that — "

Dutch cut in, "Miss McCarthy, please be calm. Lloyd is in a bit of a crisis within the department, and I'm sure he's behaving erratically."

"But you don't understand! He's talking about killing people!"

Peltz laughed. "Policemen talk about such things. Please have him call me. Tell him it's important. And don't worry."

When she heard the receiver click, Kathleen steeled herself for the next call, then dialed. After six rings a soft tenor voice said: "Teddy's Silverlake Camera, may I help you?"

"Y . . . Yes . . . Is this Teddy Verplanck?"

"Yes, it is."

"Thank God! Look, you probably don't remember me, but my name is Kathleen McCarthy, and I . . ."

The soft voice went softer. "I remember you well."

"Good . . . Look, you may not believe this, but there's a crazy policeman out to get you. I — "

The soft voice interrupted. "Who is he?"

"His name is Lloyd Hopkins. He's about forty, and very big and tall. He drives a tan unmarked police car. He wants to hurt you."

The soft voice said, "I know that. But I won't let him. No one can hurt me. Thank you, Kathleen. I remember you very fondly. Goodbye."

"G . . . Goodbye."

Kathleen put down the phone and sat on the bed, surprised to find that she was still nude. She walked into the bathroom and stared at her body in the full-length mirror. It looked the same, but she knew that somehow it had changed and would never be completely hers again.

CHAPTER FIFTEEN

Running red lights and using his siren, Lloyd drove downtown. He left the car in an alley and ran the four blocks to Parker Center, taking a service elevator to the third floor S.I.D. offices, sending up silent prayers that Artie Cranfield would be the only data analyst on duty. Opening a door marked "Data Indentification," he saw his prayers rewarded — Cranfield was alone in his office, hunched over a microscope.

The technician looked up when Lloyd closed the door behind him. "You're in trouble, Lloyd," he said. "Two I.A.D. bulls were here this morning. They said you were talking about becoming a TV star. They wanted to know if you had processed any evidence lately."

"What did you tell them?" Lloyd asked.

Artie laughed. "That you still owe me ten scoots on last year's World Series pool. It's true, you know."

Lloyd forced himself to laugh back. "I can do better than that. How'd you like your very own Watanabe A.F.Z. 999?"

"*What?*"

"You heard me. Nagler from Fingerprints has it. He's at his father's house in San Berdoo. Call the San Berdoo P.D., they'll give you the phone number."

"What do you *want*, Lloyd?"

"I want you to outfit me with a body wire, and I want six .38 caliber blank slugs."

Artie's face darkened. "When, Lloyd?" he asked.

"Right now." Lloyd said.

The outfitting took half an hour. When he was satisfied with the concealment and feedback check, Artie said, "You look scared, Lloyd."

This time Lloyd's laughter was genuine. "I am scared." he said.

Lloyd drove to West Hollywood. The body recorder constricted his chest, and each of his raging heartbeats felt like it was bringing him closer to a short-circuit suffocation.

There were no lights on in Whitey Haines's apartment. Lloyd checked his watch as he picked the lock with a credit card. 5:10. Daywatch ended at 5:00, and if Haines came home directly after getting off duty, he should arrive within half an hour.

The apartment was unchanged since his previous entry. Lloyd chased three Benzedrine tablets with sink water and stationed himself beside the door, accustoming himself to the darkness. After a few minutes the speed kicked in and went straight for his head, obliterating the smothering feeling in his chest. If it didn't take him too high, he would have enough juice for days of manhunting.

Lloyd's calm deepened, then shattered when he heard a key inserted into the lock. The door swung open a split second later, and blinding light caused him to reach up to shield his eyes. Before he could move, a flat handed karate chop glanced off his neck, long fingernails gouging his collarbone. Lloyd dropped to his knees as Whitey Haines shrieked and swung his billy club at his head. The club smashed into the wall and stuck, and as Haines tried to jerk it free Lloyd rolled onto his back and kicked out with both feet at Haines's groin, catching him full force and knocking him to the floor.

Haines retched for breath and went for his holstered revolver, wrenching it free just as Lloyd managed to get to his feet. He pointed the gun upward as Lloyd sidestepped, yanked the billy club out of the wall, and slammed it into his chest. Haines screamed and dropped the gun. Lloyd kicked it out of the way and drew his own .38 from his waistband. He leveled it at Haines's nose and gasped, "On your feet. Up against the wall and walk it back. Do it real slow."

Haines drew himself slowly upright, massaging his chest, then spread-eagling against the wall, his hands above his head. Lloyd nudged the .38 on the floor over to where he could pick it up without relinquishing his bead on him. When the gun was safely in his waistband he ran his free hand over Haines's uniformed body. He found what he was looking for in the lining of his Eisenhower jacket — a plain manila folder stuffed with paper, Craigie, Lawrence D., A.K.A. Bird, Birdy, Birdman, 1/29/46, typed on the front.

Haines started to blubber as he sensed Lloyd's eyes boring into the folder. "I...I...I didn't kill him. It...It...was probably some crazy faggot. You gotta listen to me. You got — "

Lloyd kicked Haines's legs out from under him. Haines crashed to the floor and stifled a scream. Lloyd squatted beside him and said, "Don't fuck with me, Haines. I'll eat you up. I want you to sit on your couch while I do some reading. Then we're going to talk about the good old days in Silverlake. I'm a Silverlake homeboy myself, and I know you're going to love walking down memory lane with me. On your feet."

Haines stumbled over to his naugahyde sofa and sat down, clenching and unclenching his fists and staring at the gleaming toes of his boots. Lloyd took a chair across from him, the manila folder in one hand, his .38 in the other. With one eye on Haines, he read through the pages of the Vice files.

The notations went back ten years. In the early 70s,

Lawrence Craigie had been arrested regularly for soliciting homosexual acts and had been frequently questioned when found loitering in the vicinity of public restrooms. Those early reports carried the signatures of the entire eight-man Vice Squad. After 1976, all entries pertaining to Lawrence Craigie were filed by Deputy Delbert W. Haines, #408. The reports were ridiculously repetitive, and dubious question marks covered the later ones. When he saw the report dated 6/29/78, Lloyd laughed aloud. "Today I employed Lawrence Craigie as my vice finger man. I have told the men on the squad not to bust him. He is a good snitch. Respectfully — Delbert W. Haines, #408."

Lloyd laughed; booming stage laughter to cover the sound of his pushing the activator button on his body recorder. When he felt mild electric tendrils encircle his chest, he said, "An L.A. County Deputy Sheriff running dope and male prostitutes, getting kickbacks from fruit hustlers all over Boy's Town. What are you going to do with the Birdman dead? You'll have to find yourself a new sewer, and when the Sheriff's dicks link you to Craigie you'll have to find a new career."

Whitey Haines stared at his feet. "I'm clean all the way down the line," he said. "I don't know what the fuck you're talking about. I don't know nothing about Craigie's murder or any of that other shit. This is some kind of outlaw shit you're pulling on me or you would have brought another cop with you. You're a punk cop who likes to hassle other cops. I had your number the other day when you asked me about them suicides I reported. You wanna bust me for ripping off that vice folder, then bust on, homeboy, 'cause that's all you got on me."

Lloyd leaned forward. "Look at me, Haines. Look at me real close."

Haines took his eyes from the floor. Lloyd looked into them and said, "Tonight you pay your dues. One way or the other you are going to answer my questions."

"Go fuck yourself," Whitey Haines said.

Lloyd smiled, then held up his .38 snub nose and opened the chamber. He emptied five of the six rounds into his hand, then snapped the chamber shut and spun it. He cocked the hammer and placed the barrel on Haines's nose. "Teddy Verplanck." he said.

Whitey Haines's florid face went pale. His clenched hands mashed together so hard that Lloyd could hear tendons cracking. A network of veins pulsated in his neck, jerking his head away from the gun barrel. A thick layer of dry spittle coated his lips as he stammered, "J — just — a g — guy from high school."

Lloyd shook his head. "Not good enough, Whitey. Verplanck is a mass murderer. He killed Craigie and God knows how many women. He sends your old classmate Kathy McCarthy flowers each time he kills. He had your apartment bugged; that's how I connected you to Craigie. Teddy Verplanck was obsessed with you, and you're going to tell me why."

Haines fingered the badge pinned above his heart. "I — I don't know nothing."

Lloyd spun the chamber again. "You've got five chances. Whitey."

"You haven't got the guts," Haines whispered hoarsely.

Lloyd aimed between Haines's eyes and squeezed the trigger. The hammer clicked on an empty chamber. Haines started to dry sob. His twitching hands grabbed at the sofa and ripped out hunks of naugahyde and foam.

"Four chances," Lloyd said. "I'll give you a little help. Verplanck was in love with Kathy McCarthy. He was a Kathy Klown. Remember the Kathy Kourt and the Kathy Klowns? Does the date June 10th, 1964 mean anything to you? That was the day that Verplanck first contacted Kathy McCarthy. He sent her a poem about blood and tears and hatred being spent on him. You and Verplanck and the Birdman were all at Marshall High then. Did you and Craigie hurt Verplanck, Haines? Did you hate him and bleed him and — "

"No! No! No!" Haines screamed, wrapping his arms around himself and banging his head on the couch. "No! No!"

Lloyd stood up. He looked at Haines and felt the last piece of the puzzle slip into place, fusing Christmas of 1950 and a score of June 10ths into a door that unlocked the inner sanctum of hell. He put his gun to Haines's head and pulled the trigger two times. At the first hammer click Haines shrieked; at the second he clasped his hands and began murmuring prayers. Lloyd knelt beside him. "It's over, Whitey. For you, for Teddy, maybe even for me. Tell me why you and Craigie raped him."

Lloyd listened to Haines's prayers wind down, catching the tail end of the rosary in Latin. When he finished, Haines smoothed his sweat drenched khaki shirt and adjusted his badge. His voice was perfectly calm as he said, "I always figured that someone knew, that God would tell someone to hurt me for it. I've been seeing priests in my dreams for years. I always figured God would tell a priest to get me. I never figured he'd send a cop."

Lloyd sat down facing Haines, watching his features soften in his prelude to confession.

"Teddy Verplanck was weird," Whitey Haines said. "He didn't fit in and he didn't care. He wasn't a sosh and he wasn't an athlete and he wasn't a bad ass. He wasn't a loner, he was just different. He didn't have to prove himself by doing crazy shit, he just walked around school in his fruity ivy league clothes, and every time he looked at you you knew he thought you were scum. He printed up this poetry newspaper and stuffed it into every locker on the fucking campus. He made fun of me and Birdy and the Surfers and Vatos and nobody would fuck with him because he had this weird kind of juice, like he could read your mind, and if you fucked with him he'd put it in his newspaper and everyone would know.

"There were these love poems that he used to put in his paper. My sister was real smart; she figured out all the big words and the symbolic shit and told me that the poems were ripoffs of the great poets and dedicated to that snooty bitch Kathleen McCarthy. Sis sat next to her in Home Ec, she told me that the McCarthy cunt lived in this fantasy world where she thought that half the guys at Marshall had the hots for her and the other stuck-up bitches she hung out with. 'Cathy's Clown' was a big hit song then, and the McCarthy bitch told Sis that she had a hundred personal 'Cathy Clowns.' But Verplanck was the only clown, and he was afraid to hit up on McCarthy and she didn't even know he had the hots for her.

"Then Verplanck printed these poems attacking the Bird and me. People started giving us the fisheye in the quad. I was cracking jokes when Kennedy got knocked off, and Verplanck stared me down. It was like he was ripping off my juice for himself. I waited for a long time, until just before graduation in '64. Then I figured it out. I had my sister write this fake note from Kathy McCarthy to Verplanck, telling him to meet her in the bell tower room after school. Birdy and I were there. We were only going to hurt him. We kicked his ass good, but even when he was all beat up he still had more juice than we did. That's why I did it. Birdy just followed me like he always did."

Haines hesitated. Lloyd watched him grope for words to conclude his story. When nothing came, he said, "Do you feel shame, Haines? Pity? Do you feel anything?"

Whitey Haines pulled his features into a rock hard mask that brooked no mercy. "I'm glad I told you," he said, "but I don't think I feel nothing. I feel bad about the Birdman, but he was born to die freaky. I've been revenging myself all my life. I was born to live hard. Varplanck was just in the wrong place at the wrong time. He got what he paid for. I say tough shit. I say I've paid my dues all the way down the line. I say fuck 'em all and save six for the pallbearers." It was the most eloquent moment of his life. Haines looked at Lloyd and said, "Well, Sergeant. What now?"

"You have no right to be a policeman," Lloyd said, opening his shirt and showing Haines the tape recorder hook up. "You deserve to die, but I'm not equipped for cold-blooded killing. This tape will be on Captain Magruder's desk in the morning. You'll be through as a Deputy Sheriff."

Haines breathed out slowly as his sentence was passed. "What are you going to do with Verplanck?" he asked.

Lloyd smiled. "Save him or kill him. Whatever it takes."

Haines smiled back. "Right on, homeboy. Right on."

Lloyd took out a handkerchief and wiped the door knob, the arms of the chair and the grips of Haines's service revolver. "It'll only take a second, Whitey," he said.

Haines nodded. "I know."

"You won't feel much."

"I know."

Lloyd walked to the door. Haines said, "Those were blanks in your gun, right?" Lloyd raised a hand in farewell. It felt like a giving of absolution. "Yeah. Take care, homeboy."

When the door closed, Whitey Haines walked into the bedroom and unlocked his gunrack. He reached up and took out his favorite possession—a sawed off .10 gauge double barrelled shotgun, the weapon he was saving for the close quarters apocalypse that he knew would one day come his way. After slipping shells into the chambers, Whitey let his mind drift back to Marshall High and the good old days. When the memories started to hurt he jammed the barrels into his mouth and tripped both triggers.

Lloyd was unlocking his car when he heard the explosion. He sent up a plea for mercy and drove to Silverlake.

CHAPTER SIXTEEN

Teddy Verplanck was parked across the street from his camera store sanctuary, waiting for the arrival of a tan unmarked police car. Within minutes of the incredible phone call he had thrown his entire set of consummation tools into a canvas duffle bag and had run for his safeguard unregistered car and the one-on-one combat that would decide his fate. Somehow, through chance or divine intervention, he had been given the opportunity to fight for the very soul of his beloved Kathy. He had been passed the torch by Kathy herself, and an eighteen-year-old covenant was about to be fulfilled. He thought of the armaments now resting in his trunk: silencer-fitted .32, .30 caliber M-1 carbine, two-edged fire axe, custom-made six-shot Derringer, spiked, lead-filled baseball bat. He had the technology and the love to make it work.

Two hours after the call, the car pulled up. Teddy watched a very tall man get out and survey the front of the shop, walking the length of its facade, peering into the windows. The big man seemed to be savoring the moment, collating instinctive information for use against him. Teddy was beginning to enjoy his first glimpse of his foe when the big man bolted for his car, hung a U-turn and headed south on Alvarado.

Teddy took deep breaths and decided to pursue. He waited ten seconds and followed, catching the tan car at Alvarado and Temple and keeping a discreet distance behind as it led him to the Hollywood Freeway westbound. When it hit the on-ramp, the Matador accelerated full force into the middle lane. Teddy followed suit; certain that the policeman was so lost in thought that he would never notice the headlights behind him.

Ten minutes later the Matador exited at the Cahuenga Pass. Teddy let two cars get between them, keeping one eye on the road and the other on his foe's long radio antenna. They drove into the hills surrounding the Hollywood Bowl. Teddy saw the tan car come to an abrupt halt in front of a small thatch-covered house. He pulled to the curb several doors down and quietly squeezed out the passenger side, watching his policeman-adversary walk up the steps and knock on the door.

Moments later a woman opened the door and exclaimed, "Sarge! What brings you here?!"

The voice that answered her was hoarse and tight. "You won't believe what's been happening. I don't know if I believe it myself."

"Tell me about it," the woman said, closing the door behind them.

Teddy walked back to his car and settled in to wait, weighing the dark practicalities of his situation. He knew that it had to be a vendetta waged by one man—Detective Sergeant Lloyd Hopkins—or he would have been deluged with policemen before this. It *had to be* that Hopkins wanted Kathy for himself and was willing to forego due process to get her.

Comforted by the knowledge that the force arrayed against him consisted of only one man, Teddy formulated a plan for his elimination, then thought of the path that had brought him to this point.

He had spent the days after June 10, 1964 regrouping in his art and observing the mutiny of Kathy's Kourt.

His initial outrage against his violators had become tragic validation of his art; he had paid for his art in blood, and now it was time to take his blood knowledge and reach for the stars. But the pages he filled up were turgid and hollow, timid and obsessed with form. And they were completely subservient to the drama that was taking place in the rotunda court: a betrayal so brutal that he knew it rivaled his own recent devastation.

One by one, hurling maiming prose, the girls of Kathy's Kourt attacked their leader in the very spot where she had given them every sustaining ounce of her love. They called her frigid and a no-talent shanty Mick. They told her that her no-dating policy was a cheap ploy to save them for scuzzy lesbian encounters that she was too cowardly to initiate. They called her a prissy, derivitive poet. They left her with nothing but tears, and he knew that they had to pay.

But the price eluded him, and he was too fragmented in his own life to pursue the payoff. He spent a year writing an epic poem on the themes of rape and betrayal. When the poem was completed he knew that it was trash and burned it. He grieved for the loss of his art and turned to the sad efficacy of a craft — photography. He knew the rudiments, he knew the business end, and above all he knew that it would supply him with the means to live well and seek beauty in an ugly world.

He became a proficient, unimaginative commercial photographer, earning a decent living by selling his photographs to newspapers and magazines. But Kathy was always with him, and thoughts of her brought back the terror of June 1964 full force. He knew that he had to combat that terror, that he would not be worthy of Kathy's memory until he had conquered the fear that always came with it. So for the first time in his life, he sought the purely physical.

Hundreds of hours of weightlifting and calisthenics transformed the puny body he had always secretly despised into a rock-hard machine; a like amount of time earned him a black belt in karate. He learned about weaponry, becoming an expert rifle and pistol shot. With the gathering of these worldly skills came a concurrent lessening of terror. As he grew stronger his fear became rage and he began to contemplate the murder of the Kathy Kourt betrayers. Death schemes dominated his thoughts, yet last vestiges of fear prevented him from taking action.

Self disgust was returning in force when he hit on the solution. He needed a rite of blood passage with which to test himself before beginning his revenge. He spent weeks speculating on the means, without results, until one night a phrase from Eliot jumped into his mind and stuck there: "Below, the boardhound and the boar, pursue their pattern as before, yet reconciled among the stars."

He knew immediately where that pattern was taking him — the inland regions of Catalina Island, where wild boars roamed in herds. He sailed over the following week, bringing with him a six-shot Derringer and a weighted baseball bat with sharpened ten-penny nails driven into the head. Carrying only those weapons and a canteen of water, he hiked by nightfall into the middle of the Catalina outback, prepared to kill or die.

It was dawn when he spotted three boars grazing next to a stream. He raised his baseball bat and charged them. One boar retreated, but the other two stood their ground, their tusks pointing straight at him. He was within killing range when they charged. He feinted, and they rushed past him. He waited two seconds, then feinted in the opposite direction, and when the boars snorted in frustration and turned to ram him, he sidestepped again and swung his bat downward at the closest one, catching it in the head, the impact of the blow wrenching the bat from his hands.

The wounded boar writhed on the ground, squealing and flailing at the embedded bat with its hooves. The other boar turned around, then stood on its hind legs and leaped at him. This time he didn't feint or sidestep. He stood perfectly still, and when the boar's tusks were almost in his face he raised the Derringer and blew its brains out.

On his exultant return hike he let the dozens of boars that he saw live in peace. At last "reconciled among the stars," he took the tourist steamship back to L.A. proper and began plotting the deaths of Midge Curtis, Charlotte Reilly, Laurel Jensen, and Mary Kunz, first determining their whereabouts through phone calls to the Marshall High Records Office. When he learned that all four girls were scholarship students at Eastern colleges he felt his hatred for them grow in quantum leaps. Now their motive for betraying Kathy was clearly delineated. Academically validated, and thrilled with the prospect of leaving Los Angeles, they had spurned their mentor's plans to remain in L.A. and be their teacher, attributing it to the basest of desires. He felt his rage branch out into deepening areas of contempt. Kathy would be avenged, and soon.

He compiled his college itinerary and left for points east on Christmas day, 1966. Two carefully staged accidental deaths, one forced drug overdose and one killing that matched the Boston Strangler M.O. comprised his mission.

He landed in snowbound Philadelphia and rented a hotel room for three weeks, then set out by rented car on his circuit of Brandeis, Temple, Columbia, and Wheaton Universities. He was armed with caustic agents, strangling cord, narcotics, and formidable reserves of bloodstained love. He was invulnerable at all levels but one, for when he saw Laurel Jensen sitting alone in the Student Union at Brandeis he knew she was *of* Kathy, and that he could never harm anyone who was once so close to his beloved. Glimpses of Charlotte Reilly browsing the Columbia bookstore confirmed the symbiotic thrust of their union. He didn't bother to search out the other two girls; he knew that to see them would render him as vulnerable as a child at its mother's breast.

He flew home to Los Angeles, wondering how he could have paid such a severe price and not even have his art or his mission as a reward. He wondered what he was going to do with his life. He fought fear by strict adherence to the most stringent martial arts disciplines and by the penance of prolonged fasting followed by ascetic desert sojourns where he clubbed coyotes to death and roasted their carcasses over fires he built and nurtured with desert tools and his own breath. Nothing worked. The fear still drove him. He was certain that he was going insane, that his mind was a tuning fork that attracted hungry animals who would one day eat him up. He couldn't think of Kathy — the animals might pick up his thoughts and descend on her.

Then suddenly things changed. He heard the meditation tape for the first time. And then he met Jane Wilhelm.

Emboldened by his sojourn in the past, Teddy walked over to the thatch-covered house and stationed himself behind the towering hibiscus plants adjoining the front porch. After a few minutes he heard voices coming from inside, and seconds later the door opened and the policeman was standing there, shivering against the chill night air.

The woman joined him, huddling into his arms, saying softly, "You promise that you'll be real careful and call me after you catch the son of a bitch?"

The big man said, "Yes," then bent and kissed her on the lips. "No protracted farewells," the woman said as she closed the door behind her.

Teddy got to his feet as he watched the tan police car drive off. He pulled a pushbutton stiletto from his pocket. Lloyd Hopkins was going to die soon, and he was going to die regretful of this last visit to his mistress.

He walked to the front door and drummed light knuckles across it. Joyous laughter answered the intimacy of the knock. He heard footsteps approaching the door and flattened himself off to the side of it, the knife held against his leg. The door burst open and the woman's voice called out, "Sarge? I knew you were too smart to turn down my offer. I knew — "

He jumped from his hiding place to find the woman framed in the doorway in an attitude of longing. It took seconds for her hopeful face to turn terrified, and when he saw recognition flash in her eyes he raised his knife and held it before her, then flicked it lightly across her cheek. Her hands jumped to her face as blood spurted into her eyes, and he raised a hand to her throat to silence her potential screams. His hand was at the neck of her sweater when he slid on the doormat and crashed to his knees. Joanie's sweater ripped free in his hands, and as he tried to get to his feet she swung the door onto his arm and kicked at his face. A pointed toe caught his mouth and ripped it open. He spit out blood and stabbed blindly through the crack in the doorway. Joanie screamed and kicked again at his face. He ducked at the last second and grabbed her ankle as it descended, yanking it upward, bringing her down in a flailing tangle of limbs. She scuttled backward as he got to his feet and walked inside, weaving the stiletto in front of him in a slow figure-eight pattern. He turned to close the door, and she kicked out and sent a floor lamp crashing into his back. Stunned, he jumped backward, his body weight slamming the door shut.

Joanie got to her feet and stumbled back into her dining room. She wiped blood from her eyes and banged her arms sideways, looking for weapons, her eyes never straying from the jumpsuited figure advancing slowly toward her. Her right arm caught the back of a deck chair, and she hurled it at him. He kicked it out of his way and inched forward teasingly, in a parody of stealth, his knife movements becoming more and more intricate. Joanie crashed into her dining room table and grabbed blindly at a stack of dishes, scattering them, getting her hands on only one dish, then finding herself without the strength to throw it.

She dropped the dish and stepped backward. When she touched the wall she realized that there was no place left to run and opened her mouth to scream. When a gurgling sound came out, Teddy raised his stiletto and threw it at her heart. The knife caught and Joanie felt her life burst, then seep out in a network of fissures. As bright light became darkness she slid to the floor and murmured, "Do-wah, wah-wah-do...", then surrendered herself to the dark.

Teddy found the bathroom and cleansed his split lips with mouthwash, wincing against the pain but going on to douse the wounds with the whole bottle as penance for allowing himself to be bloodied. The pain enraged him. Hatred of Lloyd Hopkins and contempt for the puny bureaucracy he represented burst out of his every pore.

Let them all know, he decided; let the world know that he was willing to play the game. He found the telephone and dialed O. "I'm in Hollywood and I want to report a murder," he said.

The stunned operator put him directly through to the switchboard at the Hollywood station. "Los Angeles Police Department," the switchboard officer said.

Teddy spoke succinctly into the mouthpiece: "Come to 8911 Bowlcrest Drive. The door will be open. There's a dead woman on the floor. Tell Sergeant Lloyd Hopkins that it's open season on police groupies."

"And what is your name, sir?" the switchboard officer asked.

Teddy said, "My name is about to become a household word," and hung up.

The bewildering phone call was relayed from the switchboard officer to the desk officer, who flashed on the name "Lloyd Hopkins" and remembered that Hopkins was a good friend of Captain Peltz, the daywatch commander. Having heard rumors that Hopkins was in trouble with I.A.D., the desk officer called Peltz at home with the information. "The operator got the message slightly garbled, Captain," he said. "She thought it was a crank, but she did mention a dead woman and your buddy Sergeant Hopkins, so I thought I'd call you."

Dutch Peltz went cold from head to foot. "What *exactly* was the message?" he asked.

"I don't know. Just something about a dead woman and your bu..."

Dutch's voice, filled with worry, interrupted. "Did the caller leave an address?"

"Yes, sir. 8911 Bowlcrest."

Dutch wrote it down and said, "Have two officers meet me there in twenty minutes and tell no one about this call. Do you understand?"

Dutch didn't wait for an answer, or bother to hang up the phone. He threw on slacks and sweater over his pajamas and ran for his car.

CHAPTER SEVENTEEN

Frock-coated figures wielding razor-edged crucifixes chased him across an open field. In the distance a large stone house shimmered in the glow of a white hot spotlight. The house was encircled by iron fencing linked together by musical clefs, and he knew that if he could hit the fence and surround himself with benevolent sound he would survive the onslaught of the cross killers.

The fence exploded as he made contact, hurtling him through barriers of wood, glass, and metal. Hieroglyphics flashed before his eyes; computer printouts that twisted into the shapes of contorted limbs and bombarded him past a last barrier of pulsating red light and into a sedately furnished living room fronted with triangular bay windows. The walls were covered with faded photographs and gnarled flower branches. As he moved closer he saw that the pictures and branches formed a door that he could will open. He was willing himself into a pitch-black trance when a succession of crosses slammed into him and pinned him to the wall. The photographs and branches descended on him.

Lloyd jerked awake, slamming his knees into the dashboard. It was dawn. He looked through the windshield and saw a half-familiar Silverlake side street, then looked at his haggard face in the rear view mirror and felt it all come back: Haines, Verplanck and his planned stakeout around the corner from Silverlake Camera. The speed had boomeranged and had combined with his nervous tension to knock him out. The killer was a block away, asleep. It was time.

Lloyd walked over to Alvarado. The street was perfectly still, and no lights issued from the red brick building that housed the camera store. Remembering that Verplanck's motor vehicle registration listed an identical business and home address, he stared up at the second story windows, then checked the parking lot next door. Verplanck's Dodge van and Datsun sedan were parked side by side.

Lloyd walked around to the alley in back of the building. There was a fire escape that reached up to the second floor and a metal fire door. The door looked impregnable, but there was an unshaded window with a deep brick ledge about four feet off to its right. It was the only possible access.

Lloyd leaped for the bottom rung of the fire escape. His hands caught iron and he hauled himself up the steps. At the second story landing he gave the metal door a gentle push. No give; it was locked from the inside. Lloyd eyed the window, then stood up on the railing and flattened himself into the wall. He took a bead on the ledge and pushed off, landing on it squarely, grasping the window runner to hold himself steady. When his heartbeat subsided to the point where he could think, he looked down and saw that the window led into a small, darkened room filled with cardboard boxes. If he could get in he could reach the apartment proper without rousing Verplanck.

Squatting on the ledge, Lloyd got a grip on the bottom of the window runner and pushed in and up. The window squeaked open and he lowered himself into a closet-sized storage space reeking of chemicals and mildew. There was a door at the front of the room. Lloyd drew his .38 and nudged it open, entering into a carpeted hallway. Using his gun as a directional finder, he crept down it until he came to an open door.

He braced himself head first into the wall and peered in. An empty bedroom with a neatly made bed. Picasso prints on the walls. A connecting door into a bathroom. Complete silence.

Lloyd tiptoed into the bathroom. Immaculate white porcelain; polished brass fixtures. There was a half-open door next to the sink. He looked through the crack and saw steps leading downstairs. He inched down them with painstaking slowness, his gun arm extended to its maximum length, his finger on the trigger.

The steps ended at the back of a large room filled with cardboard photographic displays. Lloyd felt his tension ridden body breathe out of its own accord. Verplanck was gone, he could *feel* it.

Lloyd surveyed the front of the store. It looked like camera stores everywhere: wood counter, neatly arrayed cameras in glass cases, cheerful children and cuddly animals beaming down from the walls.

Treading silently, he walked back upstairs, wondering where Verplanck had spent the night and why he hadn't taken one of his cars.

The second floor was still eerily silent. Lloyd walked through the bathroom and bedroom and down the hall to

an ornate oak door. He pushed it open with his gun barrel
and screamed. Triangular bay windows made up the front
wall. Huge photographs of Whitey Haines and Birdman
Craigie covered the side walls, interspersed with taped-on
rose branches, the whole collage united by crisscrossed
smearings of dried blood.

Lloyd walked along the walls, looking for details to
prove his dream a fake, a coincidence, anything but what
he couldn't let it mean. He saw dried semen on the photos,
crusted over the genital areas of both Haines and Craigie,
the word "Kathy" finger-painted in blood. Beneath the
photographs there were small holes in the wall stuffed with
excrement. The holes were at waist level; higher up the
white wallpaper surrounding the photographs bore
fingernail tracks and bite marks.

Lloyd screamed again. He ran back through the hallway
and bathroom and downstairs. When he reached the first
floor he crashed over a pile of cartons and stumbled out the
front door. If his dream was for real, then music would
save him. Dodging traffic, he ran across Alvarado and
around the corner to his car. He hit the ignition and
fumbled the radio on, catching the end of a commercial
jingle. His mental colors and textures were returning to
normal when an alarmed electronic voice leaped out at
him:

"The 'Hollywood Slaughterer' has claimed his third
victim in twenty-four hours, and police are gearing up for
the greatest manhunt in Los Angeles history! Last night
the body of forty-two-year-old actress-singer Joan Pratt
was discovered in her Hollywood Hills home, making her
the third person to die violently in the Hollywood area in
the past two days. Lieutenant Walter Perkins of the
L.A.P.D.'s Hollywood Division and Captain Bruce
Magruder of the West Hollywood Sheriff's are holding a
joint news conference this morning at Parker Center to
discuss the massive manhunt and to advise the Hollywood

area populace on security measures to thwart the killer or killers. Captain Magruder told reporters this morning that 'The Sheriff's department and L.A.P.D. have deployed our largest force of street officers ever in our effort to catch this killer. We firmly believe that this person's insanity is peaking and that he will try to kill again soon. There will be helicopter patrols throughout the Hollywood–West Hollywood areas, as well as a concentrated deployment of officers on foot. Our efforts will not cease until the killer is caught. Our entire detective force is tracking down every available lead. In the meantime, remember: This killer has killed both men *and* women. I urge all Hollywood residents not, repeat, *not* to stay alone tonight. Buddy up, for your own safety. We bel...'"

Lloyd began to whimper. He kicked the radio housing, then ripped the metal box free of the dashboard and hurled it out the window. Joanie was dead. His genius had become the door to a telepathic charnel house. He could read Teddy's thoughts and Teddy could read his. The dream and Joanie's death; a logic defying fraternal bonding that would spawn more and more and more horror; a horror that would only end with the killing of his evil symbiotic twin. He looked in the rear view mirror and saw Teddy Verplanck's yearbook picture. The transmogrification was complete. Lloyd drove to the old neighborhood to tell his family that the Irish Protestant ethos was a one-way ticket to hell.

Dutch Peltz sat in his office at the Hollywood Station, armed for betrayal with a Polaroid snapshot of a nude man and woman.

Since he had refused to press assault charges, the Internal Affairs officers investigating Lloyd had been swarming over him in an attempt to find other perfidies that they could bring to light to offset Lloyd's threatened media barrage. They had no idea that the L.A.P.D.'s most brilliant detective had been intimately familiar with Joan Pratt, the third victim of the Hollywood Slaughterer. The photograph was enough evidence to end Lloyd's career at best and have him shot on sight at worst.

Dutch walked to the window and looked out, thinking that he may have already signed away his own best years. His refusal to file charges would cost him his command of I.A.D., and if anyone found out that he had withheld the photograph and of his knowledge of the anonymous phone call that had mentioned Lloyd's name, he would be brought to departmental trial and suffer the ignominy of possible criminal prosecution. Dutch swallowed and asked himself the only question that made any sense. Was Lloyd a murderer? Was his protégé/mentor/son a killer brilliantly concealed by the cloak of genius? Was he a textbook schizophrenic, an academically identifiable split-personality monster? *It couldn't be.*

Yet there was a logical narrative line that said "maybe." Lloyd's erratic behavior throughout the years, his recent obsession with murdered women, his outburst at the party. *That* he had seen himself. When coupled with the traumatic aftermath of his wife and daughters' desertion and Kathleen McCarthy's phone call and the anonymous phone call and Joan Pratt's body and the nude snapshot and —

Dutch couldn't finish the thought. He looked at his telephone. He could call I.A.D. and save himself, dooming Lloyd, but maybe saving innocent lives. He could do nothing or he could track down Lloyd himself. His sleepless night, filled with images of Joan Pratt's body, had given him a good command of his options. Then Dutch asked himself the only other question that made sense. Who mattered the most? When "Lloyd" resounded through him, he tore up the photograph. He would clear the case himself.

When he got to the old wood-framed house on Griffith Park and St. Elmo, Lloyd went straight to the attic and a thirty-two-year-old treasure trove of antiquity. He traced patterns on dust-covered rosewood surfaces and marveled at his mother's foresight. She had never sold the furniture because she knew that one day her son would need to commune in the very spot that had formed his character. Lloyd felt another hand resting on his, guiding him in his artwork. The hand forced him to draw death's heads and lightning bolts. He took a last look at his past and future, then went downstairs to wake up his brother.

While Lloyd stood over him, Tom Hopkins ripped out the squares of synthetic grass that covered the ground adjoining their father's electronics shack. When he got to bare dirt he whimpered, and Lloyd handed him a shovel and said, "Dig." He obeyed, and within minutes Lloyd was hauling out wooden boxes filled with shotguns and a steamer truck containing handguns and automatic rifles. Astonished to find the weaponry well oiled and ready to use, he looked at his brother and shook his head. "I've underestimated you," he said.

Tom said, "Bad times are coming down, Lloydy. I gotta get my shit together."

Lloyd reached down into the hole and pulled out a reinforced plastic bag filled with individually wrapped .44 magnums. He hefted one, then stuck it in his waistband. "What else have you got?" he asked.

"I got a dozen A.K. 47s, five or six sawed-offs and a shitload of ammo," Tom said.

Lloyd slammed his hands onto Tom's shoulders, forcing him to his knees. "Just two things, Tommy," he said, "and then our slate will be clean. One, when you get your shit together you've got nothing but a big pile of shit; two, stay scared of me and you'll survive."

Lloyd grabbed a Remington 30.06 and a handful of

shells. Tom pulled a pint of bourbon from his pocket and took a long drink. When he offered him the bottle Lloyd shook his head and looked up at his mother's bedroom window. After a second the mute old woman appeared. Lloyd knew that she knew and had come to offer a silent goodbye. He blew her a soft kiss and walked to his car.

All that remained was to set a time and place.

Lloyd drove to a pay phone and dialed Silverlake Camera. The call was answered on the first ring, as he knew it would be.

"Teddy's Silverlake Camera, may I help you?"

"This is Lloyd Hopkins. Are you about ready to die, Teddy?"

"No, I have too much to live for."

"No more innocent ones, Teddy. You've been waiting for me all these years. I'm ready, but don't hurt anyone else."

"Yes. It's just you and me. *Mano a mano?*"

"Yes. You want to pick the time and place, homeboy?"

"Do you know where the Silverlake Power Plant is?"

"Yes, it's an old friend of mine."

"I'll meet you there at midnight."

"I'll be there." Lloyd hung up, his mind bursting with lightning bolts and death.

Kathleen woke up late and put on coffee. She looked out her bedroom window to appraise the growth of her daisies and saw that they had been trampled. She thought of the neighborhood kids, then saw a huge footprint in the dirt and felt her strategems for putting the crazy policeman out of her mind coalesce around a unifying thread. Instead of her planned day of opening the store and taking care of paperwork she would write her dream lover-betrayer into oblivion, consigning him to villainhood on the wings of a scathing broadside against weak, violence-obsessed men. She would meet Detective Sergeant Lloyd Hopkins head-on and defeat him.

After coffee, Kathleen sat down at her desk. Words fluttered through her mind, but refused to connect. She considered smoking a joint to get things going, then rejected the notion; it was too early for a reward. Feeling both her resistance and determination deepen, she walked into the front room and stared at the table by the cash register. Her own books, all six of them, arranged in a circle around a pasteboard blow-up of a four-star review in *Ms.*

Kathleen leafed through her own words at random, looking for old ways to say new things. She found passages decrying male hierarchies, but saw that the underlying symbolism centered on glass. She found acid portraits of men seeking shelter, but saw that the central theme was her own need to nurture. When she saw that her most righteously hateful prose featured crimson-flowered redemption, she felt her narcissistic nostalgia die. Her six volumes of poetry had earned her seven thousand four hundred dollars in advances and nothing in royalties. The advances for *Knife-edged Chaste* and *Notes from a Non-Kingdom* had paid off her long standing Visa card bill, which she promptly ran up again, paying off the following year with the advance for *Hollywood Stillness. Staring Down the Abyss, Womanwold* and *Skirting the Void* had secured her her bookstore, which was now skirting the edge of bankruptcy. Her remaining volumes had bought her an abortion and a trip to New York, where her editor had gotten drunk and had stuck his hand up her dress at the Russian Tea Room.

Kathleen ran into her bedroom and hauled out her glass encased rose petals. She carried them back to her bookstore-living room and one by one hurled them at the walls, the sound of breaking glass and falling bookshelves drowning out her own screamed obscenities. When the detritus of the past eighteen years of her life had devastated the room, she wiped tears from her eyes and savored the destruction: books lying dead on the floor, glass shards reflecting off the carpet, plaster dust settling like fallout. The overall symbolism was perfection.

Then Kathleen noticed that something was off. A long black rubber cord was dangling from a torn out section of her ceiling. She walked over and yanked on it, pulling loose spackle-covered wiring that extended all the way around the room. When she got to the wire's terminus a tiny microphone was revealed. She took up the cord and yanked a second time. The opposite end led to her front door. She opened the door and saw that the wire continued up to the roof, shielded by the branches of the eucalyptus tree that shaded the front porch.

Kathleen got a ladder. She stood it up on the ground beside the tree and followed the wire up to her roof. She could see that on the rooftop it had been concealed by a thin coat of tar. Squatting down, she ripped the wiring out and let it lead her to a mound of tar paper covered with shellac. She pulled the cord a last time. The tar paper ripped open and she looked down at a tape recorder wrapped in clear plastic.

At Parker Center, Dutch went through Lloyd's desk, hoping that the I.A.D. officers hadn't picked it clean. If he could find any of the homicide files that Lloyd was working with, maybe he could form a hypothesis and go from there.

Dutch rifled the drawers, prying the locks open with the buck knife he carried strapped to the inside of his gunbelt, coming away with nothing but pencils, paper clips and wanted posters. Slamming the drawers shut, he pried open the filing cabinets. Nothing; the Internal Affairs vultures had gotten there first.

Dutch emptied the wastebasket, sifting through illegible memos and sandwich wrappers. He was about to give up when he noticed a crumpled piece of Xerox paper. He held it up to the light. There was a list of thirty-one names and addresses in one column, and a list of electronic stores in the other. His heart gave a little leap; this had to be Lloyd's "suspect" list — the men that he had wanted him to detach officers to interview. It was slim — but something.

Dutch drove back to the Hollywood Station. He handed the list to the desk officer. "I want you to call all the men on this list," he said. "Lay out a *heavy* spiel about 'routine questioning.' Let me know who sounds panicky. I'm going out, but I'll be calling in."

From his office, Dutch called Lloyd's house. As he expected, there was no answer. He had called in vain every half hour throughout the night, and now it had become obvious that Lloyd had run to ground. But to where? He was either hiding out from I.A.D. and/or stalking his real or imaginary killer. He might also be —

Unable to complete the thought, Dutch recalled that Kathleen McCarthy had mentioned at the party that her bookstore was on Yucca and Highland. She had fearfully denunciated Lloyd on the phone last night, but *might* know of his whereabouts; Lloyd always sought out women when he was under stress.

Dutch drove to Yucca and Highland, pulling up in front of the *Feminist Bibliophile*, noticing immediately that the front door was half open and the porch was littered with broken glass.

Drawing his gun, Dutch walked inside. Mounds of broken glass, plaster, and books covered the floor. He walked back through the kitchen and into the bedroom. No more evidence of destruction, only the eeriness of a leather purse lying on the bed.

Dutch dug through the purse. Money and credit cards were intact, throwing the scene way out of kilter. When he found more money and Kathleen McCarthy's driver's license and car registration inside a calfskin wallet, he grabbed the telephone and dialed the desk at the station.

"This is Peltz," he said. "I want an all points bulletin issued. Kathleen Margaret McCarthy, white female, 5'9", 135, brown and brown, D.O.B. 11/21/46. Beige 1977 Volvo 1200, license LQM 957. Have the officers detain for questioning only. No force—this woman is not a suspect. I want her brought to my office."

"Isn't this a little irregular, Captain?" the switchboard officer asked.

"Shut up and issue it," Dutch said.

After checking the blocks around the bookstore unsuccessfully for Kathleen and her car, Dutch began to feel like a pent-up Judas having second thoughts. He knew that movement was the only antidote. Any destination was better than no destination.

Dutch drove to Silverlake. He knocked on the door of the old house that Lloyd had driven him by so many times, only half heartedly expecting someone to answer; he knew that Lloyd's parents were old and lived in silent solitudes. When no one came to the door, he walked around the side of the house to the back yard.

Peering over the fence, Dutch saw a man swigging from a pint of whiskey and waving a large handgun in front of him. He stood perfectly still, recalling Lloyd's stories about his crazy older brother Tom. He watched the sad spectacle until Tom dropped the handgun to the ground and reached into a packing crate next to it, pulling out a machine gun.

Dutch gasped as he watched Tom weave drunkenly, muttering, "Fuckin' Lloyd don't know shit, fuckin' fuzz don't know how to deal with the fuckin' niggers, but I know for fuckin' sure. Fuckin' Lloyd thinks he can fuck with me, he's got another fuckin' think comin'.'"

Tom dropped the machine gun and fell to the dirt along with it. Dutch drew his .38 and squeezed through a gap in the fence. He crept along the side of the house, then sprinted over to Tom, his gun aimed straight at his head. "Freeze," he said as Tom looked up, bewildered.

"Lloydy took my goodies," he said. "He never wanted to play with me. He took my *best* stuff and still wouldn't play with me."

Dutch noticed a large hole in the ground next to him. He looked into it. The muzzles of a half-dozen sawed-off shotguns stared up at him. Leaving Tom weeping in the dirt, he ran back to his car. He gripped the steering wheel and wept himself, praying for God to give him the means to indict Lloyd with pity or release him with love.

CHAPTER EIGHTEEN

Kathleen zigzagged through Hollywood side streets, destinationless, numbing the discovery of the tape recorder with silent chantings of her very best prose, the big policeman and his murder theory battling her words point counter-point until she ran a red light on Melrose and fishtailed across the intersection, narrowly missing a crossing guard and a flock of children.

She pulled to the curb, shaking, her literary holding action drowned out by the honking of angered motorists. She was past words now. Lloyd Hopkins and his conspiracies demanded to be disproved on the basis of fact. The tape recorder was evidence that would require the negation of superior evidence. It was time to visit an old classmate and let *his* words speak.

Dutch watched from the back of the room as Lieutenant Perkins, the commanding officer of the Hollywood Division Detective squad, briefed his men on the Hollywood Slaughterer case:

"Our black and white units and helicopter patrols are

going to keep the bastard from killing again, but you guys are going to find out who he is. The Sheriff's dicks are handling the Morton and Craigie cases, and may have an angle—some Deputy who used to work West Hollywood Vice blew his brains out last night at his pad, and some of his old Vice partners say he was in tight with Craigie. Robbery-Homicide downtown is handling the Pratt case, which leaves you guys the job of rousting every pervert, burglar, dope addict, and all-purpose scumbag known to use violence in the Hollywood area. Utilize your snitches, your parolee files, your brains, and the feedback of the guys from patrol. Use whatever force you deem necessary."

The men got up and headed for the door. Noticing Dutch, Perkins called out, "Hey skipper, where the fuck is Lloyd Hopkins now that we really need him?"

Kathleen pulled up in front of the red brick building on Alvarado. She noticed a "closed due to illness" sign on the front door and peered through the plate-glass window. Seeing nothing but shadow-covered countertops and stacks of boxes, she walked to the parking lot, immediately spotting a long yellow van with a license plate reading "P-O-E-T". She had her hand on the rear door latch when darkness reached out and smothered her.

Lloyd waited for darkness in the park-playground a half mile below the Silverlake Power Plant. His car was hidden from street view behind the maintenance shed, the 30.06 and .44 magnum in the trunk, loaded and waiting. Sitting on a child's swing that shuddered under his weight, he compiled a list of the people he loved. His mother and Janice and Dutch headed the list, followed by his daughters and the many women who had brought him joy and laughter. Casting out hooks of memory to sustain the loving moments, he reeled in fellow cops and engaging criminals and even passersby he had glimpsed on the street. The more obscure the people became, the deeper the feeling of love touched him, and when twilight came and went Lloyd knew that if he died at midnight he would somehow live on in the vestiges of innocence that he saved from Teddy Verplanck.

Kathleen came out of the darkness with her eyes open, chemical stench and a glaze of tears her prelude to vision. She tried to blink to adjust her focus, but her eyelids wouldn't move. When squinting with all her might brought nothing but a flood of burning teardrops, she opened her mouth to scream. Some unseen closure rendered her mute, and she twisted her arms and kicked out with her legs, gouging the air for sound. Her arms remained fixed while her feet scraped an invisible surface, and as she flailed and heaved with every inch of her sense-blunted body she heard "sssh, sssh," and then there was a soft blackness daubing at her eyes, followed by bright light. *I am not blind and deaf, but I am dead,* she thought.

Kathleen's vision centered in on a low wooden table. When squinting brought her greater clarity she saw that it was only a few feet in front of her. As if in answer, the table, with a scraping sound, moved up to where she could touch it. She twisted her arms again, pain cutting through her numbness. *I am dead, but I am not cut in pieces.*

Willing all her senses into her eyes, Kathleen stared at the table. Gradually a room came into view behind it, and then the soft blackness was on and off her like the clicking of a camera shutter, and when the light returned the table was in her face, covered with naked plastic dolls with pins stuck into their crotches and huge heads made out of black and white photographs. *I am in hell and these are my fellow exiles.*

Sensing familiarity in the photograph heads, Kathleen forced her mind to function. *I am dead, but I can think.*

She knew that the heads were somehow *of* her, somehow close to her, somehow —

Kathleen's senses snapped. Her arms contracted and her legs jerked upwards, sending her chair to the floor. *I am alive and those are the girls from my court and the policeman was right and Teddy from High School is going to kill me.*

Invisible hands picked up the chair and turned it around. Kathleen squirmed and dug her heels into a soft white carpet. *My eyelids are forced open and my mouth is taped shut, but I am alive.*

Kathleen rolled her eyes to the far edges of the periphery, memorizing the wall in front of her in hopes of combining sight and thought into something more. When she assimilated all that she saw she began to sob, and tears once again turned her blind. Blood, rose branches, desecrated photographs and excrement. The stench assaulted her. *I am going to die.*

There was a whirring sound. Kathleen followed it with her mind and what remained of her vision. She saw a tape recorder on a nightstand. She tried to scream, and felt the tape across her mouth begin to give. *If I can scream, I* —

A soft sighing came over the tape machine. Kathleen breathed in through her nose and blew out with all her strength. The tape strained against her mouth and came loose along her lower lip. The soft sighing became a soft singsong voice:

I am only worthy to love you in verse,
To spread my love on the wings of a curse;
They betrayed you and ripped you,
Buried in dread;
I avenged your heartache by killing them dead;
Then *you* betrayed me with
    Badge one-one-one-four-
You let him hurt me and make you his whore;

I cannot blame you — but tonight you must choose;
With your eyes sewn open you will watch
    him lose;
I will always love — love. . .love. . ."

The soft voice receded back into a sigh. Kathleen contorted her eyebrows and felt the stiches at the corners of her eyelids loosen. *I am going to kill him before he kills me.*

The tape recorder clicked off. Kathleen's chair was hoisted into the air and spun around in a perfect circle. She screamed and heard the faintest vibration of her own voice, then looked up at Teddy Verplanck in a skin-tight black jumpsuit. She formed words to keep from screaming and ripping the tape from her mouth prematurely. *He has become so handsome. Why are cruel-looking men always the most handsome?*

Teddy put a piece of paper in front of Kathleen's eyes. Biting down on her tongue, she read the block printed script: "I cannot speak to you yet. I am going to take out a knife and mark myself. I will not hurt you with the knife."

Kathleen nodded up and down, probing the tape with the tip of her tongue. Feeling was returning to her feet, and she could tell that she was wearing her blunt-toed wingtip flats. *Good kicking shoes.*

Teddy smiled at her nodding acquiesence and turned the paper over. The reverse side was covered with faded newspaper clippings. Kathleen's gaze zeroed in on them. When she saw that the clippings detailed accounts of women's murders she stifled a dry sob by biting her cheeks and methodically reading every word on the page. Her terror turned to rage and she bit down harder, until blood and spittle filled her mouth. She breathed deeply through her nose and thought: *I am going to maim him.*

Teddy threw the paper to the floor and unzipped the top of his jumpsuit, letting it fall to his waist. Kathleen looked at the most perfect male torso she had ever seen, transfixed by the rock-hard perfection until Teddy reached behind his back and drew out a penknife. He held the blade in front of his chest and twirled it like a baton, then pointed the blade at the area above his heart. When the tip drew blood, Kathleen twisted her hands on the arms of her chair, pushing out with her elbows, feeling her right hand bonds give way completely. *Now. Now. Now. Please God let me do it now. Now. Now.*

Teddy wiped his torso and squatted in front of Kathleen, holding his chest at her eye level. He whispered, "It's 10:30. We have to go soon. You were so beautiful with your eyes rolled back." He wiped his chest a second time. Kathleen saw that he had carved "K Mc" beside his left nipple. She gagged, but held on. *Now.*

Teddy squatted lower and smiled. Kathleen spat in his face and kicked out with both her legs, catching him in the groin, jerking her right hand free and pushing forward, toppling her chair just as Teddy crashed to the floor. She screamed and kicked again, her legs glancing off Teddy's stomach. Teddy dropped his knife and shrieked, wiping bloody spittle from his eyes. Kathleen lunged with her whole body and got her free hand on the knife, hooking her right leg around Teddy to draw her within stabbing range. Teddy twisted and flailed blindly with his arms. Kathleen brought the knife down in a swooping roundhouse at his abdomen. Teddy jerked backwards and the blade cut air. Kathleen stabbed again, the knife snagging into the carpet. Teddy got to his knees and wrapped his fists into a hammer and swung down. Kathleen bared her teeth to bite as the blow arced toward her. She screamed and tasted blood when the hammer made contact. Then there was a throbbing red darkness.

Dutch watched the muster-room clock strike eleven. He shifted his gaze out the door to the front desk. The desk officer looked up from his telephone and called out, "Nothing yet, skipper. I've made contact with twenty-three out of the thirty-one. The rest are no answers or recorded messages. Nothing even remotely suspicious."

Nodding curtly in answer, Dutch said, "Keep trying" and walked out to the parking lot. He looked up at the black sky and saw the crisscrossed beacons of the helicopter patrols light up low cloud formations and the tops of Hollywood skyscrapers. Save for a skeletal station contingent, every Hollywood Division officer was on the street, on foot, in the air or in a black-and-white, armed to the teeth and pumped up for glory. Rolling imaginary dice, Dutch calculated the odds on accidental shootings by overeager cops at ten to one, rookies and promotion happy hot dogs the most likely blood spillers. With Lloyd still missing and no clues to his whereabouts, he found that he didn't care. Blood was in the air, and nihilist rectitude was the night's prevailing logic. He had gone through cartons of Lloyd's arrest records from his Hollywood Division days, finding no indicators pointing to trauma that might have festered to the point of combustion; he had telephoned every one of Lloyd's girlfriends whose name he could recall. Nothing. Lloyd was guilty or Lloyd was innocent and Lloyd was nowhere. And if Lloyd was nowhere, then he, Captain Arthur F. Peltz, was a spiritual seeker who had gone to Mecca and had come away with unimpeachable evidence that life was shit.

Dutch walked back inside the station. He was halfway up the stairs to his office when the desk officer ran up to him. "I got a response to your A.P.B., Captain. Vehicle only. I wrote down the address." Dutch grabbed at the paper the officer was holding, then ran downstairs to the front desk and ran frenzied eyes over Lloyd's interview list. When 1893 N. Alvarado screamed out from both pieces of paper, he yelled, "Call the officers who called in the bulletin and tell them to resume patrol; this is mine!"

The desk officer nodded. Dutch ran up to his office and got his Ithaca pump. Lloyd was innocent and there was a monster to slay.

CHAPTER NINETEEN

A winding two-lane access road led up to the Power Plant. It terminated at the base of a scrub-bush dotted hillside that rose steeply to the tall barbed-wire fence that enclosed the generator facility. There was a dirt parking lot off the left of the road, next to a tool shack sandwiched between two stanchions hung with high powered spotlights. Another spotlight housing was stationed directly across the blacktop, with feeder wires connecting to the Silverlake Reservoir a quarter of a mile north.

At 11:30, Lloyd walked up from the playground, staking out the territory as he trudged uphill, the 30.06 resting on his shoulder, the .44 magnum pressed to his leg. He knew only that since assuming his position on the street side of the playground at eight-thirty, six cars had driven northbound on the access road. Two were official Water and Power Department vehicles, presumably headed for the plant's administration offices. The four remaining cars had returned within an hour, meaning that the occupants had gotten stoned or laid on the hillside and had retreated back to L.A. proper. Which meant that Teddy Verplanck had arrived on foot or was in the process of driving up.

Lloyd walked north on the dirt shoulder, hugging the embankment that branched into Power Plant Hill. When he reached the last turn in the road he saw that he was correct. Two cars were parked next to the fence beside the tool shack; both were Water and Power vehicles.

The embankment ended, and Lloyd had to walk a stretch of pavement before he could scale the hill and establish a killing ground. He treaded lightly, his eyes constantly scanning his blind side. If Verplanck was nearby, he was probably hiding in the clump of trees adjoining the parked cars. He checked his watch: eleven forty-four. At precisely midnight he would blow that clump of trees to kingdom come.

The pavement ended, and Lloyd began to climb uphill, pushing forward slowly, dirt mounds breaking at his feet. He saw a tall scattering of scrub bushes looming in front of him and smiled as he realized that it was the perfect vantage point. He stopped and unslung his 30.06, checking the clip and flipping off the safeties. Everything was operative and set to go at a split second's notice.

Lloyd was within a yard of his objective when a shot rang out. He hesitated for a brief instant, then hurled himself head first into the dirt just as a second shot grazed his shoulder. He screamed and burrowed into the ground, waiting for a third shot to give him a direction to fire in. The only sound was the pounding of his own chest.

An electrically amplified voice cut the air: "Hopkins, I have Kathy. She has to choose."

Lloyd rolled into a sitting position and aimed his 30.06 at the sound of the voice. He knew that Verplanck was a conjuror who could assume shapes and voices and that Kathleen was safe somewhere in her web of fantasies. Clenching his bloodied shoulder into a huge ache to allow for the recoil, he fired off a full clip. When the shattering echoes died out, a laughing voice answered them. "You don't believe me, so I'll make you believe me."

A series of hellish shrieks followed, noises that no conjuror could artifice. Lloyd muttered "No, no, no," until the electronic voice called out, "Throw down your weapons and come out to meet me or she dies."

Lloyd hurled his rifle at the road. When it clattered onto

the pavement he stood up and jammed his .44 magnum into the back of his waistband. He stumbled downhill, knowing that he and his evil counterpart were going to die together with no one but the strident woman poet to write their epitaph. He was murmuring "rabbit down the hole, rabbit down the hole," when white light blinded him and a white-hot hammer slammed him just above the heart. He flew back into the dirt and rolled like a dervish as the light bored into the ground by his side. Wiping dirt and tears from his eyes, he crawled for the pavement, watching the spotlight's reflections gradually illuminate Teddy holding Kathleen McCarthy in front of the toolshed. He tore through his blood-drenched shirt and felt his chest, then twisted his right arm and pawed at his back. A small frontal and a crisp exit wound. He would have the juice to kill Teddy before he bled to death.

Lloyd pulled out his .44 and spread himself prone, his eyes on the two spotlights next to the toolshed. Only the top light was on. Teddy and Kathleen were right below the housings, forty feet of blacktop and dirt away from the muzzle of his handcannon. One shot at the spotlight; one shot to take off Teddy's head.

Lloyd squeezed the trigger. The light exploded and died at the precise second that he saw Kathleen break free of Teddy's grasp and fall to the ground. He got to his feet and stumbled across the pavement, his gun arm extended, his left hand holding his trembling wrist steady. "Kathleen, hit the other light!" he screamed.

Lloyd moved forward into his last gauntlet of darkness, a red-black curtain that masked all his senses and enveloped him like a custom-made shroud. When the spotlight went on Teddy Verplanck was ten feet in front of him, coming to meet his destiny with a .32 automatic and a nail-studded baseball bat.

Both men fired at the same instant. Teddy clutched his chest and pitched backward just as Lloyd felt the bullet tear into his groin. His finger jerked the trigger and recoil sent the gun flying from his hand. He fell to the pavement and watched Teddy crawl toward him, the spikes on the baseball bat gleaming in the white-hot light.

Lloyd pulled out his .38 snub nose and held it upright, waiting for the moment when he could see Teddy's eyes. When Teddy was on top of him and the bat was descending and he could see that his blood brother's eyes were blue he pulled the trigger six times. There was nothing but the soft click of metal on metal as Lloyd screamed and blood burst from Teddy's mouth. Lloyd wondered how that could be and if he was dead, and then just before losing consciousness he saw Dutch Peltz wipe the blade that stuck out of his steel-toed paratrooper's boot.

CHAPTER TWENTY

The long transit of horror ended, and the three survivors began the longer process of healing.

Dutch had carried Lloyd and Teddy to his car, and with Kathleen weeping beside him had driven to the home of a doctor under indictment for dealing morphine. With Dutch's gun at his head the doctor had examined Lloyd, pronouncing him in need of an immediate transfusion of three pints of blood. Dutch checked Lloyd's driver's license and the I.D. cards he had taken from the body of Teddy Verplanck. Both men were type O+. The doctor performed the transfusion with a makeshift centrifuge to stimulate Teddy's heartbeat while Dutch whispered over and over that he would kill all the charges against him, regardless of the cost. Lloyd responded favorably to the transfer of blood, regaining consciousness as the doctor sedated Kathleen and removed the catgut stitches that anchored her eyelids to her brows. Dutch didn't tell Lloyd where the blood had come from. He didn't want him to know.

Leaving Lloyd and Kathleen at the doctor's house, Dutch drove the remains of Teddy Verplanck to their final resting place, a stretch of condemned beach known to be rife with industrial toxins. Hauling the body over a series of barbed wire fences, he had watched as the poisonous tide swept it away on the wings of a nightmare.

Dutch spent the next week with Kathleen and Lloyd, convincing the doctor to oversee their medical recovery. The house became a hospital with two patients, and when Kathleen came out of her sedation she told Dutch of how Teddy Verplanck had gagged her and slung her over his back, carrying her through the Silverlake hills on his way to ambush Lloyd.

He told her of how verse notations on Teddy Verplanck's calendar had led him to the reservoir and how if Lloyd was to survive as a policeman and a human being she would have to be very gentle and never talk to him about Teddy. Weeping, Kathleen agreed.

Dutch went on to say that he would destroy every official trace of Teddy Verplanck, but it would be her job to blunt Lloyd's terror-driven memory with love. "With all my heart," was her answer.

Lloyd was delirious for over a week. As his physical wounds healed, his nightmares took over, and gradually, between the gentlest of caresses, Kathleen succeeded in convincing him that the monster was dead and that mercy had somehow prevailed. Holding a mirror to his eyes, she told him tender stories and made him believe that Teddy Verplanck was not his brother but a separate entity who was sent to close out the books on all the anguish in his first forty years. Kathleen was a good storyteller, and tenuously, Lloyd started to believe her.

But as Kathleen pieced together the story of Teddy and Lloyd her own terror began. Her phone call to Silverlake Camera had caused the death of Joanie Pratt. Her reluctance to believe Lloyd and smash her own pitiful illusions had resulted in the destruction of a living, breathing woman. She felt it with *her* every breath, and when she touched Lloyd's devastated body it felt like a death sentence. Writing about it compounded the grief. It was a life sentence with no parole and no means of atonement.

A month to the day after the Silverlake *walpurgisnacht,* Lloyd discovered that he could walk. Dutch and Kathleen had discontinued their daily visits and the indictment-free doctor had taken him off his pain medication. He would have to retrieve his family and face his I.A.D. inquisitors soon, and before he did that there was a place that he had to visit

The cab dropped him in front of a red brick building on North Alvarado. Lloyd picked the lock on the door and walked upstairs, not knowing if he wanted the worst of his nightmares confirmed or denied. Whatever he saw would determine the course of the rest of his life, but he still didn't know.

The nightmare room was empty. Lloyd felt his hopes soar and shatter. No blood, no photographs, no body waste, no rose branches. The walls had been painted a guileless light blue. The bay windows were boarded shut. He would never know.

"I knew you'd come."

Lloyd turned around at the voice. It was Dutch. "I've been staking the place out for days," he said. "I knew you'd come here before you got in touch with your family or reported back to duty."

Running light fingertips over the wall, Lloyd said, "What did you find here, Dutch? I have to know."

Dutch shook his head. "No. Not ever. Don't ever ask again. I doubted you and I almost betrayed you, but I've made my amends and I won't tell you that. Everything that I could find pertaining to Teddy Verplanck is destroyed. He never existed. If you and Kathleen and I believe that then maybe we can live like normal people."

Lloyd slammed the wall with his fist. "But I have to know! I've got to pay for Joanie Pratt, and I'm not a cop anymore, so I've got to figure out what it means so I can know what to do! I had this dream that Jesus God I just can't ex — "

Dutch walked over and put his hands on Lloyd's shoulders. "You're still a cop. I went to the Chief myself. I lied and I threatened and I groveled and it cost me my promotion and my I.A.D. command. Your trouble with I.A.D. never happened, just like Teddy never happened. But you owe me, and you're going to pay."

Lloyd wiped tears from his eyes. "What's the price?"

Dutch said, "Bury the past and get on with your life."

Lloyd got Janice's new address and flew up to San Francisco the following night. Janice was gone for the weekend, but the girls were there with her friend George, and when he walked through the door they pounced on him until he was certain that they would bruise every inch of his battered body. He had a brief moment of panic when they demanded a story, but the tale of the gentle lady poet and the cop satisfied them until it burst apart in a torrent of tears. Penny was the one to supply the conclusion. Holding Lloyd tightly, she said: "Happy stories are a new mode for you, Daddy. You'll get the hang of it. Picasso switched his style late in life, so can you."

Lloyd got a hotel room near Janice's apartment and spent the weekend with his daughters, taking them to Fisherman's Wharf and the Zoo and the Museum of Natural History. When he dropped them off Sunday night George told him that Janice had a lover, an attorney specializing in tax shelters. He was the one Janice was spending the weekend with. Brief thoughts of wreaking havoc on the affair crossed his mind and he reflexively balled his hands into fists. Then images of Joanie Pratt rendered his blood thoughts stillborn. Lloyd kissed and hugged the girls goodbye and walked back to his hotel. Janice had a lover and he had Kathleen and he didn't know what he felt, let alone what it all meant.

On Monday morning Lloyd flew back to Los Angeles and took a cab to Parker Center. He walked up to the sixth floor, feeling the sore muscles around his groin wound stretch and tighten. It would still be weeks before he could make love, but when old doc dope pusher gave him the word he would sweep Kathleen off for a whole shitload of weekends.

The sixth floor corridors were empty. Lloyd checked his watch. 10:35. Morning coffee break. The junior officers' lounge was probably packed. Dutch had undoubtedly covered his prolonged absence with some sort of story, so why not get the reunion amenities out of the way in one fell swoop?

Lloyd pushed the lounge door open. His face lit up at the sight of a huge roomful of shirt-sleeved men hunched over coffee and donuts, laughing and joking and making good-natured obscene gestures. He stood in the doorway savoring the picture until he felt the noise recede to a hush. Every man in the room was looking at him, and when they all rose to their feet and began to applaud he looked back into their faces and saw nothing but awe and love. The room swayed behind his tears, and shouted "bravos" coupled with the applause to drive him back out into the corridor, dashing more tears from his eyes, wondering what on earth it all *meant*.

Lloyd ran toward his office. He was fumbling in his pocket for his keys when Officer Artie Cranfield came up beside him and said, "Welcome back, Lloyd."

Lloyd pointed down the hallway and wiped his face.

"What the fuck was that all about, Artie? What the fuck did all that *mean?*"

Artie looked puzzled, then wary. "Don't shit a shitter, Lloyd. There's a rumor all over the department that you cleared the Hollywood Slaughterer case. I don't know where it started, but everyone in Robbery-Homicide believes it, and so does half the L.A.P.D. The word is that Dutch Peltz told the Chief himself and that the Chief pulled the Internal Affairs bulls off your ass because keeping you *on* the Department was the best way to keep your mouth *shut.* You want to tell me about it?"

Lloyd's tears of bewilderment became tears of laughter. He opened his door and wiped his face with his sleeve. "The case was cleared by a woman, Artie. A left-wing cop-hater poet. Dig the irony and enjoy your tape recorder."

Lloyd closed the door on Artie Cranfield's baffled face. When he heard him walk away muttering to himself he switched on the light and looked at his cubicle. Everything was the same as when he had last seen it, except for a single red rose sticking out of a coffee cup on his desk. There was a piece of paper next to the cup. Lloyd picked it up and read:

Dearest L. — Protracted goodbyes are terrible, so I'll be brief. I have to go away. I have to go away because you have given me back my life, and now I have to see what I can do with it. I love you and I need your shelter and you need mine, but the mortar that binds us is blood, and if we stay together it will own us and we will never have the chance to be sane. I have given up the bookstore and my apartment. (It belongs to my creditors and the bank, anyway.) I have my car and a few hundred dollars in cash, and am taking off sans excess baggage for parts unknown. (Men have been doing it for years.) I have much on my mind, much writing to do. Does "Penance for Joanie Pratt" sound like a good title? She owns me, and if I give her my best then maybe I'll be forgiven. I hurt for our past, L. — But I hurt for your future most of all. You have chosen to stalk ugliness and try to replace it with your numbing kind of love, and that is a painful road to follow. Goodbye. Thank you. Thank you. Thank you.

K.

P.S. The rose is for Teddy. If we remember him, then he'll never be able to hurt us.

Lloyd put the paper down and picked up the flower. He held it to his cheek and juxtaposed the image with the spartan accoutrements of his trade. Floral-scented terror merged with metal filing cabinets, wanted posters, and a map of the city, producing pure white light. When Kathleen's words turned the light into music he drew the moment into the strongest fiber of his heart and carried it away.

About The Author

James Ellroy was born in Los Angeles in 1948. He is the author of two previous novels, *Brown's Requiem* and the Edgar-nominated *Clandestine*. He lives in Eastchester, New York, where he is working on a new novel.